WILDFIRE PEGASUS
FIRE & RESCUE SHIFTERS: WILDFIRE CREW - BOOK 4

ZOE CHANT

AUTHOR'S NOTE

Wildfire Pegasus is a complete romance without cliffhangers, and can be enjoyed as a standalone. However, the *Wildfire* series is intended to be read in order. Each book features a different couple, but characters reoccur throughout, and there is an overarching plot that is gradually revealed over the course of the entire series.

Wildfire Pegasus takes place a few months after *Wildfire Sea Dragon*. The shifters of the Thunder Mountain Hotshots have spent another hard summer battling wildfires, bodysnatching demons, and rogue hellhounds—with the help, and sometimes the hinderance, of the mysterious, erratic Thunderbird. Now, as fire season comes to an end, the firefighters are looking forward to a well-deserved break.

But someone is heading to their base. And she's bringing a surprise...

CHAPTER 1

This is a terrible idea. It's going to go wrong. He'll hate you.

Diana knew better than to try to silence that nagging inner voice. She kept her eyes on the twisting mountain road, steering her car through each bend as smoothly as possible despite the pounding of her heart.

He'll be angry. He'll shout. He'll call the cops and have you escorted away in handcuffs and they'll throw you in jail and—

"I haven't done anything *illegal*, Gertrude," Diana said out loud. "I'm not going to get arrested."

Naming her anxiety disorder and treating it like a separate person helped her to control her runaway worries. Even if it did make her sound like a loon to be talking to thin air. She just had to be careful not to slip up and do it in public.

You're going to forget, Gertrude promptly piped up. *You'll talk to yourself in front of him, and he'll decide that you're utterly mad and want nothing to do with you. Or he'll have you committed. Or he'll call child services and they'll come and declare you unfit and take her away.*

Diana drew in a long, deep breath and let it out slowly, counting to five. She slowed down, making sure that the road was clear before risking a glance over her shoulder. The baby mirror she'd rigged over the back seat showed Beth was still lost in sleep, one chubby little fist clutching her comfort blanket.

As always, her daughter's baby-round cheeks and rosebud mouth made Diana's heart expand, even as her chest tightened in worry. She took a firmer grip on the steering wheel despite her sweating palms.

"I have to do this for Beth," she told both herself and Gertrude. "She deserves to have a chance to know her father."

He could be terrible. A bully. A sexist pig. You hardly know anything about him.

"That's true," Diana acknowledged. "But I know that he was kind to me. I know that he made me laugh, at a point when I thought I would never laugh again. I know that he's quick-witted and sweet and funny. Beth deserves to have someone like that in her life."

What if that was all an act, though? Gertrude fretted. *What if he was just lying to get into your pants? What if he's a drug addict?*

Diana had to laugh at herself for coming up with *that* one. "He's a wilderness firefighter. I don't think people addicted to crack cocaine can work nineteen-hour days cutting line."

Steroid abuse, Gertrude suggested. *He'll have mood swings and rages. He must spend all his money on illicit injections. No one looks that good naturally. Remember his body?*

Oh, how she remembered his body. It had only been one night, and they'd both been drunk to the point of irresponsibility, but she could still visualize every inch of his perfect physique. She could still feel the hard planes of his chest under her palms, the bold confidence of his mouth on hers, the thick length of his—

Diana gave herself a mental shake. *That* was all in the past. She was a mother now. She couldn't even contemplate a relationship, not with Beth needing all her attention.

This wasn't about her. This was all for Beth.

Gertrude subsided to a background murmur of dire predictions of disaster and heartbreak. Diana let the intrusive thoughts roll past, acknowledging but not engaging the way that her therapist had taught her to do.

She focused on the road instead, which had degenerated to a dirt track. Her little car jolted over ridges and furrows left by much larger vehicles. Diana guessed that no one must come up this way much apart from the hotshot crew members themselves. She did her best to soften the ride, hoping that Beth wouldn't wake up. The chance of this meeting going well wouldn't be improved by handing a shocked hotshot a screaming, red-faced baby.

She needed everything to go perfectly. She owed it to Beth.

She ran through her pre-prepared speech as she drove. She'd spent days agonizing over every word, writing it out again and again until it was burned into her brain. Maybe she should have just sent it to him as a letter...but no letter, no picture could convey the sheer breathtaking wonder of *Beth*. He couldn't fall in love with cold, hard facts. She had to *show* her to him, in person. It was the best chance that he would see his surprise daughter as the living, breathing miracle she was, rather than as a mistake.

Even if that meant driving from California to Montana, wrestling diapers in dingy gas stations and spending hours disinfecting every surface in cheap motels. Road trips were considerably less fun when you had a ten-month-old baby that had fully mastered the art of crawling. Diana was grateful that Beth always dropped off to sleep in the car, but it did mean that Beth was wide awake and raring to explore *all night*.

What if you're making poor decisions due to sleep deprivation? Gertrude whispered.

If that was the case, then Diana probably hadn't made a good decision all year. No matter how she tried to let the worry slip by, it clung stubbornly, like a burr in her mind.

She wound down the window a crack, hoping the breeze would help to clear her head. The habitual tight knot in her chest eased a little as she breathed in the gloriously clean mountain air. The sunlight filtering through the tree canopy was still summer-warm and golden, but hints of red in the foliage showed that fall was just around the corner. It was a long way from her own crowded, run-down, smoggy corner of L.A.

Diana's heart thumped as she spotted a hand-lettered sign

proclaiming THUNDER MOUNTAIN HOTSHOTS - CREW BASE. It pointed down an even narrower track, leading higher up the mountain. Diana had to slow to a crawl, her lightweight tires struggling on the rough terrain.

Just as Diana was starting to wonder if her little car could cope with the steep gradient, the track gave out into a wide clearing. A group of wooden buildings clustered at the far end. Most of them were small, rough log cabins, set back near the tree line, but there were a couple of larger structures set around a wide, flat parking area.

Which was completely empty.

The entire base had a still, shuttered feeling. Every door was closed, every window dark.

Diana couldn't help feeling like she was trespassing as she parked her car and got out. Leaving Beth still asleep in her car seat, she took a few hesitant steps toward the largest building.

"Hello?" The word came out as a squeak. She cleared her throat and tried again. "Um, hello? Is anyone around?"

Her voice sounded too loud in the silent base. A bird made a call of alarm from the forest off to her left, making her jump. She held her breath, listening, but only heard the gentle whisper of wind through leaves. No sound of chainsaws or men working; not even a hint of distant traffic.

The Thunder Mountain Hotshots weren't at their base.

She'd read on the crew's website that the end of September was the close of fire season. She'd assumed that they'd *have* to have been here, storing all their gear and shutting everything down for the winter. But the hotshot crew must have been called out again on one final, late assignment.

Her stomach plummeted, even as guilty relief flooded through her. It had taken her literally days to psych herself up for this confrontation and now…now she'd have to find the nerve to do it all over again.

She wasn't sure she'd be able to. Not even for Beth. Just the thought of putting herself through all this *again* had her pulse spiking.

"Hello?" she called again, in futile hope. "Is anybody here?"

"You looking for someone?"

She nearly wet herself—*thanks, post-pregnancy pelvic floor*—at the unexpected male voice. Heart in her mouth, she spun round. A burly, bearded man lounged near her car, watching her with his head cocked to one side.

"Wh-where did you come from?" she stammered.

He jerked his head casually in the direction of the forest. "Saw you drive in. You lost?"

It was ridiculous—he was being perfectly polite, even if he did look a bit unkempt—but a hammer-blow of adrenaline hit her as she realized he was standing between her and Beth.

"Hey, don't look like that, Little Red Riding Hood. I don't bite." The man grinned, exposing startlingly white teeth. "Except in special circumstances."

"Um." As unobtrusively as she could, Diana edged around him, putting her back to the vehicle. The man didn't move, although his grin widened, as though he was enjoying her obvious discomfort. "Are you one of the hotshots here?"

"Might be." The man shoved his hands into his pockets, still smiling. "Depends who's asking. You looking for one?"

"Y-yes." Diana tried to ignore the way that all her instincts were screaming at her. "I, um, I need to talk to Callum Tiernach-West. Do you know him?"

The man's eyes narrowed. His smile dropped away, revealing intent, predatory focus. "Oh yes. I know him. Question is, how do *you* know him, Little Red?"

There was no way she was going to blurt out to a complete stranger that she'd had a secret baby with a sexy firefighter. Especially not to someone as creepy as this guy.

"Oh, it's not important." Nerves got the better of her. She could hear her voice going high and thin, words pouring out in a panicked torrent. "I can see he's not here right now. No big deal, honest. I'll come back another time. Really sorry to bother you. I'll just be going now."

She fumbled for the car door as she babbled. She got it open—and shrieked as a rough hand closed round her wrist.

"I don't think so, Little Red." Somehow the man had closed the distance between them in an eye-blink, so fast she hadn't even been aware of him moving. His rank, wet-dog smell choked her. "I think you should come with me."

Oh God, he's not a hotshot! A dozen horrific possibilities whirled through Diana's mind. She kept her eyes fixed on his, not daring even the slightest flicker of a glance in Beth's direction. It didn't matter what happened to her, not as long as her baby was safe.

The man's nostrils flared. He sniffed the air like an animal. To Diana's horror, he turned his head, his eyes fixing on Beth.

"Holy shit," the man breathed. "He's got a kid."

"No, no, please!" Diana dug in her heels, trying to hold the man back. It was no use. He dragged her effortlessly in his wake as he peered through the car window. "She's not his, I swear! I'll go with you, do whatever you want, just leave her alone!"

"Calm down, Little Red. I'm not going to eat her." Despite his words, the man was staring at Beth as if she was a dozen glazed donuts. He let out a short, ugly laugh of triumph. "Nobody will get hurt...as long as your boyfriend does *exactly* what we want. Oh, man. I'll be the golden boy for this. Even that bitch Lupa will have to kiss my ass."

He was so caught up in gloating, his grip on her wrist slackened. With the strength of desperation, Diana broke free. He turned, snarling, but she was already pivoting. It had been years since she'd last played soccer, but her body still knew exactly what to do.

Her foot connected with the man's crotch with enough force to drive a ball across an entire pitch.

Thank you, thank you, thank you! She blessed her old college coach for all those hours of practice as the man crumpled. She scrambled into her car, slamming the door shut and locking it. By the time the man rolled to his feet, she was already roaring away.

She caught a last glimpse of him in the rear-view mirror as she sped out of the parking lot. He was still down on his hands and knees, crouched in the dirt. His features were so distorted in rage that he barely seemed human. He threw back his head, letting out a feral howl.

Still, he was on foot. Even if he had a car or motorbike hidden somewhere nearby, it would take him time to get to it and come after her. She held the accelerator down, taking the bends in the road as fast as she dared, and prayed that she had enough of a head start.

A sleepy, grumpy wail rose from the backseat. The breakneck, bumpy ride had woken Beth up. She sounded more indignant than upset, but her cries still stabbed through Diana.

"It's okay, baby, it's okay." She spoke as soothingly as she could, despite the rapid pounding of her heart and the constant *oh my God oh my God oh my God* running through her head. "Mommy's here. Everything's going to be—"

A wall of flame cut her off.

CHAPTER 2

"Six months until we have to see anything else that's on fire," Blaise said with intense satisfaction. "Bliss."

Rory chuckled from the front passenger seat. "You said that last year too. And by Christmas, you were complaining how bored you were, and counting down the days until fire season started again."

Blaise took one hand off the steering wheel to flip off their hotshot squad boss. "Not this time. After the season we've had, I for one am looking forward to peace and quiet and a total lack of demons and hellhounds."

Fenrir, riding in the back of the vehicle, stuck his pointed muzzle over the last row of seats to shoot Blaise a wounded, puppy-eyed look.

"Not *all* hellhounds," Rory's mate Edith said, reaching over to scratch behind Fenrir's ears.

"Present company excepted, of course." Wystan rolled his neck, stretching cramped muscles with a wince. "It has been rather a summer, hasn't it?"

"Are you going for the gold medal in English understatement, Wys?" Joe said. The sea dragon shifter was lounging across the middle seats with one arm around his mate Seren, shamelessly taking up far more than his fair share of space in the crowded crew vehicle. "You do remember that I was nearly eaten by a giant snake monster, right?"

"To be fair, that was mostly your fault," Seren murmured to him.

"Even without all the supernatural events, it's been quite a ride," Rory said. "We've logged a record number of hours this season. We all deserve a break. What are everyone's plans for off-season?"

"Hot showers," Blaise said promptly. "*All* the hot showers. I may just become aquatic."

"Hey, if it's water you want, you should come hang out with me and Seren," Joe said. "We've got all the water you could want in Atlantis."

"I said *hot* showers." Blaise kept her attention on the road as she spoke, though she could no doubt have navigated the twisting roads leading up Thunder Mountain with her eyes shut. "Anyway, I already promised my parents I'd spend off-season with them in Brighton. I'm going to help my mom out at the pub. It'll be nice to see all the old faces again. You're coming too, aren't you Rory?"

"Wouldn't miss it for the world." Rory grinned, his golden eyes brightening. "Danny and Morwenna are coming over with baby Charlie, so the whole family will be back together for the holiday season. I'm just grateful Edith agreed it was okay for us to spend all winter in England."

"It's more than okay," Edith said, still petting Fenrir. "I like your family a lot. I'm looking forward to spending more time with them. Especially your sisters. I promised Skye I'd help her with her application for fire academy."

Rory's forehead wrinkled. "And suddenly, I'm wondering if we should go to Atlantis instead."

"Ross would hunt you down and drag you back by your tail-feathers," Blaise told him. "What about you, Wys? Are you and Candice coming home too?"

Wystan smiled. "Yes, but not in the way you mean. Thunder Mountain is my home now, not England. Candice and her friends have been doing marvels with the ranch while I've been away for fire season, but there's still a great deal to be fixed and restored. Besides which, someone needs to stay in Montana, just in case our supernatural friends make an unexpected move."

"You think that's likely?" Rory asked. "I thought your research showed that the Thunderbird never showed up outside of fire season. Doesn't that mean that the demons must be hibernating or something?"

"They do indeed seem to go dormant over the winter," Wystan replied. He cocked a significant eyebrow at Joe. "But as we've learned, the demons aren't working alone. They might not be able to emerge when the weather cools down, but that Lupa woman and her hellhound pack could still be very much active."

Bad Bitch, Fenrir growled. *Don't trust her. Must guard the den until pack returns.*

"Oh, you're staying too?" Edith said, looking a little disappointed. "I thought maybe you'd come with me and Rory."

"Fenrir has kindly agreed to help me keep an eye on things," Wystan said. "But don't worry, you won't be parted for the entire winter. We're all going to fly over to England for Christmas."

"So will we," Seren put in. "The Pearl Empress has already decreed that Winter Court shall be held on land this year. We too shall be in Brighton."

Joe sat bolt upright, banging his head against the ceiling of the truck. "Wait. Wait. You know what this means?"

Edith eyed him side-long. "No. What?"

Joe flung his arms wide, as best he could in the packed space. *"Epic party!"*

"For once, Joe actually has a good idea," Blaise said. "Well, since we'll all be back—"

"Not all."

It was the first time Callum had spoken during the six-hour journey, and he regretted it immediately. The rest of the squad turned to stare at him, looking as startled as if the chainsaws loaded in the back had started whistling the Star-Spangled Banner.

"What do you mean, Callum?" Rory said, his brow creasing. "You're coming back home for Christmas at least, aren't you?"

Their attention pinned him in place like a spotlight, no matter how much he wanted to slink back into the shadows. Discomfort made it harder to shut out the rest of the world. The back of his mind was a constant strobe-flicker of the life-forms streaking past as the vehicle as it barreled along—*rabbit, rabbit, sparrow squirrel lizard jay jay sparrow jay mouse rabbit mousemousesparrowsparrowsnakemousemousejay—*

Callum had never been able to shut off his talent. And in the past couple of years, since he'd moved to America, it had only gotten worse. It was like his pegasus was constantly reaching out, searching for something…

He ignored the insistent stream of information as best he could, trying to concentrate only on his ordinary senses. "Can't."

Rory's gaze raked across his face. "Can't, or don't want to?"

Damn it, the griffin shifter had always been too perceptive. *Squirrelsquirreljayhawk*—Callum dug his fingernails into his palm for focus. "Like Wystan said. Someone needs to stay to keep guard."

"Over what?" Edith said. "I mean, that Lupa woman was targeting Joe, right? Even if she still wants to get at one of us, she can't do that if we're all on the other side of the ocean."

"Edith's got a point, Cal," Wystan said. "I'll be leaving the base and ranch warded while I'm away, of course, but you'll still be safer with us than on your own."

Pack stays with pack, Fenrir agreed. *Sometimes must hunt alone, true. But important to come back to den, too, otherwise forget why one is hunting at all. Shadowhorse should come with pack. Sleep fur to fur. Gnaw sweet bones. Sing to the moon.*

Blaise snorted with laughter. "There's no party like a Fenrir party. This will be quite a Christmas. Come on, Cal. You can't seriously want to spend the holidays on your own."

Actually, Callum could think of nothing better. Unfortunately, even alone at the hotshot base, he would still be sharing the surroundings with countless woodland creatures. But that was still infinitely preferable to going to a city.

Especially his home city.

"Wait. Wait! I…I'm seeing something." Joe put one hand to his forehead in an over-dramatic gesture, as though he was about to fall onto a fainting couch. "I'm having a vision...of Callum...wearing a paper party hat..."

"No, you aren't," he said flatly.

Joe let his hand drop again, shrugging unrepentantly. "It was worth a try."

"We all want you to come home, Callum," Rory said softly. "Even just for a day or two. And we're not the only ones, you know."

Callum clenched his teeth, hating the sad, pitying look on Rory's face. Wystan, Blaise, and Joe wore similar expressions. It was all too familiar. Over the years, they'd often regarded him with the same baffled concern, ever since they'd been little kids together.

Even his oldest friends didn't understand him. They were all so close to their own families, they simply couldn't comprehend anyone who wasn't. Anyone who didn't *want* to be.

If he was better with words, maybe he could have explained it to his friends. But he'd always been the quiet one. The one who wasn't good with people. The one who struggled to filter out the world, always distracted by *crow crow jay mouse mouse mouse rabbit THERE—*

Callum jerked, attention utterly derailed. Amidst the shimmering constellations of life-forms all around, one blazed like a supernova. No, not one—two, as close as binary stars. They were like nothing he'd ever sensed before. They were...they were...

OURS. His inner pegasus reared in his soul, wings spreading wide. *OURS, THERE, THEY NEED US, GO!*

"Stop," he blurted out.

Rory held up his hands. "We're not trying to pressure you into doing something you don't want, Cal. But we're your friends. We're just worried—"

"No," he interrupted. He fumbled for his seatbelt, releasing the catch. "Stop the truck. Now!"

Wystan looked concerned. "Is something wrong?"

"I'd say there is." Blaise leaned over the steering wheel, peering up through the windscreen. "Uh, guys? Is it just me, or is our base on fire?"

Urgency beat in his chest like a drum. Callum didn't need the thick plume of smoke rising on the horizon to know that something was wrong, badly wrong. The two lives he could sense called out to him like beacons in the night, calling to him across the mountain.

And they weren't alone. There was a third life circling them, blood-red and malevolent, closing in...

"Hellhound." Callum struggled free of his seatbelt at last, accidentally elbowing Wystan in the ribs in his haste. "Attacking—they need me—*stop!*"

Rory nodded to Blaise, reaching for his own seatbelt. "Do it. Callum, hang on. We'll go together—"

Callum was already opening the door. He hurled himself out, even though the truck hadn't yet fully come to a halt. He hit the ground hard, rolling, shifting.

He came up on four hooves, his pegasus surging eagerly up from his soul. With a single leap, he was in the air. The world dropped away beneath him. Out of the corner of his eye, he glimpsed Rory leaping down from the truck, his stocky form blurring into his golden griffin —but nobody could beat a pegasus for speed.

CALLUM. Rory's telepathic roar blasted through his mind. *Wait for me! It's not safe to go alone!*

No time, he hurled back, his flame-red wings never slowing. *And there's only one hellhound.*

That you can sense now, Rory retorted. His telepathic voice was getting fainter as the distance between them increased. He was doing his best to keep up, but his hawk-like wings weren't built for rapid acceleration like his own. *You can't detect hellhounds when they're using their invisibility power. There could be dozens of them waiting to ambush you!*

The griffin shifter was right, but Callum didn't care. He stretched himself out, tucking up his legs and sweeping his wings back into a streamlined arrowhead. He cut through the sky like a knife, leaving Rory behind.

Smoke burned in his sensitive equine nose. As he shot toward the mountain, he could see that it wasn't the hotshot base itself that was ablaze. Only a small section of the forest was on fire, in an unnaturally straight line. The flames were spreading much faster than should have been possible in the wet conditions, burning with an evil red glare.

Hellfire, Callum thought. It wasn't a curse, just simple recognition. The hellhound had breathed a fireball across the track, setting fire to the trees on either side of the road.

The reason why was immediately apparent. A car was nose-down in the ditch, airbags filling the windscreen. The driver had managed to avoid hurtling straight into the flames, but the crushed vegetation around the tires was starting to smolder as sparks fell into it.

A burly man was yanking at the driver side door. He could have been trying to rescue the people trapped inside—but Callum knew better. The man's life-force crackled in his senses, sharp and feral.

Rage filled him. He didn't shriek, didn't give voice to it. He simply folded his wings and dropped, silent and swift and deadly.

Only shifter instincts saved the hellhound. He glanced up just in time to throw himself to one side. Callum's front hooves clipped him in the shoulder rather that striking him square in the head as he'd intended.

He still hit the hellhound with enough force to send him hurtling through the air. The man flew into the forest, disappearing into the smoke. A *crunch* and a sharp scream indicated that a tree had interrupted his brief flight.

Callum was going too fast to land and go after him. He soared back into the sky, flaring his wings to execute a tight turn. He sensed the hellhound struggling to his feet, wisely staggering deeper into the cover of the trees rather than facing him out in the open. His life-force blurred, going thin and wispy like fog before vanishing utterly.

Gone invisible. As Rory had reminded him, he couldn't detect hellhounds when they did that.

It would have been safer to stay in the air, but Callum dropped to the ground. If the hellhound did try to ambush him, he'd just have to rely on his own reflexes. The creature would have to return to corporeal form to attack him, giving him a split-second to react and counterattack.

Right now, that was the least of his worries.

Flames licked at the tires of the crashed car. An ominous dripping sound came from the car's engine, indicating a fuel leak. In his previous career as an urban firefighter, he'd attended enough car collisions to recognize the danger signs. The whole vehicle could go up at any moment.

The two lives inside the vehicle beat strong and steady, but one was unconscious and the other was just an infant. Neither would be able to get out on their own in time.

Callum didn't waste time trying to shift and force the driver's door. Hellhounds were just as strong as any other type of shifter; if the burly man hadn't been able to get it open, it was unlikely that he himself could.

Instead, he galloped around to the far side of the vehicle. A quick assessment of the positions of the people inside; then he spun, kicking both back hooves into the front passenger-side door. Metal crumpled. Shifting back into human form, he yanked the now-destroyed door off its hinges, hurling it away.

The smoke was getting thicker. Coughing, he crawled into the crashed car. To his relief, the air in here was clear. Neither of them could have suffered any damage from smoke inhalation yet.

In fact, the infant's lungs were definitely healthy. Her high, outraged screams cut through him. His pegasus surged forward, nearly mad with the need to comfort and protect the young one.

Be quiet, Callum shouted—not at the baby, but at his unruly animal. Turning into an enormous winged horse in the middle of a Ford Fiesta would *not* help the situation.

A dark-haired woman slumped over the airbag in the driver's seat. Instinct screamed at him to grab her and get her out of the car, but the baby had to come first. He crawled through the gap between the front seats, having to contort himself like a pretzel to reach the baby car seat clipped into the back.

"Shhh, shhh," he murmured as he tried to work out how the hell the damn harness unfastened. Giving up, he pulled his utility knife out of his belt and started sawing through the straps. "It's okay. I'm here."

To his surprise, her wails faded into hiccups. Her wide green eyes fixed on his face. Callum didn't know the first thing about babies, so he couldn't guess at her age, but she seemed to understand that he was trying to help her.

"That's it. Everything will be fine." For once, words came easily. He kept up a stream of soothing, meaningless babble as he untangled her from the harness. "There's my girl. Up you come."

Her little hands fisted in his shirt. Something in his chest seemed to crack open as her small body nestled trustingly against him. He suddenly felt as though the most precious treasure in the world had been placed into his arms. Cradling her in the crook of one elbow, he wriggled back into the front of the car.

Freeing the woman turned out to be much easier, thankfully. *Carrying* her, on the other hand, was considerably more difficult. She groaned, stirring, as he bodily dragged her out of the vehicle.

"Sorry." With a grunt, Callum heaved her over his shoulder in a fireman's hold. Sparks swirled through the smoke. Even through his protective gear, he could feel the heat of the rising flames licking at his legs.

He sprinted for the drainage ditch, diving into it just in time. Heat blasted across his back with the force of an angry dragon. He covered the woman and the baby with his own body, sheltering them as the car went up in a blazing fireball.

CALLUM! Rory's mental shout echoed the explosion.

I'm fine, he sent back. *We're all fine.*

Callum risked a glance over the top of the drainage ditch. Now that the fuel had burned off, the car had settled into a crackling nest of flames. From experience, he could tell that there was little risk of further explosions. On his old crew, this would have been the point where they'd close in to put out the fire.

No immediate danger here, he reported to Rory. Several trees were still burning, but this far into fall, the forest was too wet for the fire to spread easily. *Can't sense the hellhound. Went invisible.*

Fenrir's going after him. Seren too. Rory's broad-winged shadow swept over his head. *I'll stay in the sky just in case our firebug friend is still hanging around. The others are coming to handle the fire. I take it you got anyone in the car out in time. What's their status?*

Callum looked down at the bundle of baby in his arms. *Adorable.*

There was a moment of deafening silence from Rory. *Uhhh...what?*

He hadn't meant to send that thought telepathically. He mentally shook himself, trying to focus. *Woman and a baby. Both stable, but the woman is unconscious.*

Wystan's on his way. A hint of amusement rippled through the griffin shifter's telepathic communication. *And we'll rescue you from the baby as soon as we can. Just sit tight, okay?*

Callum sent a wordless acknowledgement and cut the connection. He sat back on his heels, giving the baby a more careful inspection. She stared back at him just as intently, as though she was evaluating him too. There was something strangely familiar about that focused, unwavering green gaze.

Ours, whispered his pegasus.

He snorted. *That seems unlikely. Particularly if that is indeed her mother.*

Surely he would have remembered making love to such a stunning woman. And yet, and yet...there was something familiar about her. As though he'd met her in a dream, or another life...

He shook his head free from the fanciful thought. Shifting the baby to a more comfortable position on his hip, he knelt to check on her mother.

Even though he knew it was inappropriate, he couldn't help appreciating the woman's lush curves as he rolled her into the recovery position. A strange thrill ran up his arm as he brushed her glossy, raven-black hair back from her striking face. There was a mark on her forehead showing where she must have hit her head, but otherwise she seemed uninjured.

His fingers ached to trace the curve of her cheek. He had a sudden mad, burning need to discover whether her lips were truly as soft as they looked.

What was *wrong* with him? It had been a long time since he'd been intimate with anyone other than his own right hand, but that didn't excuse ogling a trauma victim.

Even if she made his inner stallion paw at the ground...

Getting a firm grip on his inner animal, he reached for the woman's wrist to take her pulse. She stirred at his touch, letting out a low moan. Her fingers flexed, clutching anxiously at him, then letting go. Her hand swept across the ground as if she was searching for something.

In a flash of intuition, Callum understood. He caught her hand, guiding it to her child. The infant made a happy chirp of recognition, gripping her mother's fingers.

"It's all right." He folded his own hand over both of theirs, holding them together. "She's safe. You're safe. You're both safe now."

The woman gasped in relief. Her eyelashes fluttered.

"Beth?" she whispered. Her fingers twitched under his. In a sudden convulsive movement, she tried to sit up. "Beth!"

"Lie still." Callum put his free hand on the woman's shoulder, holding her down. "You were in a car crash. You could be injured."

She shook her bruised head, though he could tell the movement had to hurt. Her eyes never left her daughter. "I don't matter. Beth's the one that's important. Is she all right?"

"She's fine." She was, in fact, becoming increasingly wiggly. He adjusted his grip, holding her out so that the woman could see her better. "Look, here she is."

"Beth, oh, my baby, my baby." The woman clutched at the child, her breathing going ragged. Shock must be catching up with her. Her voice wavered, then firmed. She was clearly forcing herself to be calm for the sake of her daughter. "It's okay, sweetie, everything's fine. Mommy's just, just having a little rest. You need to let the nice man hold you for a minute, okay?"

The woman lifted her head, finally tearing her attention away from her daughter long enough to meet his eyes.

MINE

He'd heard his friends talk about that first shock of recognition when they'd met their mates. Rory had said it was like being hit by lightning; a primal force of unimaginable power coursing through every cell in his body. Wystan had described it as the whole world tilting, suddenly revolving around his mate instead of the sun. Joe, for once short on words, had simply said: *Everything changed.*

He'd always thought they'd been exaggerating.

Now, looking into the infinity of her eyes, Callum knew that they hadn't. They'd been struggling to explain something unexplainable, with metaphors that were pale, feeble shadows of the real thing. No words could capture the immensity of the shift in his soul.

She was his, and he was hers. Would always be hers. *Had* always been hers. He just hadn't known it until now.

She froze as well, eyes locked onto his face. "*You.*"

"Yes," he breathed.

Sheer joy filled him like light. She *knew* him. Recognized him as the other half of her soul, just as she was his.

But…she wasn't a shifter.

Despite the way that she was staring at him, her life-force was completely human. Incandescently bright in his senses, true, blazing with vitality…but human. She didn't have the distinctive two-tone duality that marked someone who shared their soul with an animal.

So how could she be looking at him with such unmistakable recognition?

"Oh no." The woman's face had gone pale. She shook her head again, sharp and urgent, as though she could deny his entire existence. "No, no, no. It *is* you."

Dismay sliced through his joy. Somehow she knew he was her mate, and…she didn't want him?

The woman's eyes flicked from him to the baby. She let out a high, somewhat hysterical laugh, and buried her face in her hands. "Oh God. Your expression…you already know, don't you?"

He knew that his heart beat only for her. He knew that he would die for her, and her child—no, *his* child now. His pegasus had been right after all. He might not share genes with the baby in his arms, but he would share everything else, his whole life, always.

Callum wanted to explain all that to his mate, to wipe away the apprehension in her face. But he was the one who was bad with words. Bad with people. He would get it wrong.

"This isn't what I planned," the woman muttered to herself. "This is all wrong. You weren't supposed to meet her like this."

And now Callum was even more baffled. He glanced down at the baby, who was sucking on one fist, still watching him with that rather unnerving focus.

"You mean your daughter?" he asked.

The woman dropped her hands. She took a deep breath, as though having to steel herself.

"Our daughter," she said. "You're her father, Callum."

CHAPTER 3

Oh no. I broke him.

It was like her words had been some sort of magic curse, turning Callum from a living man into a stone statue. Diana didn't think he was even still *breathing*.

A truly horrific possibility occurred to her. He was looking so blank, as though he didn't remember…

"Oh no," she breathed. "Um. You do know who I am, right? Los Angeles, last March?"

"Los Angeles," he whispered, his lips barely moving. "I was in Los Angeles. The charity event."

He *had* seemed to recognize her. But she still had a horrible suspicion that he didn't know how the night had ended. *She* was foggy enough on the details, and he'd drunk at least four times what she had.

"I, I'm so sorry," she babbled, anxiety loosening her tongue. "I mean, you seemed enthusiastic enough when I barged into your hotel room and jumped you, but in retrospect you were *really* not in a fit state to be making decisions. Neither was I, not that I'm trying to make any excuses. And I absolutely don't expect you to just take my word for it that you're Beth's father. Of course I'll pay for a paternity test, if you want."

"No." His shell-shocked expression didn't change. "No need."

It *was* pretty obvious. Now that Diana could finally see Beth side-by-side with her father, there could be no doubting that they were related. Beth got her warm bronze skin tone from Diana's side of the family, but her green eyes and thick, curly red-gold hair were pure Callum. Even with the baby fat rounding her cheeks and plumping out her chin, the shape of her face was eerily similar to his.

"I'm really sorry to spring this on you like this," Diana said. "It's just, just that I thought it was wrong to hide something this big from you. And it's important to me that Beth has a chance to know her biological father. I know this must be a heck of a surprise."

From his frozen rigidity, that was the world's biggest understatement. She might have been the one who had just been in a car crash, but he was the one who seemed to have gone into shock. She was honestly starting to get worried that he might go down like a cut tree at any moment.

"I'm sorry I didn't tell you earlier. I wanted to, I really did. But I, um..." She could feel her face heating. "I didn't know how to find you. I didn't even know your name until a few weeks ago."

He blinked, once.

"I did try, I really did," she hurried on. "I must have called every fire station in California, but nobody recognized your description. It never occurred to me that you were on a hotshot crew in another state. I didn't even know that sort of thing existed. But then I happened to turn on the TV, and there was this piece on the news about the firefighters battling the latest wildfires, and there you were. Doing an interview."

Well, it had been kind of an interview. The reporter had been doing most of the talking. Diana still couldn't figure out why the editor had cut out most of Callum's responses. He was so witty and charismatic, it seemed a waste to just have him standing around looking brooding and stoic and devastatingly attractive.

Much as he was doing now. Maybe it was just her still-wild post-pregnancy hormones, but holy hotness, he was even better-looking than she'd remembered. When they'd last met, his easy smile had charmed her socks off, but that was nothing compared to the way the straight, serious set of his jaw had her panties melting now.

There was a kind of fierce, burning intensity to him that she could have sworn hadn't been there before. If she hadn't already been lying on the ground, she was pretty sure her knees would have given way from the sheer masculine power he exuded.

Fun-off-duty Callum had been sexy enough to get her knocked up. At this rate, there was serious danger that at-work-in-uniform Callum was going to leave her impregnated with octuplets.

"Interview," he murmured. He drew in a sharp breath, as though something had just clicked in his head. "So *that's* why Joe..."

"Why Joe what?" Diana asked, when he didn't go on.

He shook his head, very slightly. "Never mind. So you saw me on TV."

"I know, right? What are the odds?" She forced a smile, hoping to spark one in return. "It almost makes you believe in fate, doesn't it?"

Her attempt at levity shriveled in the face of the unwavering furnace-blast of his stare. His face was still utterly frozen, emotionless, giving away nothing of his thoughts.

In contrast, Diana felt stripped naked. Those penetrating green eyes seemed to look straight into her soul.

"Anyway," she said nervously. "I finally got your name, and the reporter said that you were with the Thunder Mountain Hotshots, and well…here I am. With Beth. Who's your daughter."

She wished that he would smile, or frown, or *something*. Anything. She didn't have a clue what was going on in his head.

She swallowed hard. "Please say something."

He took a deep breath, mouth opening—but then his head snapped to one side, as though someone had called his name. For the briefest instant, she thought she saw relief flash across his face.

"They're here," he said.

Diana started to sit up to see who he meant, but he pushed her flat again. The fierce look he shot her suggested that he was fully prepared to pin her down with his own body to hold her still if necessary.

The mental image of exactly what *that* would be like made embarrassing heat shoot through her. She stayed still, hoping that Callum couldn't tell how the mere contact of his hand on her shoulder made her pulse pound.

You probably have a concussion, Gertrude informed her. *You're acting like an idiot, and he can totally tell. As soon as he can, he's going to run for the hills. You've made a complete mess of this.*

The earth under her cheek vibrated. Distantly, she heard the roar of a car engine—no, something bigger than a car, a truck—then slamming doors and raised voices. From her position flat in the ditch, she couldn't see what was happening, but from the sounds of booted feet the rest of Callum's hotshot crew had turned up.

"Oh!" Diana gasped, her heart thudding for an entirely new reason. In all the shock of seeing Callum, she'd entirely forgotten about the previous events. Now it all came crashing back. The creepy man, her car skidding out of control, the *fire—*

Callum's hand tightened on her shoulder, as though he'd read her mind. "It's all right. He's gone. My crew will contain the fire. You're safe now." He straightened, raising his voice. "Wystan!"

A man jumped down into the ditch, joining them. Like Callum, he wore beige firefighter gear, but he also had a medical case marked with a red cross clipped to his belt. Sunlight gleamed from his white-blond hair as he knelt down next to Diana.

"Hello." The newcomer offered her a polite, professional smile. His fingers were cool on her wrist as he took her pulse. "I'm Wystan. I'm a paramedic. Do you have any pain?"

"I'm fine," Diana said, though in truth her skull was pounding like someone had been using it as a kettledrum. "Please, you have to check on Beth first. Is she okay?"

"I'm certain that she's fine," Wystan said soothingly. His swift hands moved lightly over her neck and spine, then ran down her arms. "Baby car seats are marvelous at protecting infants through this sort of thing. But I know you're worried, so as long as you promise not to move, I'll check up on her now."

Diana tried to look exceedingly meek and co-operative. "I promise."

Wystan gave her another smile, then turned to Callum. He held out his hands. "I'll take it from here, Cal. You can go help the others with the fire."

Callum hesitated. It might have been her imagination, but his arm seemed to tighten around Beth, holding her possessively out of the paramedic's reach for a moment.

Then his shoulders dropped. He passed Beth over.

The instant she left his arms, her face crumpled. Her bottom lip started to tremble.

From the way Wystan's eyes widened, he was fully aware that he'd just been handed a grenade without the pin. He held Beth at arm's-length, his rising voice betraying his panic. "Oh dear. It's all right, little one. Please don't—"

"WAAAAAAAAAAH!"

Diana instinctively tried to reach for Beth, but Callum got there first. Shooting Wystan a vicious glare, he plucked the wailing baby out of his arms. He propped her up against his shoulder, patting her back. Her screams morphed into hiccupping, betrayed sobs.

"I'm so sorry," Diana said to Wystan. "She's not very good with strangers."

Wystan, who was looking somewhat shell-shocked, nodded in the direction of Callum. "She seems fine with *him*."

"Not a stranger," Callum grunted.

Wystan's eyebrows rose. "Oh, you know each other?"

"Um." Diana could feel a blush rising in her cheeks again. "Sort of. It's a long story."

Wystan's gaze moved from Beth's face to Callum's. He did a distinct double-take. "My word. That's uncanny. Callum, is that…your niece?"

Callum hesitated, and Diana's heart jumped into her mouth. Of course he would be tempted to claim that Beth was a more distant relative. He'd only just found out about her, after all, and now here he was being put on the spot by his colleague. He wouldn't want to publicly acknowledge her, not so soon—

"No," Callum said firmly. He unzipped his jacket, shifting Beth from one shoulder to the other so he could shrug out of each sleeve in turn. "She's my daughter."

He'd claimed her. Despite everything, a jolt of pure happiness went through her. *He'd claimed her.* Beth had a daddy.

Wystan, for his part, could not have looked more flabbergasted if Callum had announced Beth had been fathered by the Pope. "*What? How?*"

"The usual way," Callum said curtly. With a deft flick, he spread the thick material out on the ground like a blanket. "Be gentle with her."

"But—wait, what? You—she—when—er. Yes. Well." Wystan cleared his throat, regaining some of his previous professional attitude, although his eyebrows were still up in his hairline. "This is clearly going to require some time to explain. For now, perhaps you could help keep—Beth, was it?—calm while I examine her."

Callum nodded. He laid Beth down on his jacket. Beth squirmed, trying to flip herself over to her front.

"Careful," Diana warned. "She's a champion crawler. If you give her the slightest opening, she'll bolt. I swear she must be part racehorse."

She'd meant it as a joke, but both men twitched. She distinctly saw Wystan side-eye Callum, who made the slightest head-shake in response. The paramedic blew out his breath, returning his attention to Beth. The whole thing took less than two seconds, but Diana had the oddest sense that the two men had just had an entire silent conversation.

Beth kicked in protest as Wystan attempted to check her legs. Callum bent down lower, his forehead nearly touching Beth's. His solemn expression never changed, but Beth gurgled in delight, as if he'd made a silly face at her. She grabbed at his nose. Callum winced, but let her maul him as she pleased while Wystan quickly checked her over.

"Well, she's certainly as healthy as a, er, horse, in any event," the paramedic announced after a few moments. He straightened. "Now let's see about you...I'm sorry, I don't know your name. Callum, won't you introduce your, um, lady friend?"

This time, she definitely *wasn't* imagining the panic that flashed across Callum's face. He froze, looking at her helplessly.

Diana burst into giggles, relieved that for once she wasn't the only one feeling awkward. "I'm sorry. I forgot to tell you *my* name, didn't I?"

Wystan looked even more confounded. "I'm sorry, you have a child together but...you don't know each other's names?"

"*Very* long story," Callum said, in a tone that promised immense woe unto anyone who dared to inquire further.

Diana smothered her giggles. She held out her hand to Wystan, as best she could from flat on the ground. "I'm Diana. Diana Whitehawk. That's Beth."

"A pleasure to meet you," Wystan replied, taking her hand and dipping his head in an honest-to-God old-fashioned bow. He cast a slightly pained look at Beth, who was now enthusiastically attempting to ascend Mount Callum. "At least, as long as you don't feel the need to scream in my face."

Diana pressed her lips shut on another giggle. Oh no, she was definitely teetering on the border of hysteria. Even the pain in her head was starting to feel vaguely unreal. She had to hold herself together, for Beth's sake.

Callum shot her another of those sharp, peculiar glances. She had a sudden mad hunch that he knew what she was feeling, no matter how she tried to hide it.

He turned to Wystan. "Head injury. And she's going into shock."

"Thank you, I *am* a trained paramedic," Wystan said, a little tartly. He was once again examining her neck, fingers probing at each vertebra. "But I agree with your diagnosis. Diana, you don't seem to have any spinal injuries. I'm going to help you sit up now, but I need you to take it slowly, and tell me if you experience even the slightest dizziness or discomfort, all right?"

He started to slip an arm around her—and a sudden, sharp sound made Diana jump. Wystan paused, not quite touching her. He stared at Callum, startled bafflement written across his features.

"Sorry." Callum's expression was as blank as a wall, but one of his boots scraped against the ground in an odd, repetitive motion, like an agitated horse pawing at the ground. He stilled the instant he realized she was watching. "Let me help."

Wystan looked like he was now wondering if *Callum* could be suffering from a concussion, but he moved over to give his colleague room. Callum shifted Beth to his other hip, crouching down so he could assist as well.

A little thrill went through Diana as she curled her arm around Callum's strong neck. It was weird, because objectively Wystan was just as attractive, but she didn't have to fight a crazy urge to slip her fingers under *his* collar.

Callum's muscles flexed under her palm. The two firefighters helped her up, supporting her so carefully that it felt like she floated to her feet. The world spun for a moment, then steadied.

"All right?" Callum asked her.

She nodded, cautiously at first, then with more certainty. "I think so. I have a headache, but it's not too bad."

"I'll give you something for that, but let's get you somewhere more comfortable first." Wystan kept his shoulder braced under her arm, though Callum was the one taking most of her weight. "Do you think you could walk a little? Our crew transport is parked just over there. Or would you prefer someone to carry you?"

"I can walk," Diana assured him.

At the same time, Callum said, "I'll carry her."

"But you need to carry Beth," Diana pointed out.

"I'd offer to do that, but I don't think she likes me very much," Wystan said, one eyebrow quirking in self-deprecation. "For the sake of all our ears, I think we'd better not disturb her."

Beth had settled against Callum's shoulder, her curly head nestled against his neck. Diana had never seen her trust anyone so readily before. It was as if she somehow knew, by scent or touch or some deep animal instinct, that he was her father.

In return, Callum seemed to know just how to hold her. For all his grim face, there was a clear tenderness in the way he cradled Beth, one hand underneath her, the other spread protectively across her back.

Some of the hard lump of anxiety she'd been carrying around melted away. Beth and Callum looked so natural together. She'd done the right thing. It was going to be okay.

Then her gaze fell on the burned-out shell of her wrecked car, down the road behind Callum. A small group of people in firefighter uniforms were working around it, beating out the smoldering fires in the vegetation surrounding the crashed vehicle. She remembered the jet of flame shooting out of nowhere, her sheer terror as she desperately stomped on the brakes...

And the words of the burly man: *Nobody will get hurt...as long as your boyfriend does exactly what we want.*

Her attacker had been lurking around the base in order to target Callum. He'd gone after her because he'd thought he could use her as some kind of hostage. He'd gone after *Beth*.

Ice-cold fear crystallized into a sharp, spiky mass in her chest. She'd worried that Callum might reject Beth, or that he wouldn't be a good, loving father to her. Not even in her worst anxiety-spiral had she ever imagined that she might be bringing her baby into danger.

What have I done?

CHAPTER 4

"Callum, what the hell is going on?" Blaise barged into the crew kitchen, with Rory, Edith, and Joe hot on her heels. They were all still sweaty and soot-stained from putting out the car fire. "Wystan has this crazy notion that you're that baby's *dad?*"

He didn't pause in chopping up carrots. "I am."

"Oh no." Blaise jabbed an accusing finger at him. "It is not possible. There is not a single universe in which you have a secret baby. Joe, I would believe. You? Never."

"Hey!" Joe protested. "Okay, I admit, I was a man-slut. But I was always an *ethical* man-slut. The only thing I ever left a woman with was a satisfied smile. No broken hearts. No accidents."

"And if even *you* could manage to be careful, there's no way Callum wouldn't be," Blaise said. "Come on, Cal. That can't possibly be your kid."

There were times when having a reputation for taciturnity was a distinct advantage. He shrugged one shoulder and carried on chopping.

Finger-sized, lightly steamed, Diana had instructed. She hadn't said what size finger. Her finger? His finger? Average-length fingers? What *was* the average length of a finger? Maybe he should Google it.

Rory also seemed to have fingers on his mind. He was counting backward on his own, folding them down one after another. He looked up again, brow furrowed. "Cal, I have enough younger siblings that I know babies. And that one is at least ten months old. That means she has to have been conceived sometime around last March."

"Busted!" Blaise crowed. "Cal, you weren't even in *America* then."

"I was. Los Angeles."

It was, in fact, entirely true. And from what Diana had said about barging into a hotel room, he really *could* be Beth's father.

Which only made matters worse.

"—not buying it," Blaise was saying. He hoped he hadn't missed too much of her sentence while he'd been lost in thought. "You never mentioned going to Los Angeles."

He slid the carrots into the simmering water. "I don't tell you everything."

Diana, he had to find something for Diana as well. She might be hungry. What would she like? There was too much to do. He cast around for a piece of paper. A list, he needed to make a list.

"You're not telling us *anything*," Blaise said, interrupting his switch-backing train of thought. She planted herself firmly in his path, arms folded. "Callum! Stop running around and talk to us!"

"Can't." He could barely keep enough focus on the conversation to form coherent replies. His attention kept skipping to Diana and Beth. They were tucked away in the infirmary, being treated by Wystan. Were they safe?

His mind skittered like a spider over the web of lives all around. He could detect Seren and Fenrir combing through the forest down by the road. Both the hellhound and the shark shifter had special senses of their own. Rory must have sent them out to follow the trail of the man who had attacked Diana. From the way they were moving —a methodical, sweeping search pattern—it was clear they hadn't managed to pick up his scent yet.

Callum cast his own senses wider, searching for any hint of threat. Mice, squirrels, deer, a distant bear—

"*Cal.*" The hint of alpha power in Rory's voice snapped him back into the kitchen. The griffin shifter's eyes were concerned, but his jaw was set in his *I am your boss as well as your friend* expression. "I'm sorry, but you really do have to explain yourself. Who is that woman? Why is she here in the first place? Why does she think you're the father of her child?"

He needed to cook the carrots. He needed to guard the base. He needed to baby-proof a cabin and come up with a plausible story to tell them all and persuade Diana that she could trust him and take her in his arms and kiss her until she saw stars.

Yes, his pegasus interjected. *That last one.*

There were a million and one things to do. His head was a swarm of angry bees. He couldn't *concentrate*. He just wanted them all to go away and give him space.

"Rory." Alone out of all of them, Edith wasn't staring at him with accusing eyes. She tugged on her mate's sleeve. "One question at a time. Can't you tell Cal's barely holding it together? You're just making things worse."

Anyone who thought autistic people couldn't be empathic was flat-out wrong. Somehow, she always seemed to understand him even better than his friends who'd grown up with him.

It was probably because she *hadn't* grown up with him. She'd only ever known him as an adult. An individual.

She saw who he was. Not just who he wasn't.

"Edith's right," Joe said. "Back off, bros. Cal, your pan's boiling over."

He spun round. Foaming water was cascading out from under the lid, threatening to douse the burner beneath. He hastily yanked off the rattling lid.

"Let me help, bro." Joe came over to the stove, peering over his shoulder. "What are you making, anyway?"

"Carrot fingers. They're for Beth. Diana said she doesn't like purees. Beth, I mean. Not Diana." He turned in a circle, opening a cupboard as yet another task occurred to him. "Tea. I have to make tea as well. And the carrots have to cool, so Beth can pick them up. Buck's car just turned up the road. B and C squad are with him. Crackers,

Diana said crackers were good too. Herbal tea, peppermint. For Diana. I think Seren and Fenrir just found something. Peppermint tea. Wystan said he might have some."

Rory and Blaise exchanged glances.

"Okaaaaay." Blaise plucked the mug out of his hands. "I'll make the tea. Joe will take care of the food. And for once he won't put chili in it, *will you*, Joe."

"Well, I read that you're meant to introduce babies to as wide a range of tastes as possible," Joe started—then broke off, holding up his hands as Blaise glared at him. "Okay, okay! Bland it is. No chilies. Sea dragon's honor."

"I'll find some crackers." Edith started poking through the cupboards. "You just sit down and rest, Callum."

"Can't. Too much to do. All Beth and Diana's things burned in the car. I have to—"

"Callum." Rory's hands closed firmly over his shoulders. The griffin shifter steered him into the chair. "Sit down before you fly apart. We'll help you. You don't have to do everything alone."

He pressed the heels of his hands into his eye sockets, trying to calm the storm raging within his head. He could sense the rest of the crew heading up the mountain in their vehicles. Soon, there would be even more lives assaulting his senses, human souls, bright and distracting. Trying to concentrate with all *that* going on around him would be like trying to take a calculus exam in a disco.

He had to take care of Beth and Diana. Even if that meant admitting his own limitations.

"I do need help." It was hard to say the words, but a weight lifted from his chest the instant they left his mouth. "Thank you."

"Anytime." Rory took the seat opposite him, resting his forearms on the table. "Callum, why didn't you tell us about Beth?"

"I didn't know about her until today."

Rory nodded, as though he'd been expecting this. "I couldn't imagine you'd just abandon a woman in need. Even if she isn't your one true mate."

He hesitated, but this was one truth that would be impossible to hide. And he found that he didn't *want* to hide it.

"Diana *is* my mate," he said.

Blaise looked up sharply from the box of tea bags she was rummaging through. "*What?*"

"But I thought shifters couldn't live without their mates," Edith said. "Once they've met, I mean."

"We can't." Joe was also staring at him as though he'd just announced that he was a small pink bunny. "At least, not without going stark raving nuts. Believe me, I should know. I mean, I'd only *dreamed* about meeting Seren, and forcing myself to stay away from her all those years still made me a few bananas short of a fruit salad."

"Just a few?" Blaise muttered.

"Cal, I don't believe that you've been hiding the fact that you met your mate eighteen months ago," Rory said. "Even you aren't *that* stoic."

He was worried about that too. Surely, if he'd really met Diana before, if he really was Beth's father, he should *remember*?

"I didn't know that I'd met her." He made himself say the awful possibility out loud. "I don't know *if* I met her."

Blaise blinked. "Huh?"

He put his head in his hands, as though he could somehow forcibly squeeze the memory out. "Apparently Diana and I were in Los Angeles, at the same hotel, on the same night. You know I don't do well with big cities. I was angry about…things, which made it even harder to control my talent. So I took sleeping pills. I don't remember anything that happened after that."

Edith looked horrified. "You think she came into your room and —*without your consent?*"

"No!" He didn't want anyone thinking such a terrible thing about Diana. "Diana had good reason to think that I was fully consenting. I *was* fully consenting, if it actually happened. But *she* might not have been. If, if I truly am Beth's father, it's because Diana came into the wrong hotel room and mistook me for someone else."

"And if you're not, it's because she really *was* with someone else,"

Blaise said slowly. He could tell that pieces were starting to connect in her head.

"Which means..." Rory trailed off, his golden eyes widening as he too came to the obvious conclusion.

"Oh," Joe breathed. For once, words seemed to have deserted the eloquent sea dragon. "Oh, *shit*."

That was exactly his sentiment too.

"Do you know which one it was?" Rory asked him.

He shook his head. "She didn't know his name. Just that he was a firefighter."

"Well, that narrows it down," Blaise said. Then she frowned. "Or, actually, maybe not. Given what they're like."

"Oh come on," Joe said. "Yeah, it's a hilarious trick, but I'm sure they wouldn't take it *that* far."

Knowing them as he did, he didn't share the sea dragon's confidence. "They would."

"Wait, time out. What are you all talking about?" Edith was still looking puzzled. "I'm admit that I'm not great with faces, but that baby looks exactly like you, Callum. How is that possible if you might not be her father?"

Of course, she'd never met either of them. "Someone show her."

Blaise pulled her phone out of her back pocket. She thumbed at the screen for a moment, then, without a word, passed the device to Edith.

"Why are you showing me a picture of Callum?" Edith's brow creased. She peered at the picture more closely. "Wait a sec. Is this Photoshopped?"

"No," Rory, Joe, and Blaise said in unison.

Edith's gaze flicked from the photo to his face and back again. Her own face was baffled. "But then how can there be two Callums in this photo?"

"That's not a picture of me," he said grimly. "That's Connor and Conleth. My brothers."

CHAPTER 5

After all the trauma of the day, Diana could tell that Beth was running on fumes. Normally Beth's favorite thing in the world was her late afternoon cuddle and milk. Today, however, she was fussy and distractible. One moment she would be latched on, sucking as though there was no tomorrow; the next, she would be doing a top-class owl impression, head swiveling and eyes wide.

Diana's voice was going hoarse from singing Beth's favorite lullaby over and over. She desperately wished that Beth would settle, even if just for five minutes. Jumbled questions whirled through her head, all wound about with worry.

Why was that man hanging around the base? Why was he looking for a way to get at Callum? Will he come back? Did he get my license number? Will he be able to track us back home? Why is Callum so different? What on earth is he mixed up with? What's he hiding? Does he really want to be Beth's father, or is it all an act for some awful reason? Should I leave right now? How could I leave? What am I going to do for diapers? Am I the world's worst mother, bringing Beth into all this?

She was too on edge to unpack her anxieties or externalize them. She needed time to process events and her own emotions. If only Beth would give her a few minutes to herself to *think*.

"Come on, baby," she crooned, shoving down the urge to scream. She rocked Beth, trying to keep her turned away from all the distractions in the office. She'd drawn the blinds and turned off the lights to try to encourage Beth to go to sleep, but even in the dimness Beth seemed to find the paperwork scattered across the desk and the dog-eared maps tacked to the rough wooden walls fascinating. "There's nothing interesting to see. It's nap time. You need to sleep. Please, Mommy needs you to go to sleep. *Please.*"

Beth started to settle at last. Her sucking grew slower and sleepier. Her eyelids fluttered.

The office door creaked open.

Diana had never in her life so badly wanted to throttle someone.

"*Go away,*" she whisper-snarled, hunching over Beth and praying that Callum would take the hint and retreat quietly.

"It's *my* office, thank you very much," growled an unfamiliar male voice. "Who the motherloving monkey nuts are you?"

Diana yelped, spinning round. Beth popped off her breast, giving the man in the doorway an eyeful of nipple. *He* yelped and spun round.

"U-um." Diana clutched at herself, covering her chest with her free arm. Beth, seeing the precious boob disappear from view, howled like a banshee. "Callum said I could breastfeed here."

"Did he," the man said in flat tones. He kept his back resolutely turned.

Callum had mentioned earlier that the rest of the crew would be returning that afternoon. Now that she was no longer preoccupied with trying to settle Beth, Diana became aware of the sounds outside —booted feet, car doors slamming, tools rattling as they were unloaded. This man must be the boss. And he obviously had no idea what she was doing in his office.

Diana struggled to do up buttons one handed, juggling an increasingly furious Beth. "I'm so sorry. I'll just—"

"Sit your butt back down," the man interrupted her. He half-turned, still shielding his eyes with one hand. "And for the love of dog, will you give that baby what she wants before my eardrums rupture?"

Diana hesitated. The man shot her a fierce glare from under his hand—or rather, he glared at a point somewhere just above the top of her head, since he was still carefully not looking at her exposed chest.

"I'm not used to having to repeat myself," he snapped. "Feed your kid. Ma'am."

Face hot with embarrassment, Diana got Beth back into position. Beth latched on as if she'd been deprived of sweet, sacred boob for ten months rather than ten seconds. The frantic sucking made Diana wince, but at least Beth's head meant she was no longer flashing the grumpy firefighter.

She drew her shirt as far over her chest as she could. "I really am sorry. I would have fed her somewhere else, but Callum insisted on bringing me here. He said this was the most comfortable chair on the base."

"Being the boss has its perks." The man dropped his hand at last, revealing a weather-beaten, hawkish face. "And at least you're giving me a novel excuse to avoid starting on my paperwork. I'm Superintendent Buck Frazer. I'm in charge around here."

"Diana Whitehawk." Diana spent a second trying to work out how to offer the Superintendent her hand without disturbing Beth, then gave up. "And this is my daughter, Beth."

"Whitehawk," Buck muttered. He studied her face for a moment. "Any relation to Elizabeth Whitehawk?"

"My mother," Diana said, startled. "You knew her?"

"A bit. She was good friends with my sister Wanda, years and years ago. I was sorry to hear that she'd passed away. Mirror Lake disaster, wasn't it?"

The old stab of pain went through Diana as she nodded. She'd only been eight when her mother had died, but some hurts never entirely healed.

Old grief shadowed Buck's fierce face. "Tribe lost a lot of good people that day. The police ever catch the bastard that started the fire?"

"No sir. It was definitely arson, but they never found any leads. They ended up declaring it a random hate crime."

Buck grunted. "Wouldn't be the first time we were targeted like that."

She'd been wondering if he had Native heritage like herself, from the set of his eyes and cheekbones. "Are you Lakota too?"

"On my mother's side. Oglala. Don't really have any contact with the tribe, though, these days. Wanda was always the one who was into that stuff. Kept bugging me to get involved, but I always thought I had better things to do, young jackass that I was. Too late now." Buck shook his graying head, reverting to brisk, business-like tones. "That your burned-out car down the road?"

"Yes, sir. I'm so sorry."

Buck grunted. "No need to 'sir' me. Buck'll do. And what have you got to be sorry about?"

"Everything, sir. I mean, um…Superintendent." Diana had never before met anyone who so effortlessly exuded authority. She couldn't bring herself to be so familiar as to use his given name. She rushed on, "Um, that is, I'm sorry for intruding."

Oh no, I'm just making things worse. From the way Buck's dark eyebrows drew together, her repeated apologies were only annoying him even more.

"I-I'm sorry!" And now she was apologizing for apologizing. *Way to go, Diana, at this rate he'll kick you out before you even have a chance to explain.* "I'll get the wreck towed away as soon as I can. But my cellphone was in the car, and everything burned up, and I haven't had a chance—"

"Stop." Buck held up a hand. "Explain later. You've clearly got more important things to do right now. And so do I."

"I'm sorry," Diana said, and winced.

Buck gave her a curt nod. "Let me know when I can have my chair back. Now, if you'll excuse me, apparently I have to go murder a man."

"Superintendent!" Callum appeared behind Buck, so suddenly he seemed to have materialized out of thin air. "I'm sorry!"

Diana had thought that the glare Buck had given *her* had been fierce enough, but it had been butterflies and rainbows compared to the one he turned on Callum now. "That seems to be a common sentiment around here."

"I meant—to call." From Callum's heaving chest, he must have been sprinting flat out. "But I—forgot."

"You forgot," Buck repeated, in dangerous tones. "You're normally a stickler for following protocol. Yet somehow reporting a serious fire right on our doorstep just *slipped your mind?*"

It was barely perceptible, but Diana thought she saw Callum wince. "It's…been a day."

"It's my fault," Diana said, prompted by an odd urge to defend the firefighter. "Callum's been looking after Beth and me ever since he saved us from the crash. I was a mess after the attack. Please don't blame him for being preoccupied."

"Attack?" Buck said sharply. "This wasn't an accident?"

"No," Callum said. He caught Buck's eye, holding his gaze. "One of Lupa's men."

Lupa. The man who'd attacked her had mentioned that name. But…she hadn't told Callum that yet. How had he known?

He's involved in some kind of gang warfare, Gertrude whispered. *Organized crime. He's wanted by the mob. And now they know you exist, they'll hunt you and Beth to the ends of the earth. She'll never be safe again—*

"Motherfucker," Buck said—then grimaced, glancing at her apologetically. "Sorry. Didn't mean to swear in front of the kid."

"She's ten months old. It's not like she can understand you." Still, Diana appreciated the sentiment. "Who is this Lupa person? A gang leader?"

Buck and Callum exchanged a brief glance. "Something like that," Buck said. "We had some trouble with her lot earlier in the year, at the start of fire season."

"What sort of trouble?"

"Arson," Callum said, succinctly.

She supposed that explained the fireball. No doubt an experienced arsonist knew all sorts of ways to improvise a flamethrower. And if Lupa's gang burned things down for money—or even just for fun—

she could see how they could end up clashing with a hotshot firefighting crew.

Still...she had a feeling in her gut that there was more going on here. Everyone was just being too furtive. Even Callum was barely talking. She smelled a rat, and it made her nervous.

"So those turd-eating dogs *have* been watching us," Buck said to Callum. "You find the motherlover?"

Callum shook his head. "Seren and Fenrir picked up his trail, but lost him at the road. They're still searching. Rory is fl—" He checked himself, flashing the briefest glance at Diana. "Rory's out looking too."

"Hmm. And you don't...?" Buck left the sentence hanging.

Callum shook his head again.

Diana was starting to feel like she was missing half the conversation. Of course, people who worked closely together under difficult conditions *did* tend to have a lot of in-jokes and private references, but this was getting ridiculous.

Buck was frowning again. "I can understand Lupa setting one of her hounds to keep an eye on us, but not why he'd blow his cover to chase after a random visitor. What in the seven bells were you doing all the way up here anyway, Diana? This is a working hotshot base, not a motherloving picnic spot."

"Um." Diana's face heated again. "I was looking for Callum, actually."

One of Buck's eyebrows twitched upward. "You two an item?"

"Not exactly," Diana said, just as Callum said, "Yes."

Buck started to say something, then paused. He looked at Diana as if he was only truly seeing her for the first time. Then he switched his raking stare to Callum. His expression shifted into aggrieved disbelief.

"Oh, for the love of fuzzy little squirrel balls," Buck said in tones of deep disgust. "*Another* one?"

Callum seemed mildly embarrassed. He avoided Buck's eyes.

"How is this my life?" Buck muttered, apparently to himself. "How does this *keep happening?*"

Diana's heart lurched. Of course someone as charismatic and charming as Callum would have women throwing themselves at him.

And evidently she wasn't the first casual fling to track him down to his base in the hope of more.

She couldn't help feeling a pang of jealousy at the thought. Which was utterly ridiculous and unfair of her. They'd only shared a single night, after all. It wasn't like she had any claim to his heart.

Though…why had he told Buck that they were an item?

Buck let out a heavy sigh. "Well, at least it's the end of fire season. Feel free to have all the emotional drama you want on your own time. Just don't make me watch."

"Ah." Callum fidgeted, shifting his weight from side to side. "Diana and Beth need to stay here for a while."

Buck gave him a level look. "What do you think I'm running here? A motherloving motel for lonely hearts?"

"I'm not staying," Diana said quickly. "Don't worry, I understand this is a working facility. I won't be bothering you again. I only came here in the first place so that Callum could meet Beth."

Buck's brow furrowed. "Why would—?" He cut himself off, studying Beth more closely. Then he did the now familiar double-take, staring from Beth to Callum. "Wait. That's *your* kid?"

"Yes." Callum spoke with odd emphasis, like he was expecting someone to contradict him. "She's mine."

Buck contemplated this. When he next spoke, his tone was flat and cold as an arctic plain. "Callum Tiernach-West, the next words out of your mouth had better be 'I didn't know about her.'"

"He *didn't* know about her," Diana put in. "Not until today."

"Good," Buck said. "These are my best boots. I'd hate to have to extract them from an asshole's butt. Now that you *do* know about your kid, Callum, I trust that you'll do the right thing."

"Yes. Which is why Diana and Beth need to stay here." Callum's mouth set in a grim, flat line. "Because I'm not the only one who found out about them today."

Buck's breath hissed between his teeth. "Lupa. Shit."

Callum nodded. "You see now."

Diana's pulse picked up. She'd been trying to tell herself that she was overreacting, that her fears were just her anxiety disorder talking. But Callum and Buck were both clearly taking the threat seriously.

She hugged Beth tighter. "You really think that your enemies will go after me and Beth again in order to get to you?"

"I wouldn't put it past them. They're a nasty bunch." Buck rubbed the back of his neck, thinking. "Where do you live, Diana? Are you local?"

"No. Los Angeles."

Buck's eyebrows rose a little. "Long way." He glanced at Callum. "Maybe it would be far enough."

"Can't risk it," Callum replied. "The pack tracked Joe to Las Vegas, remember."

"Good point." Buck blew out his breath. "What about taking her back to *your* home for the winter? Your folks are in Ireland, right?"

"England. City of Brighton." Callum's lips thinned. "Not an option."

"I should say not!" Diana was getting irritated by the way the two men were talking over her head. "Stop trying to rearrange my entire life without even consulting me. I can't just drop everything and fly overseas!"

"This is the safest place for them," Callum said to Buck. "Wystan's here. Fenrir. The rest of the squad too, at least for a while. They'll all help."

Buck let out another heavy sigh. "Motherloving shif—uh, shifty-eyed weasels. Fine. They can stay."

"No, we can't!" Diana protested. "A firefighter base is no place for a baby."

"I'm in complete agreement with you there," Buck muttered. "What are we going to do, stash her with the chainsaws?"

"Diana." Callum came forward, kneeling so that they were face-to-face. She found herself captured by the intense green of his eyes. "Please. I need to keep you and Beth safe. This is the best place."

This close, his charisma was overwhelming. The late afternoon light caught in his hair, revealing a hundred subtle shades of copper and auburn. She remembered what it had felt like to run her fingers through those short, soft curls as that sensuous mouth trailed kisses down her neck…

She thrust down the memory. "But I can't hide here forever. I have a life back in California."

"Not forever. Just until I've dealt with Lupa." He leaned even closer. One of his hands lifted, then dropped, as if he'd started to reach out to her but then thought better of it. "Once you're safe, we can come up with something more long term. Together."

She broke away from the hypnotic emerald depths of his eyes, looking down at Beth instead. She couldn't let herself be influenced by her own desires. She had to do what was best for her daughter.

Still…if this Lupa woman was as dangerous as Callum and Buck seemed to think, perhaps this really *was* the best place to stay at the moment. An entire crew of muscular hotshots had to be a deterrent to even the boldest arsonist.

And it would give her the opportunity to learn more about Callum. If he was going to be involved in Beth's life, she needed to know everything about him.

"All right," she said. "Just for a while. Until we've figured things out."

"Then that's settled." Buck rubbed his forehead, looking like he was fighting a migraine. "Now where in the name of all that's holy can we put a baby?"

CHAPTER 6

His cabin was a deathtrap.

Callum had never before fully appreciated just how many ways there could be to injure a baby in three small rooms. He was starting to think it was a miracle that *he'd* managed to survive living here this long.

"Bro, chill." Joe switched off the vacuum cleaner he'd been running over the worn carpet. "You don't have to obsess over every square inch of wall. It'll be fine."

He didn't stop his slow, methodical examination. "Have you seen that?"

"You mean in a vision? No." Joe shrugged. "But I haven't seen it *not* being fine. I'm pretty sure I would have gotten a warning if your baby was going to choke on a stray splinter or something."

"Can't take that risk."

Joe's talent for scrying the future in water was useful, but it had its limits. There had been more than a few occasions in the past when the squad had run into difficulties that Joe hadn't foreseen.

His awareness flicked over the surroundings, touching each nearby life—*BuckTannerJessicasquirrelmousemousemouseFenrir*—before settling on one particular cabin, a little way off from his own. He could sense Diana and Beth inside, along with Blaise and Edith. The two women had offered to lend Diana some clothes from their own wardrobes, since most of her own things had been destroyed in the car fire.

With an effort, Callum pulled his attention away from his mate. Much as he wanted to bask in the diamond sparkle of Diana's energy, he had to finish baby-proofing the cabin before they got back.

His searching fingertips found a rough spot on the planed log wall. He rubbed at it with his sandpaper until it was silky-smooth. "Here."

Joe sighed, but obligingly vacuumed up the scattering of sawdust. "Sometimes you can be just a little OCD, you know."

Callum did know. But given the choice of obsessively scheduling every minute of the day to make sure he didn't miss anything, or wandering around in a distracted daze thanks to the life-forms all around, there was only one option.

He still couldn't believe that he'd forgotten to call Buck. He couldn't afford to make any more mistakes.

Finishing his slow circuit of the room, Callum pulled his notebook and a stub of pencil out of his pocket. He wished that he'd had more time to sit down and work through everything properly, but even a scrappy, hastily-scribbled plan was better than nothing.

He ticked off *Check walls*, and consulted the next item. *Block sockets*.

"Electrical sockets," he said to Joe. "Did you bring the tape?"

"Yep." Joe dug into the bag he'd brought with him, emerging again with a roll of duct tape. "Here you go. Hey, what have you got there?"

Callum reflexively hid the small notebook in his hand...and then hesitated. Normally he was careful not to let anyone witness his odder habits. Years of childhood teasing—mostly from his brothers—had taught him that lesson all too well.

But Beth's safety was more important than his pride. He handed Joe the book, swapping it for the duct tape. "To-do list. Can you check it for me?"

"Mop bathroom floor...dry bathroom floor...put away mop and bucket..." Joe's eyebrows ascended as his eyes moved down the list. "Wow, bro. This is, uh, thorough."

Callum tore off a wide strip of tape, and knelt to stick it over the nearest electrical socket. "Let me know if there's anything missing."

Joe's brow creased as he finished scanning the list. He looked up again. "You've forgotten the most important thing."

Now he was glad he'd asked for help. "What?"

Joe handed the notebook back to him. "'Tell Diana the truth.' You know you have to."

"I will." He shoved the notebook back into his pocket. "At the right moment."

Joe gave him a distinctly skeptical look. "And when will that be? As you're ice-skating hand-in-hand through Satan's Winter Wonderland?"

"I *will* tell her," he insisted. "Once…once she knows me. Trusts me."

Joe pinched the bridge of his nose as if he had a sudden headache. "Oh, Sea. Cal. I tried to hide the truth from *my* mate. And I was lucky Seren just whacked me over the head with a blunt object when she found out. How do you think Diana will react when she discovers you've been lying to her about something this important?"

"I'm not lying." Despite his words, a pang of guilt stabbed through his gut. "No matter what happened that night, I *am* Beth's father. Or at least, I will be."

"You'll be cooling in a shallow grave, if Diana has any self-respect. And I'll happily pass her the shovel." Joe dropped his hand, revealing an uncharacteristically serious expression. "Bro. You really have to tell her. Today. And more than that, you have to tell Connor and Conleth too. You three need to compare notes and work out which of you really fathered that baby."

Callum stuck tape over the last socket and straightened. He took out his list again. He needed to update it and move on to the next item before he got distracted and forgot.

"*Bro.*" Joe plucked the notebook out of his hand, using his full six-foot-eight height to keep it out of reach. "Are you listening to me?"

His fists clenched. For a second, he was a child again, furious tears burning his eyes, snatching futilely at thin air as his brothers laughed and tossed his book between them…

"Give that back." With huge effort, he kept his voice level. "I need it."

Joe hesitated, then lowered his arm to offer him the notebook. "Sorry, bro. That was a dick move."

Callum nodded curtly, not trusting himself to speak. Reclaiming his list, he drew a line through *Block sockets*.

Joe let out a long sigh. "Listen, Cal. I don't have to have a vision to know that even if you *are* that kid's dad, things are going to go badly, badly wrong for you if you don't come clean with Diana."

There was only one item remaining on his list: *Make bed*. He *literally* needed to make a bed. Since they didn't have a cot or crib, Diana had said it would be safest for her to sleep on the floor with Beth.

He'd borrowed a couple of camping mats from the storeroom. They weren't exactly comfortable, but maybe if he piled up a few of them…

"Cal." Joe's voice made him start. "I know we haven't always been best buds, but I thought we'd grown closer since we started working together. If something's worrying you, I've got your back, I promise. Talk to me?"

Belatedly, Callum realized that it had been his turn to contribute to the conversation. "Not good at talking."

"Then perform an interpretive dance." Despite Joe's light-hearted words, the sea dragon's turquoise eyes revealed genuine concern. "Or I could fetch some semaphore flags."

"You know semaphore?"

Joe promptly waved his long arms in a sequence that might have indicated *Yes, of course I do*. Then again, given that *he* didn't know semaphore, it could just as easily mean *Help, we're being attacked by giant aquatic squirrels*.

"You have many hidden talents," Callum said, amused.

"Talents, yes. Hidden, no. I've learned my lesson there." Joe picked up a sheet, shaking it out. "Seriously, bro. Why are you so scared of telling Diana about your brothers?"

Callum took the end of the sheet, tucking it under the mattress. "You said yourself that we haven't always been friends."

The sea dragon blinked at him. "I think you skipped a few links in that chain of thought, bro."

"You were *their* friend." Callum met Joe's eyes, steadily. "Before."

Joe fidgeted, looking a little embarrassed. "Yeah, well…back then I had more in common with Conleth and Connor. I mean, let's face it, I was something of a playboy. And you were never exactly keen on coming out partying. Sorry."

"Not blaming you. You just preferred their company. Like everyone."

Joe started to speak—and then paused, staring at him. "Hang on. Are you trying to say that you're worried that Diana might like your brothers better than you?"

Callum looked down, smoothing out a tiny wrinkle in the sheet. "She already liked one of them well enough to *want* to sleep with him. Even if she really did accidentally sleep with me instead."

"But *you're* her true mate. Did you consider the possibility that she was only attracted to your brother because he's like you?"

He made a hollow laugh. "We're nothing alike."

"Apart from, you know, literally being identical."

"Just on the outside." A restless energy filled him. He needed to do something, but he'd finished his list. His hands twitched. "You know them, Joe. They're witty and charming and charismatic. And I'm…me."

Joe looked at him for a long moment. "Yes. And you're Diana's mate. Her perfect match. Not Connor or Conleth. *You.* Maybe you should trust fate on this one, bro."

Much as Callum tried, he couldn't stay still any longer. He restlessly paced the room, sweeping his fingertips across every flat surface to make sure he hadn't missed any dust.

"Maybe," he said. "Or maybe she was attracted to my brother because that's how *I'm* supposed to be. If my talent wasn't…" He gestured at his forehead and heart, indicating his inner animal. "So distracting."

Most pegasus shifters had the ability to sense living creatures, though there were variations in how it manifested. But everyone else was able to turn it off. His brothers and father had never seemed to be the slightest bit bothered by the constant clamor of life-energy.

"Maybe meeting Diana will help with that," Joe suggested. "After all, Wystan only found out how to control his shield talent after he mated Candice."

This hadn't occurred to Callum before. He stilled, hope rising in his chest as he realized Joe was right. Thinking back on it, he was certain that his pegasus's sensitivity had become even worse after that fateful night. Perhaps his pegasus had been subliminally searching for the mate that they'd lost. Didn't that mean that he *had* to be Beth's father?

We are her father, his pegasus insisted. And then, ruining his rising hope, it added, *No matter what happened that night.*

That was less than reassuring, but Callum didn't have time to quiz his pegasus further on the matter now. He could sense Diana approaching the cabin. He hastily did a last sweep, gathering up the cleaning supplies and shoving them back in the bag. "They're on their way back. Is everything ready?"

"You got this, bro." Joe gave him two thumbs up, beaming with confidence. "Just be yourself, okay?"

That was exactly what he *couldn't* be. Not when Diana thought he was one of his brothers.

They went outside to meet the women. Callum's eyes skipped straight over the others to instantly fix on Diana. To his delight, he saw that the haunted, shell-shocked look was gone from her dark eyes. There was more of a spring in her step as she walked between Edith and Blaise, chatting animatedly with them both.

"So you all live here during fire season?" he overheard her ask Blaise.

"That's right," Blaise replied. "Though we're not actually here all that much, apart from at the very beginning and very end of fire season. We get deployed out to fires all across America."

"Sounds intense," Diana said. "And like it doesn't leave much time for family."

That wasn't a line of thought Callum wanted her pursuing too far.

He reached out to Blaise, thrusting an urgent message into her mind. *REASSURE HER!*

Blaise winced, giving him a pained glance. She turned back to Diana, adopting a bright, somewhat over-cheerful tone. "Oh, it's not so bad. I mean, we get a couple of days off every few weeks throughout fire season. And then we get a whole five months of vacation over autumn and winter. Wystan's married to the woman who runs the animal sanctuary just down the road, and they manage to make the schedule work for them."

"Though it's easier for me and Seren," Edith put in. "Since we're on the squad along with our mates, we get to be with them all the time."

Diana looked quizzically at Edith. "Mates?"

"I-I mean," Edith stuttered, flushing. "Uh—um."

"She means partners." Blaise waved at him before Diana could inquire further. "Look, we're here. Hi guys! Did you get the cabin ready?"

"You would not *believe* how ready the cabin is," Joe said. "The only way it could get more ready is if Callum tore it down and rebuilt it from scratch. And I'm pretty sure he's still contemplating doing exactly that."

In fact, what Callum was contemplating was Diana. She'd swapped her torn blouse for a Thunder Mountain Hotshots crew t-shirt that clung to her ripe curves. Her long black hair, now smooth and glossy, hung down her back.

"Hi," she said to him, smiling.

He wanted to fall at her feet and worship her. He wanted to memorize every inch of her perfect body. He wanted to sweep her up in his arms and carry her back into the cabin and lay her down on the mats and—

Her smile was fading fast. With a jolt of horror, Callum realized that he'd just been staring at her in silence.

"You look…" He stalled, unable to think of a word that did justice to her magnificence.

She grimaced, tugging self-consciously at the fabric straining across her glorious breasts. "Like a milk cow stuffed into Spandex. I know. Blaise's clothes would have been tight on me even before I had Beth. All you people are outrageously fit. Maybe I should take up fire-fighting."

"It's the best job in the world," Edith said, beaming. Then she looked down at Beth, who was sleeping in her arms, wrapped up in a blanket. Her smile flickered a bit. "Though...not exactly compatible with having a baby."

"I was joking. I could never do what you do." Diana patted Edith on the arm, then took Beth from her. "Thank you for watching her while I showered. You're really good with her."

"Well, she was asleep." Edith's expression didn't change, but her left hand moved in a short, repetitive motion, rubbing the fabric of her jeans. It was one of her subtler stims, which she used when she was feeling self-conscious. "I just had to keep rocking her. If she'd woken up, I wouldn't have known what to do. I don't know the first thing about babies."

"I'll tell you a secret." Diana leaned in close, dropping her voice into a whisper. "Neither do I. I'm just making it up as I go along."

Joe laughed. "I think everyone does."

That wasn't very reassuring. Improvisation had never been his strong point.

Diana's gaze flicked to him. Callum became aware that he was hanging back on the edge of the group, outside the circle of conversation. He made himself step forward, and cleared his throat.

Connor would have made some awful joke to make her eyes sparkle. Conleth would have charmed her with a smile and a clever compliment.

All he could manage to get out was, "Ready for dinner?"

"I'm *always* ready for dinner." Diana made a face, plucking again at her tight t-shirt. "Breastfeeding is supposed to help you lose weight, but apparently my body didn't get that memo. I'm constantly ravenous."

Snacks. He had to lay in snacks. He didn't dare get out his list and make a note. He tried to fix the reminder in his mind. The life-forms of the rest of the crew tugged at his awareness, distracting him.

"Everyone's gathering in the mess hall," Callum said, gesturing at the large building. "That way."

Diana hesitated. "Um…maybe it would be better if I just had a sandwich or something in the cabin."

"Coming right up," Joe said. "I'll just go and—"

"No," he interrupted. "Diana, you need a proper meal after the day you've had."

"Really, I'm fine," she insisted. "I'm sure it will be easier for everyone if I just eat privately in my room."

"There's no table. You won't be comfortable."

Joe caught his eye. *Bro,* the sea dragon sent telepathically. *What are you doing?*

He couldn't juggle two conversations at once. He blocked out the mental communication, concentrating on Diana. He *had* to persuade her to join the squad.

Diana was still looking dubious. "But Beth might wake up."

"I'll hold her while you eat." Callum was already missing the warm, baby-scented weight of his daughter in his arms. "Please. You've had to look after her on your own for so long. You need a break."

Diana bit her lip. "I don't want to intrude on your work colleagues."

"They're not just my colleagues." He gestured round at Blaise, Edith, and Joe. "They're my family. I want you to meet them."

Diana's shy smile dazzled him. "Well, in that case…I'd love to."

Callum offered her his arm. She slipped her hand through—just the slightest weight, yet it nearly knocked him to his knees. He tried not to give any indication of the heat raging through him at that tiny contact.

Behind Diana, Blaise flashed him a quizzical look. *What was that all about?*

I really do want her to meet everyone, he sent back as he led Diana toward the mess hall. *But more importantly…I need your help.*

CHAPTER 7

The men of the Thunder Mountain Hotshots were everything Diana had expected. Tough. Rugged. Full of confident, masculine power.

What she *hadn't* expected was that every single one of them would go absolutely ga-ga over a baby.

As soon as she walked into the mess hall with Beth in her arms, she was ringed by a crowd of adoring firefighters. It was like starring as the Virgin Mary in a Christmas nativity pageant, if the wise men and shepherds were all being played by improbably muscular men.

"Lookit the little critter," crooned a hulking man who looked like he wrestled grizzly bears as light entertainment. "Who's a precious sweetie bunny?"

"Shh," hissed a short Latino man, elbowing the other firefighter in the ribs. "Can't you see she's sleeping?"

"Let us know if you need anything, ma'am," a third man said to Diana. He too was gazing at Beth like she was the Second Coming. "Anything at all."

Callum's arm flexed under her hand. He drew her closer to his side. Maybe he was just trying to shield Beth from the worshipping horde, but the possessive gesture made an illicit thrill shoot through her.

"What she needs is food," he said, glaring around at his colleagues. "And space."

The crowd broke up with clear reluctance. The firefighters tiptoed back to the long tables lining the room, with many longing backward glances. Diana was rather amused to notice that the few woman in the crew had remained at their places throughout. Apparently it was only the *male* firefighters who melted into puddles at the sight of an infant.

Callum led her to a table in the corner of the room. The paramedic she'd met earlier, Wystan, was already seated there, along with a stocky man and a woman with short blonde hair and burn scars on one side of her face.

"Hello again," said Wystan, smiling. "You're looking better."

"I'm feeling better," Diana replied, taking a seat on the bench that Callum had drawn out for her. "Everyone's been very kind."

"Just doing our job." Wystan gestured at the woman sitting next to him. "I hope you don't mind, but I took the liberty of inviting my wife Candice to join us for dinner."

"Which is Wystan's way of saying I bullied him into it," Candice said, flashing a grin as she held out a hand. "When I heard that Callum had a surprise baby, there was no way I could sit at home and wait to hear the gossip second-hand."

Diana shifted Beth to one arm so she could shake Candice's hand. The woman had a *very* firm grip, and a palm rough with calluses. "I think Blaise mentioned you. You aren't a firefighter?"

"Nope. I run the horse sanctuary at the base of Thunder Mountain." Candice's bright, sharp gaze swept over Diana like a laser scanner. "Pleased to meet you. And also very surprised."

"As are we all," said the stocky blond man on the other side of the table. He had the most arresting eyes Diana had ever seen; tawny gold, like some great bird of prey. He too was studying her with intense interest. "I'm Rory. Callum's squad boss, as well as his childhood friend."

Diana shook his hand too, smiling back. "So you're the one I should ask to find out all his secrets?"

She'd meant it as a joke, but Rory twitched, his own smile turning a little fixed. His gaze flickered to Callum for the briefest instant. "Have a seat. We fixed you a plate. Hope you aren't expecting gourmet cuisine, though."

What is Callum hiding? The warm glow Diana had been feeling chilled, worry curdling once more in the pit of her stomach. It was clear that Rory knew something, and was covering for his friend.

She'd have to press harder later. Right now, she had more urgent matters on her mind—or rather, her stomach. The rich smell of chicken stew and dumplings had her mouthwatering, but the backless bench made it difficult to hold Beth and eat at the same time. She squirmed, trying to find a way to support her arm.

"Here." Callum held out his hands. "I'll take her."

Don't give her to him. You can't trust him. He'll drop her or run off or—

Diana tuned out Gertrude. Whatever Callum was hiding, he'd already proven that he was gentle and caring with Beth. After all, he *was* her father.

Carefully, she transferred Beth into Callum's arms. Beth stirred a little, snuggling closer into his chest, then fell back into deep, peaceful slumber.

"Now there's a sight I never thought I'd see," Rory said, the corner of his mouth hooking up in wry amazement. "Callum with a baby."

The opening was too good to pass up. She hastily swallowed the bite of chicken stew she'd just taken, clearing her mouth. "Why's that?"

"Because we all thought Callum's love life was nonexistent," Blaise said before Rory could respond. "As far as I know, he's never had a girlfriend."

Diana blinked in surprise. "Really?"

Callum rocked Beth, his expression unreadable. "Waiting for the right woman."

That was sweet. And also kind of weird, given that he'd been perfectly willing to hop into bed with *her*. He'd flirted so effortlessly, she couldn't believe she was his only one night stand.

Maybe he just doesn't tell his friends about meaningless random encounters, she decided. He'd called his squad mates his family. You didn't bring casual flings home to meet your family.

But he'd invited *her*.

She didn't know what to think about that. She applied herself to her dinner instead, letting the topic drop. After ten months of bolting down her food one-handed in snatched, scattered moments, it felt weird to be holding a knife as well as a fork.

Everyone else seemed to feel awkward too. Rory hunkered over his plate, shoveling food into his face as if worried that she would start cross-interrogating him if he didn't keep his mouth occupied at all times. Edith's fingertips drummed nervously on the table. Wystan and Candice kept glancing at each other in the silent, meaningful way of a married couple who knew each other well enough not to need words.

"Seren!" Joe jumped up, a relieved grin splitting his handsome face. He bounded over to a woman who'd just entered the mess hall, flinging his arms around her in an enthusiastic embrace. "You're back!"

From the way the tall firefighter swept the woman clean off her feet, spinning her round, Diana guessed they were a couple. "I take it they haven't seen each other for a while."

Blaise wrinkled her nose. "They've been apart for a whole afternoon. Sickening, isn't it?"

Personally, Diana thought it was nice to see two people so clearly head-over-heels in love. She would have given a lot to have someone look at her the way Joe looked at Seren.

Joe set the woman back down on her feet, but kept hold of her hand. He led her over to the table, chest puffed out like a rooster, pride shining in his eyes.

"Diana, this is Seren," he introduced. "Seren, meet Diana."

Seren dipped her head in greeting, making her mane of long, narrow braids shift over her shoulders. Her hair was silvery gray, even though she couldn't have been older than Diana herself. Her smile was more reserved than the other firefighters' had been, but Diana had a feeling it was no less genuine.

"Enough of that. Come on, Seren." Joe tugged his partner away before Diana had a chance to say hello. "Look. Look! It's…*a baby*."

Seren dutifully examined the bundle in Callum's arms, her solemn expression never changing. "It is indeed."

"*Look* at her." Joe gestured at Beth like a tour guide pointing out sights of historic interest. "Look at her baby fingers. They're like real fingers, only smaller! Can you believe how tiny her ears are? Look at her perfect chubby cheeks! Isn't she amazing? Don't you just want to squeeze her and cuddle her and incidentally make one of your very own?"

Seren flung Diana an amused look. "Please excuse him. We've only been together one summer, and he's already impossibly broody."

"Hey, guys have biological clocks too," Joe protested. "And we peak younger, sexually speaking. I mean, you'll just get better and better, but I'm in my prime right now. It's all downhill from here."

"What a terrifying thought," Blaise muttered.

Edith was looking around as though searching for someone. She turned to Seren. "Where's Fenrir?"

Callum answered, although the question hadn't been addressed to him. "Still out searching."

Fenrir, as in the Norse legend? The giant wolf that kills the gods at the end of the world? Diana wondered if it was a nickname, and if that was better or worse than it being some guy's *actual* name.

"Another member of your team?" she asked.

"Yes," Edith replied. "I hope he gets here soon. I really want to find out what he calls you."

Rory cleared his throat, his arm bumping against Edith's. "Did you find anything, Seren?"

The intimidating woman shook her head as she took a seat next to Joe. "Nothing immediately useful, alas. We followed the trail to the road, but our foe seems to have fled on a motorbike. We couldn't discern anything other than that he was heading north, and at speed."

Rory grimaced. "Pity. I was hoping we could track down where Lupa's lot are hiding out."

"Isn't that a job for the police?" Diana asked.

The entire squad exchanged glances. "It's not that simple," Rory said, sounding like he was choosing his words with care. "Lupa's gang are...tricky."

"We've alerted the cops, of course, but we can't depend on them to catch your attacker," Blaise said. "Which is why we've all agreed to stay at the base as long as you need us. If Lupa *does* dare to make another move, we'll be here waiting for them."

Wystan nodded. "I promise you, no one will get through us."

"Especially Seren," Joe said proudly. "She's a professional bodyguard, actually. Among other things."

Seren inclined her head. "I do have some experience when it comes to personal security and protection. You have my sworn word that no harm will come to you or your daughter."

"That's very kind of you," Diana said. "But isn't the end of fire season? You can't want to give up your vacation time."

"Actually we do." Rory's voice was a deep, soft rumble. "Anything for Cal."

The others nodded, murmuring agreement. Looking round the circle of tough, hardened firefighters, some of Diana's tight-wound anxiety relaxed. It wasn't just their obvious physical strength that made her feel safe. It was the unity and loyalty that they displayed. Without a single hesitation, they'd accepted her into their midst, embracing her as one of their own.

She'd been alone for so long, the sense of being *protected* brought a lump to her throat. Whatever Callum might be hiding, it couldn't be *too* awful, if he had friends like these ready to drop everything to help him.

She swallowed, blinking back the sting of tears. "Thank you. I don't know how I can ever repay you."

"I do," Blaise said, in the bright tones of someone who had been waiting impatiently for a chance to crowbar the conversation onto a particular topic. "You can tell us how you and Cal met. Believe me, we're all desperate to know."

"Some of us more than others," Joe muttered, his gaze flicking to Callum.

"Oh, well." Diana could feel her face coloring. "That's kind of embarrassing, actually. Callum, you tell them."

"Can't." Callum stood up abruptly. "Beth's restless."

"She is?" Diana hadn't heard the slightest peep out of her. "Here, give her to me. I'll settle her."

Callum put a hand out, pushing her gently back down as she started to rise. "No. You stay and finish your dinner. I'll take her for a walk."

A surge of anxiety swept away her previous relaxation. The chicken stew she'd eaten felt like rocks in her stomach. She couldn't just let him walk off with Beth. She'd never been apart from her baby, not for a second, *never—*

Callum's fingers tightened on her shoulder, as if he'd sensed her sudden tension. "I'll just walk her round the room. I won't go out of sight. Okay?"

No, no no! howled Gertrude. *Grab her! Protect her! Run!*

Diana made herself take a deep breath. She'd come this far already. If Beth was ever going to have a proper father, she had to take another small baby step toward trusting Callum.

She could only hope that he would trust her in return.

She exhaled her anxiety, letting go. "Okay."

As if he knew what it had cost her to say that word, Callum's green eyes softened. For the first time that day, he smiled properly. For a moment, he looked exactly as he had the night that they'd met.

"Tell them everything," he said. "Please."

He strode off, heading for the other side of the long room. True to his word, he didn't leave her line of sight; just paced slowly back and forth along the far wall, rocking Beth. A few firefighters immediately left their places, trailing after him. They were too far away for Diana to make out what they were saying, but from the way Callum's shoulders hunched, she guessed that they were begging for a glimpse of the baby.

Callum dispersed Beth's would-be admirers with a few sharp words. As they slunk back to their tables, he caught her watching him. His head dipped in a solemn nod, as though to say: *See? I'll protect her.*

Blaise rapped on the table, drawing her attention back. "Okay, now that he's gone, spill the beans. We want to know every detail." She flashed a wicked grin. "Especially the embarrassing bits. *Especially* especially the embarrassing bits Callum wouldn't want us to know."

A giggle escaped her. "I'm not sure anything *can* embarrass him, given how we met."

Rory's eyebrows rose. "Oh? How so?"

Oh, Lord. She was certain she must be bright red. But…he *had* told her to tell them everything.

"Well." Diana cleared her throat. "I kind of bought him."

CHAPTER 8

"A bachelor auction?" Diana balked at the sight of the lurid banner hung above the hotel entrance. "Sal, you know this isn't my kind of thing."

Her best friend tugged her onward mercilessly. "Which is exactly why we're here. You need something which is completely different to your normal life. Something to make new, positive memories rather than stuff that reminds you of your dad."

It had been six months since her dad had passed away, but the sharp stab of pain hadn't dulled at all. Diana wasn't sure she *wanted* it to ever dull. If she didn't feel that moment of utter, hollow loss in her chest every time someone mentioned him, would it mean that she was forgetting him?

You'll forget his face, her anxiety disorder whispered in her mind. *You're already forgetting how he used to hug you, exactly how he smelled, how safe he made you feel. You'll never feel that safe again. You'll be sad and alone and lost forever and ever and ever—*

Sal gave her hand a brief squeeze. They'd known each other ever since they'd been toddlers tipping mud-pies over each other's heads at daycare. Sal understood her silences, even better than her words.

Nonetheless, Sal continued to haul her up the steps in front of the hotel. "Come on. Pretend you're someone else, just for one night. The sort of person who comes out to drink overpriced cocktails and ogle oiled-up men. It'll be good for you."

Diana had to laugh, despite the ache in her heart. "I don't think that's one of the official stages of grief."

"Sure it is," Sal said. "Denial, Arguing, Bargaining, Depression, Sexy Encounters With Ridiculously Hot Men, Acceptance. I'm sure I read that on the Internet."

Diana looked at the banner above the door. The man sprawled across it *was* ridiculously hot. Unrealistically so. No one actually had hair that perfect autumnal red-gold, or abs that defined. He lounged, winking sexily at the camera, wearing nothing except a strategically-placed helmet.

"That's never a real firefighter," she said. "He's got to be an underwear model. Are you *sure* this is legit?"

"Positive. I come every year with my sisters. It's a great charity, they raise money for people who lost their houses to wildfires. They get the hottest firefighters from across the whole state." Sal squinted up at the banner as they went through the door. "Though I'll grant you, poster boy up there has been Photoshopped to within an inch of his life. But I promise, the real guys will be more than hot enough to take your mind off things."

Sal was, much as Diana hated to admit it, absolutely right. The moment they stepped into the hotel lobby, they were confronted by a glistening wall of pecs. Even Diana's ever-present worries flew out of her head. Mouth suddenly dry, she tracked the intricate spiraling tattoos upward.

The shirtless firefighter tipped his helmet at them with a saucy wink. "Ladies. Hope you have an *unforgettable* night. And if you've got a situation which is getting too hot, I'll be happy to help. Just bid on Rocky. Lot number five."

He sauntered off to greet the next new arrivals, revealing a back as impressively muscled as his front. Other firefighters were also working the room, flirting with groups of giggling women.

"Oh my." Sal fanned herself with her free hand. "I'd certainly like to handle his hose. Unless you want to call dibs?"

With a guilty start, Diana wrenched her gaze away from the tattooed firefighter's back. "Sal! I'm not buying a firefighter!"

"Why not? You can afford it. And it's for a good cause." Sal gave Diana a friendly shoulder-bump. "Your dad would have approved."

He probably *would* have approved. Diana doubted her father had ever attended a charity bachelor auction, but the ridiculousness of it would have appealed to his wicked sense of humor. And he'd always given generously. No fundraiser who'd knocked on their door had ever gone away empty handed. Whether it was raising money for local schools or famine relief on the other side of the world, he'd always been ready to donate.

At least, he had been when he'd been well. Over the past three long, horrible years—when every oncologist had perpetually given him two months to live, only for him to beat the odds again and again—he'd slowed down his charitable giving, more worried about investing in her future. Now, thanks to the small inheritance he'd left her, she was more financially secure than she'd ever been. But so far she'd barely been able to look at the bank statements, let alone think about spending any of it.

"Even if it's for charity, I can't touch my inheritance," she said. "He wanted me to use that money to go back to school and finish my doctorate."

Sal cast her a not-buying-your-bullshit look. "And how's that going? Have you even contacted your old college yet?"

She hadn't, of course. Yet another thing that she wasn't ready to start thinking about. She'd dropped out in order to care for her dad when he'd gotten sick. She hadn't so much as opened an academic journal for two years.

You've forgotten your own thesis, Gertrude murmured. *You've lost all your work as well as everything else. How can you presume to understand the stories of your people when you're so empty inside? You didn't deserve to be accepted onto the post-grad program in the first place. You aren't as good as all the other students—you're too close to the material, you can't be objective.*

They only let you in as affirmative action, because it looked good to have a Native student studying Native history. They'll never take you back.

Ever since her dad had died, it had been harder to manage her anxiety disorder. With an effort, Diana pulled her attention back to the present, away from that nagging, whispering negativity.

"I'm not going to let you guilt me into buying a firefighter," she said firmly. "I can't believe that you're *trying* to guilt me into buying a firefighter."

"Hey, what are best friends for?" Sal bumped her shoulder against Diana's again. "Which is why *you* should be egging *me* on to buy Mr. Tattoos over there."

Diana smiled, grateful for her friend's irrepressible enthusiasm. "You hardly need any encouragement."

"True," Sal conceded. She tapped a bright purple nail against her lower lip, scanning the room like a lioness surveying the savannah. "What do you think? I mean, that Rocky guy was smoking, but check out the butt on that blond guy over there."

Diana wished she had her friend's confidence. She couldn't even look at all the swaggering beefcake on display, let alone openly check out a firefighter's ass. She was probably as red as a tomato already.

"What would you even do with a firefighter?" she asked. "I mean, they're not actually…you know. For *sale*. Are they?"

"Of course not. You're just buying a bit of arm-candy at the party after the auction. The guy dances with you, brings you free drinks, and poses for selfies. All good clean fun." Sal waggled her eyebrows meaningfully. "Though sometimes the fun can go on late into the night, if the guy is willing. And in my experience, the guys are *very* willing."

"*Sal!*" Diana laughed despite her embarrassment. "That's terrible!"

Sal shrugged unrepentantly. "There's nothing wrong with a bit of consensual, careful, casual sex. And you could do with some of that, if you ask me."

Diana shook her head, amused. "Not my style."

"Always good to mix up your style every now and then." Sal

checked her watch. "The auction's starting soon. Let's go check out the merchandise up close and personal while we can."

"You go." She couldn't possibly go any closer to the shirtless, muscled hunks, let alone talk to one. If her face got any hotter, one of the firefighters would have to turn a hose on her. "I'll...I'll go get us some cocktails."

She hurried off before Sal could object. Unfortunately, the bar didn't turn out to be the peaceful refuge she had hoped. It was swarming with women, all looking effortlessly gorgeous and confident. The intimidating crowd brought out the worst of her social anxiety.

You don't fit in. You're not skinny and blonde and stylish. They'll know you don't belong here. They'll all stare at you.

She shrank into the shadow of a large potted fern. She couldn't go out there and elbow her way to the bar, she *couldn't*—

"You look like you're in need of rescue."

She just about died. She whirled around, and found herself nose-to-nipple with an impossibly cut chest. Wearing firefighter suspenders.

The man quirked an eyebrow at her, a small smile tugging at his mouth. "Lovely lady enters a room and dives behind the shrubbery, something's got to be wrong. Thought I'd better check if there was any way I could help."

It was *him*.

The firefighter from the poster.

And dear sweet heaven, it turned out he had not been Photoshopped *at all*.

In the flesh, he was even more ridiculously attractive than his photo. He winked at her, leaning back against the wall in a casual pose that showed off every single ridge of his abs. A bottle of whiskey dangled casually from one hand.

"You're real," she blurted out.

"Last time I checked." Even his *voice* was devastatingly sexy—teasing, melodic, with a hint of Irish lilt. "Are you hiding from someone?"

"Um. Everyone."

"Ah." He looked at her more closely. "I see. Not your cup of tea, this sort of thing?"

"Not at all. A friend dragged me out here. I didn't know where she was taking me until it was too late. Now I'm stuck." Belatedly, it occurred to her that he might find this offensive. "I mean, not that this is a bad event! It's great. Really great. Very, um, stimulating."

Oh God. She wanted to sink through the floor.

He laughed, as though her awkwardness was charming rather than humiliating. "It's all right. It's not *my* cup of tea either. Not that I don't love a good party. Just not when I'm the main course."

Despite her embarrassment, she found herself smiling back at him. His easy, genuine humor was infectious. For all his male model good looks, he wasn't at all intimidating. He felt oddly like a friend. "But aren't you literally the poster boy for this thing?"

He grimaced, scrunching up his movie-star face in a boyish, unselfconscious way that only enhanced his appeal. "Alas. Let's just say that I'm regretting several life decisions at the moment."

He took a drink from his bottle again, watching her over the rim the whole time. When he lowered the bottle again, only an inch of amber fluid still sloshed at the bottom. He either had to have a cast-iron constitution, or he was a lot drunker than he appeared.

His head cocked to one side. A crease appeared in his brow, as if he was trying to work something out.

"You know, you seem oddly familiar," he said slowly.

"I was thinking the same thing about you, actually." She *never* found it easy to talk to strangers, but somehow he felt like she'd known him all her life. "If you actually *are* an underwear model, then maybe I've seen your abs on the side of a bus or something."

He flashed a grin. "Not a model, underwear or otherwise. Thanks for the compliment, though." He took another drink, still studying her with that unnerving interest. "Huh. Do you believe in fate?"

"What?"

He shook his head, like he hadn't really meant to say that. "Never mind. So, anyone take your fancy tonight?"

"No!" she yelped. *Way to go, Diana, now he'll think that you find him and his buddies repulsive.* "I, I mean, all the men here are very, um, very nice. And I think you're very attractive."

He grinned again. "But not attractive enough to spend your money on?"

Kill me now. "I, uh, I've never done anything like this. And..."

She hesitated. Normally, she would have kept her grief private. But something about this total stranger made her feel like she could trust him.

"My father passed away recently," she said. "Well, six months ago, but it still feels recent to me. I'm not exactly in the mood for partying. I know that I should be picking myself up and moving on, but-_"

"There's nothing you *should* be doing," he said gently. "Except what feels right to you. Listen, if you want to get out of here, I can call you a cab."

"No," she said, surprising herself. "Thank you, but I couldn't just abandon my friend. And I'm actually starting to enjoy myself."

It was true. Sure, part of her still wanted to run home and hide under the covers, but she found she had an even stronger urge to stay. It was probably just hormones—the firefighter *was* ridiculously, panty-meltingly hot, after all.

But maybe Sal had been right. Maybe getting out and trying something new *was* good for her.

"Hmm." He pursed his perfect lips. "In that case, would you do me a favor?"

Diana couldn't imagine what on earth this walking sex god could possibly need from *her*. She had no doubt that every single woman in the room would throw herself at his feet if he so much as twitched an eyebrow. "You need *my* help?"

"If you don't mind." He tossed the now-empty bottle into the fern's pot, and dug in his pocket. "Would you bid on me?"

She stared at him. "I don't think you need to be worried that no one will bid on you."

"No." He pulled a wallet out of his pocket, counting out bills. "But I'd like you to win me."

"Me?" she said stupidly, as he thrust the money into her hand. "Why me?"

"Because I like you, and I think you could do with an evening of laughter and silliness." His smile turned a bit wistful. "And this might sound crazy, but...because something inside me thinks that this is meant to be."

Before she could question him further, a chime rang out. From the way all the women at the bar started to eagerly hurry in the direction of the ballroom, Diana guessed that the auction was about to start.

The firefighter blanched, looking like a man about to be thrown into a pit of wolverines. Given what Diana had seen of the thirsty crowd, she couldn't blame him. "I've got to go. Listen, you can keep the change. Just make sure you win the auction, okay? I'm counting on you."

With a final wink, he hurried off. Diana stared after his retreating back, then down at the roll of money he'd given her. They were hundred dollar bills. There had to be at least a couple of thousand dollars there.

He'd handed her a small fortune and *walked off*.

It was either the world's weirdest con, or he was very, *very* drunk.

Or...

He'd been serious.

∽

"And now it's the one you've been waiting for!" the hostess announced, flourishing a hand like a magician revealing a trick. "Our final bachelor for sale, the poster boy himself...Stallion!"

Stallion? Diana covered her mouth, fighting down a giggle as the red-haired firefighter sauntered onto the stage. All of the men had been auctioned off under fake names—she presumed to protect their real identities—but this one was the most ridiculous yet. She wondered if he'd picked it himself.

Sal squealed, bouncing up and down. "Omigod! Omigod! Di, it's him! Get ready!"

"I told you already! I'm not bidding on him!"

She had to yell into her friend's ear over the screams of the crowd. The audience had been enthusiastically lecherous throughout the auction, but Stallion's appearance had sent them into new heights of frenzy.

A bra came sailing out of the throng. Stallion caught it neatly, winked, and draped it around his neck like a scarf. He strutted around, abs flexing, playing shamelessly to his audience. It was hard to reconcile this cocky, flirty man with the one that she'd met behind the potted plants.

"You *have* to bid on him," Sal shouted back at her. "He even gave you the money!"

"It's probably counterfeit! Or stolen! Or this is a really weird money laundering scam!"

Her friend gave her an exasperated look. "So what are you going to do? Keep it?"

Diana had no intention of keeping it. She was uncomfortably aware of the thick roll of bills, stuffed into the bottom of her purse. She'd counted it in the bathroom, and discovered that her initial estimate had been way off.

He'd handed her *five thousand dollars*. On the basis of one short conversation.

No one in their right mind did that. Not with good intentions. She kept expecting a cop to crash through the door and arrest her.

I'll just give it back to him after this is all over, she vowed. Whatever was going on, it was way too weird for her.

The bidding was fast and furious. Most of the previous guys had raised a few hundred dollars each, but Stallion had already passed five hundred, with no sign of the auction slowing down.

"Six hundred!"

"Seven hundred!"

"Seven fifty!"

"One thousand dollars!" screamed the woman who'd thrown the bra. She looked on the verge of ripping off the rest of her clothes and having her way with the firefighter right there on stage.

Diana glanced at Stallion. He was still posing and flexing, putting on a show for the crowd. But she remembered how nervous he'd looked right before the auction had started, how he'd admitted he regretted having volunteered for the gig. No matter how well he was faking it now, she knew that he didn't want to be up on that stage.

He'd trusted her to save him.

Also, the four large cocktails Sal had forced on her whispered, *he's really, really hot.*

She raised her paddle. "Five thousand dollars."

She regretted it immediately. She shrank back as every face turned toward her. Even Stallion seemed surprised that she'd actually gone through with it.

"Goingoncegoingtwice*sold!*" the auction hostess said all in one breath, as though worried Diana might change her mind. "Sold to the lucky lady in the green dress! Let's hear it for our *very* generous benefactor!"

Sal whooped, pumping her fist into the air, as applause broke out all around them. "*Yes!* I can't believe you actually did that, Diana!"

Neither could she. Cheers and whoops rang in her ears. She'd expected death-glares from the women that she'd beaten, but looking around, all she could see were smiling faces. Sure, there were some envious glances mixed in, but on the whole everyone seemed genuinely delighted by the unexpected drama she'd provided.

Stallion cut through the crowd, grinning broadly. His wide, oiled chest filled her field of view as he bent over her.

"Personally, I would have just kept the cash," he murmured into her ear, as hoots and catcalls rang out around them. He drew back a little, studying her face. That strange, thoughtful expression flicked across his own again. "Huh. There *is* something about you."

Then he grinned, all seriousness chased away by playful wickedness. "Well, my goddess-for-an-evening. Looks like I owe you five thousand dollars of laughter and fun, huh? Fabulous. I do like a challenge."

Before she could utter so much of a squeak of protest, he scooped her up in a fireman's hold. She clutched at his oil-slick shoulder, head spinning, feeling like she'd been turned clean upside-down. The crowd cat-called and hooted even louder.

"It was *your* money," she protested as he carried her to the dance floor. Other couples were following, as the other firefighters also swept up their giggling auction winners. "You bought yourself."

"I'm more of a gift, really. Or an apology. It's complicated." He shifted his grip, letting her slide down his body. "Anyway, you can't just walk off and leave me here on my own. It'll look terrible if you abandon me thirty seconds into our date. My boss already thinks I'm an awful reprobate. Dance with me, my goddess. For the sake of my mid-year review."

He was so ridiculous, she couldn't help laughing even as she shook her head. "I don't dance. I don't do this sort of thing. This isn't me at all."

"Then be someone different for a little while," he suggested. "Someone who *does* dance, who walks with her head held high and a swing to her hips, without a care in the world. Just for a little while, my goddess-for-an-evening."

"My name is—" she started.

He put a finger across her lips, silencing her. "Don't tell me. I'm not supposed to tell you mine, after all. And it's fun to take a break from being yourself sometimes. So you call me Stallion, and I'll call you my goddess and worship you as you deserve. Be someone else with me. Please. Just for one night."

That mad, not-like-her-at-all impulse bubbled up again. She put her arms around his bare neck, for once letting go of all worry. "Okay, Stallion. You win. Just for one night."

After all, she thought, *what harm could it do?*

CHAPTER 9

"And, well, one thing led to another," Diana concluded. Callum's shifter-sharp hearing let him pick up every word, as clearly as if he was still sitting next to her. "Which nine months later, led to Beth."

"Wow. And I thought that *I'd* had some wild nights out." Joe sounded impressed.

Callum gave Blaise a mental nudge. *Still not enough details. Ask her what she remembers about the actual night.*

Blaise shot him an appalled glance across the hall. *I am not quizzing your mate for details about her sex life. Ask her yourself.*

Edith, with her typical bluntness, saved him from having to think of a way to do *that*. "So he took you up to his room, but didn't stick around in the morning?"

"*I* didn't stick around," Diana replied. "And please don't think that he took advantage of me. At the end of the evening, I helped him up to his hotel room because he was clearly out of it. And then *I* was the one who stupidly decided to turn around and knock on his door again instead of going home. When I woke up the next morning, I was so mortified that I fled before he opened his eyes. And it wasn't until *much* later that I found out that my birth control had failed. Don't think badly of Callum. None of it was his fault."

"Oh, we're not blaming Callum," Blaise muttered.

Callum was blaming himself. He'd been mentally kicking himself all through Diana's story. His suspicion had been correct. He and Diana *had* both been at the same hotel that night, along with his two brothers.

It had been yet another of their 'hilarious' practical jokes. Connor had signed him up to the bachelor auction, and had even impersonated him at the publicity photoshoot beforehand, so that 'his' image would be plastered all over the posters. Then Conleth had pretended that there was an urgent family crisis in Los Angeles to lure him to the hotel.

He'd dropped everything and rushed over, expecting to find his mother sick and in need of his help…only to discover that he was supposed to be stripping off and oiling up for charity.

Trying to explain to the event organizers that he was one of a set of absolutely identical triplets and this was all a set-up…hadn't gone well. He'd come perilously close to just giving up and agreeing to go through with it. Now he wished that he *had* gone through with it. Then Diana would have met *him* that evening.

But he hadn't, and apparently Connor or Conleth had ended up taking his place while he'd been fuming in his hotel room. Callum was slightly surprised by that. He guessed they must have been caught by one of the terrifying ladies on the charity committee and forced to participate.

At any other time, Callum would have taken deep satisfaction in their practical joke backfiring like that. But as it turned out, one of them might have had the last laugh.

And he still didn't know which one.

Connor was genuinely a firefighter—he was a smokejumper on an Alaskan crew. But he couldn't imagine his cocky, wild brother noticing a shy woman behind a pot plant at a party. Let alone handing her five thousand dollars to bid on him.

That sounded more like Conleth. The suave, sophisticated businessman certainly had money to burn. But then, he couldn't picture Conleth ever strutting half-naked across a stage in front of a crowd of drunken, screaming women.

Unless…they'd been tag-teaming all night.

It wouldn't be the first time they'd impersonated each other. Ever since they'd been kids, they'd delighted in fooling people. Of course, most of the time they'd pretended to be *him*, in order to get him into trouble.

In any event, he was certain that they'd both be able to convince Diana that they were a single individual. Which meant either one of them could have taken her to bed at the end, with her never suspecting a thing.

Callum clenched his teeth at the thought, a deep, boiling rage building in his chest. It was one thing for them to try to humiliate *him*. To play such a despicable prank on any woman, let alone his *mate*…it was beyond unforgivable.

Beth's little legs kicked in protest. He realized that he'd tensed his arms around her. He made himself relax again, rocking her until she fell back into peaceful slumber.

Of course, there was still the third option, unlikely as it was. He *had* been there. Diana might have come into his room that night by accident, thinking he was Connor or Conleth. But it was only the tiniest thread of hope. In all likelihood, he wasn't Beth's father.

We are, his pegasus insisted.

How can that be, if we don't even remember meeting Diana? he asked his inner animal. *How do you know?*

His pegasus rippled its hide in an equine shrug. *Our mate. Our foal. Ours now. Nothing else matters.*

"So now that I've told you all my embarrassing story, I think it's only fair that you should share some in return." Diana's voice jerked him out of his introspection. "Tell me about Callum. You must have some good tales about him, since you've all been friends for so long."

That was his cue. Callum strode back to the table, at slightly less than a run.

"It's getting late," he said, just in time. He glared at Joe, who was opening his mouth. "If you've finished eating, Diana, we should get you and Beth settled into the cabin."

Joe pouted, but subsided.

"I am getting tired," Diana admitted. She rose, smiling around at everyone. "It was nice to meet you all. I hope we can continue this conversation tomorrow."

Callum fully intended to do everything in his power to prevent that from happening. He steered Diana away, as fast as he could without bodily carrying her.

"Here, give her to me." Diana took Beth back from him. Her voice dropped into a loving, maternal croon as she snuggled their daughter. "Hi baby. Were you good for Daddy?"

His heart seemed to spontaneously grow three sizes. No accolade, no award or title, could ever compare to the honor of that name.

Callum tried not to show how much that simple word had moved him. "May I take a picture of you?"

"What, right now?" She touched her glossy black hair self-consciously. "Like *this?*"

How could she think there was something wrong with the way she looked? "Yes. I want to capture this moment. Please."

A slight blush colored her cheeks. "All right."

Callum *did* want to capture the moment—his mate holding their daughter, the golden rays of the setting sun bringing out the rich tones of her skin, crowning her with light—but he had an ulterior motive too. Pulling out his cellphone, he snapped two quick pictures.

The first one was for him. The second, for the plan that was coming together in his head.

"Thank you," he said, pocketing his phone again. He gestured her onward, toward his cabin. "I hope this is okay for tonight. I can do better tomorrow, with more time."

"I'm sure this will be fine." Despite Diana's words, her expression betrayed a hint of doubt as she eyed up the small, rustic log building. She opened the door, going in.

Callum didn't get any warning. One moment there were only two life-forces in the immediate vicinity—Diana and Beth—and the next, a *third* blazed in his senses, appearing out of nowhere in the middle of the cabin. Simultaneously, Diana's scream split the air.

He was through the door and between his mate and the interloper in a heartbeat. His pegasus surged up, ready to fight—and then he realized who the intruder was.

"It's all right," he said, straightening. "It's just Fenrir."

The hellhound was plastered to the floor in full submission, looking like a very large bear skin rug. Diana had her back pressed into a corner. She clutched at Beth, instinctively shielding the baby with her own body.

"*That's* Fenrir?" she said in a high, breathless squeak. "I thought he was a firefighter!"

Am, Fenrir said in his head.

From Diana's complete lack of reaction, she couldn't hear the hellhound's telepathic voice. Most humans couldn't. Fenrir wouldn't be able to communicate with her until she was both aware of his true nature, and become friends with him.

Which, from the way things were going so far, would be never.

"He is on the crew," Callum said. He fixed the contrite hellhound with a glare. "He's a service dog. He's very obedient. *Usually.*"

Fenrir whined like a puppy. His copper eyes stayed fixed yearningly on Beth. *Just wanted to see pack's first cub.*

"He's completely harmless." Callum normally respected Fenrir's personal space as much as if the shifter was in human form, but he had to show Diana that there was nothing to fear from the hellhound. He leaned down to ruffle Fenrir's ears, simultaneously sending him a mental *Sorry*. "See? You can trust him. And he's an excellent guard dog."

Diana pressed her back further into the corner. "I'm sure he is, but I'm really not comfortable with him being in the same room as Beth. Look at how he's staring at her."

"That's just because he loves babies. He only wants to get to know you both." He stood up, reaching for her hand. "Here. Stroke him. Let him get your scent."

Diana jerked her hand away. Her voice was still high and tight. "I—I really don't like dogs."

Fenrir whimpered. He flattened himself even further to the ground, as though attempting to make himself as small and harmless-looking as possible. Given that even in *this* form—which was half his true size—he would have dwarfed a Great Dane, this was not terribly successful.

"Don't worry. He won't come near you again." Callum held the door open. "Fenrir, out."

Fenrir's pointed ears drooped. Reluctantly, belly flat to the ground, he inched toward the door. *Understand. Nursing bitches always guard young fiercely, snap at any who get too close. But takes whole pack to raise strong pups. Tell Sky Bitch that.*

Sky Bitch? Callum blinked, wondering what had made Fenrir pick *that* one. The hellhound usually had very good reasons for the nicknames that he gave people. Even if they weren't always obvious.

This wasn't the moment to quiz him on it, though. He closed the door, shutting Fenrir out. He could sense that the hellhound didn't go far—just round the corner of the next cabin—but at least it was far enough that Diana wouldn't catch sight of him if she glanced out the window.

Diana let out a shaky breath, easing away from the wall. "I'm sorry. I'm sure he's a lovely dog. It's just that I had a bad experience when I was seven. A feral pack chased me and my mother while we were on a camping vacation. I was too young to properly remember it, but sometimes I still get nightmares of all these snarling teeth, and my mother standing between me and them. Somehow she managed to fight them off with her bare hands."

"She sounds like quite a woman."

Like you, Callum nearly added. He bit back the words. The less he spoke, the better. He'd never been able to tell the difference between a perfectly reasonable comment, and one that would make everyone stare at him and then awkwardly change the subject.

"She was." Diana looked down at Beth, her hair swinging forward to hide her face. "She passed away when I was eight, a year after the dog incident. She was a civil engineer, specializing in eco-friendly developments for tribal reservations, so she was away from home a lot. She was at a special gathering of Oglala Lakota leaders, talking about a new project, and...there was an accident. A fire. Nearly everyone there died. The police never caught the person who did it."

Callum wanted to put his arms around her. He wanted to tell her that she wasn't alone anymore. He wanted to stroke her hair and ask her more about her family; learn her sorrows and her joys, everything that had made her *her*.

Instead, he stood there. He couldn't find anything to do with his hands.

She looked up again, with a rather strained smile. "I named Beth after my mom, actually. I'm sorry you didn't get a chance to have any input."

"Beth is perfect. She's perfect." He managed to stop himself before *You're perfect* slipped out as well.

Diana's smile brightened, turning more genuine. "Well, I think she is. But then I'm biased. I suppose you are too."

"Ask the crew. Impartial judges. They'll agree."

Diana giggled. "I never imagined big, tough wilderness firefighters would be so into babies." She looked around the cabin, her eyes widening. "And this is much nicer than I expected. I assumed your crew quarters would be, you know, like military barracks or something. But this is actually cozy."

Callum stood back to allow her to look around, watching anxiously as she inspected the small common room between the two bedrooms. All he could see were the flaws—the carpet too worn to be fit for her feet, the chairs not comfortable enough, the window too small—but Diana seemed genuinely pleased.

She opened the door to her room, revealing the bed he'd made up for her on the floor. Thanks to Rory, who'd flown down to the nearest store, there were diapers and wipes set out for Beth. Callum had left a fresh t-shirt—one of his own—on the pillow for Diana to use as a nightgown, along with clean folded towels. He wished he'd been able to find better flowers for her than the mason jar of simple daisies on the nightstand.

It all wasn't enough. Connor or Conleth would doubtless have been able to convince her that the simple amenities were somehow chic and trendy, but he'd never had their gift for words.

He should have done better. She deserved the finest silks, luxury soaps, a huge bouquet of roses—

Diana turned back to him, eyes shining. "You really have thought of everything."

"I can do better." Snacks, he'd forgotten the snacks. What if she got hungry in the night? He made a mental note to raid the storeroom. "I *will* do better. I promise."

"Honestly, Callum, it's fine. More than fine. Stop looking at me like you're afraid I'm about to throw some kind of diva fit because there isn't a bowl of green M&Ms or something." Rather timidly, she touched his arm. "I think maybe you're still a little bit in shock. You don't have to tear around trying to sort everything out immediately, you know. Relax. We have plenty of time to get to know each other, and figure out how this is going to work."

"I hope so."

Oh, how he hoped. But he was sitting on more than one ticking time bomb. Lupa's pack, his brothers, the uncertainty over Beth's parentage…one of his secrets was going to explode in his face before long.

He had to win Diana's heart before that happened.

"Callum…" Diana bit her lip, as though debating with herself whether to continue. "If this *is* going to work, we have to be honest with each other. So I need to tell you…I have general anxiety disorder."

Did she think that was somehow going to put him off? "If there's anything I can do to help you feel more comfortable, please tell me."

"There is." Her shoulders straightened, as if she was steeling herself. "Please just tell me what's going on. I know you're trying to hide something. Believe me, whatever it is, it can't possibly be half as bad as all the stuff I'm imagining. What aren't you telling me?"

You're the love of my life. I don't know if I'm Beth's father. And even if I am, I've still been lying to you all day.

Also, sometimes I turn into a flying horse, his pegasus put in, helpfully.

"I...I'm not the man you think I am," he said, picking his words with care. "The charming, carefree guy that you met at the charity auction...that's not really me. And I'm scared that you aren't going to like the real me as much as him."

"Well, I'm not really the sort of confident, adventurous woman who'd buy a bachelor at a charity auction," Diana said. She blushed. "Let alone fall into bed with him. We were both acting out of character that night, Callum. Just because I liked you when you were smashed out of your mind doesn't mean I don't like you when you're stone-cold sober."

"*Do* you like me?"

Oh, for pity's sake. Someone take me behind the barn and shoot me. He sounded like a fourteen-year-old with his first crush. Then again, he *felt* like a fourteen-year-old with his first crush.

At least Diana also seemed to be having something of a regression to awkward adolescence. Her blush deepened to a charming rose pink. But despite her evident embarrassment—and the fact that she'd claimed not to be confident—she looked him straight in the eye.

"Yes. I do like you, Callum." She broke into an impish smile. "After all, you know I have a thing for firefighters. Especially ones that rescue me from burning cars."

"Can't keep rescuing you though." Wait, that had come out wrong. He rushed on, desperately trying to rectify his gaffe. "I mean, I *will* keep rescuing you. If you need. But I don't *want* you to need me to. I don't want you to be in danger. Even if that would help you to like me more. Though I *do* want you to like me more. This isn't helping, is it? See, this is why I don't talk."

Diana's eyes sparkled. "I think you just gained at least three points."

She'd...*liked* that outflow of social ineptitude?

Diana patted his arm again as he stood there in baffled confusion. "Get some sleep, Callum. It's been a long day for both of us."

"Yes. You need to rest." And he had other matters to attend to, once she was settled. "If you need anything, I'll be right here."

"Thank you, but I'm sure I'll be fine." Diana started to close the bedroom door between them—then hesitated, peering out at him round the crack. "And Callum? Stop worrying so much about showing me the real you. We're bound together now, no matter what. I'm not going to keep Beth away from her own father."

And that was exactly what he was afraid of.

CHAPTER 10

Callum waited until he could sense by the dimming of their life-forces that Diana and Beth were both asleep. Then, barefooted, he silently crept out of the cabin.

Fenrir lifted his head as he softly closed the door. The hellhound was lying across the front steps, like a very intimidating welcome mat.

Trouble, Shadowhorse? Fenrir said in his mind. The thick fur along the back of his neck bristled. *Scent enemies?*

He motioned the hellhound back down again. "No. Nothing's wrong. There's just something I need to do. Won't go far. Watch over them for me?"

Fenrir dropped his massive head back down, resting it on his crossed paws. His ears stayed on alert though, constantly flicking to monitor the surroundings. *Always. Cubs are heart of the pack. Will be on guard.*

"Thank you." He started down the path, then hesitated, turning back. "Fenrir? Why did you call Diana 'Sky Bitch'?"

Because is, the hellhound replied, predictably but not entirely helpfully.

Callum sat down next to him on the step, resting his elbows on his knees. "I know it's difficult, but can you try to explain?"

Fenrir made a disgruntled *whuff*. *Two-leg words are bleached bones in the mouth. Dry and hard. No meat on them.*

He sighed, looking up at the night sky. "Agree with you there."

Yes. Fenrir leaned into him, a hot, friendly weight against his hip. *Shadowhorse would make a good wolf.*

"If only." His life would have been a lot simpler, certainly. "Sometimes I think you have the right idea, refusing to ever shift."

Fenrir's soft growl rumbled through his side. *No two-legs inside. Just wolf. Only ever wolf.*

That was impossible, since no hellhound had ever been born that way. They were one of the few shifter types that didn't breed true— any offspring hellhounds produced were always just regular humans. New hellhounds were *made*, by hellhounds biting people, just like in the old legends about werewolves. And hellhounds couldn't turn animals. No matter what Fenrir claimed, he *had* to have been a man once.

But pressing the hellhound on his past always just made him show his teeth and back away. Callum dropped the subject. He leaned back on his hands, watching the flicker-dance of bats overhead; invisible to the eye, but swirling like sparks in his awareness.

He tried a different tack. "Is Diana a night sky? Or a day-time sky?"

Fenrir gave him a sidelong look, as though the question had made no sense at all. *Empty sky. No clouds.* He seemed to struggle for a moment, searching for words, and then added, *Waiting.*

"Waiting?"

For the storm.

Callum wondered if the hellhound was picking up on Diana's anxiety disorder. Standing under bright, clear skies, but always worried that a storm was coming.

Fenrir interrupted his chain of thought. *Asking wrong questions, Shadowhorse.*

"What should I be asking?"

The hellhound's copper eyes met his, bright in the dark. *What your name means.*

He frowned in confusion. "I thought that was obvious. *Horse* because of my animal, and *Shadow* because I'm quiet and stay in the background."

Fenrir huffed again. *Two-legs. Can't smell what's right under their noses. Shadowhorse sees a lot outward. Should look inward sometime.*

"All right, so why *do* you call me Shadowhorse?"

Fenrir started grooming one front paw, spawning out his toes to nibble at the thick fur between his pads. *Because shape is not your own. Made of absences. Defined by others.*

That seemed distinctly unfair, as well as unflattering. "But I've spent my whole life trying to be seen as an individual."

Yes. Fenrir licked his fur smooth, looking entirely unruffled. *Is the problem.*

Well, that was less than productive. And he had better things to do than to continue to try to wrap his head around the hellhound's peculiar point of view.

See, this is what happens when you don't take the time to make a proper list, Callum chastised himself. *You set off to do something important, and instead end up sitting on a porch debating linguistic philosophy with a dog.*

"Thanks for the input." He got to his feet, brushing off his pants. "I think. I won't be long. Call if you need me. Or howl, I suppose."

Miss howling, Fenrir said, his mental tone uncharacteristically wistful. He rested his head on his paws again, eyes fixed on the half-full moon. *Pack is pack now, but sometimes still hear them singing, in dreams...*

Must mean his old pack. From what they'd managed to piece together from Fenrir's jumbled, confusing statements, he'd spent years running with wild wolves. But he'd been alone when Rory had found him. Whatever had happened to his previous 'family', he'd never wanted to talk about it.

Leaving Fenrir to his enigmatic reverie, Callum strode down the path. He pulled out his cellphone as he walked, waiting for a bar of signal to flicker into life. He'd deliberately chosen the most remote cabin on the base in order to be as far as possible from all the other human lives, but it did come with the downside of being in a phone dead zone.

Not that he'd ever *wanted* to make many calls. He'd always found using the phone to be a distinctly unnerving experience. Having someone talking to him without being able to sense their life energy was like having a conversation with a ghost.

He was all the way back to the main buildings when his phone grudgingly acknowledged a signal at last. Sinking down onto a bench next to the fire pit outside the mess hall, he checked time zones. It would be early in England, but he couldn't wait any longer.

There were only seven contacts in his address book, and six of them were here at Thunder Mountain. He dialed the only one who wasn't.

It rang for a while. He was just about to give up when she finally picked up. "Callum? Is that really you? Are you okay? Is there an emergency?"

Guilt stabbed him. Had it really been *that* long since he'd last called his mother?

"I'm fine. Nothing's wrong." He heard rustling sounds, and guessed that she was sitting up in bed. "I'm sorry, did I wake you up?"

"Don't worry about that," she said firmly. "I'm thrilled to hear from you at any hour. But there must be *something* wrong if you're calling home."

His mother knew him all too well. She was the only person in his family who ever had.

"No. It's good news." Despite everything, he found himself smiling, the sheer joy of Diana's existence too great to contain. "I met my mate."

There was a beat of silence from the other end of the line.

Then his mother—the toughest woman he'd ever met, the crack stunt pilot who made macho idiots eat her tailwind, his take-no-prisoners childhood champion who could even bring his brothers to heel, his *mother*—burst into tears.

Horror struck through him. "No—wait—I said it was *good* news!"

"It's the *best* news!" crowed a new voice. The sounds of his mother's sobs faded as someone snatched her phone away from her. "No wonder you called! You need advice!"

Callum hadn't thought it was possible for him to feel any more dismayed. He'd been wrong.

"Oh," he said flatly. "Dad. You're there too."

"Of course I am! And never fear, son, I am ready and eager to help. I am an expert on all matters of the heart." Despite the early hour, his father sounded as bright-eyed and bushy-tailed as a squirrel on crystal meth. As always. "I persuaded your mother to marry *me*, after all. And I only had to propose six times! Though you have to be prepared for the fact that it will probably take you much longer."

Callum finally managed to jam a sentence of his own into the torrent of words, like hammering a piton into a glacier. "What's wrong with Mom?"

"Oh, don't mind her," his father said sunnily, not sounding the slightest bit concerned. "They're just tears of joy."

Callum's tense shoulders relaxed a little. For all his father's flaws, the one thing he was *never* careless about was his mate. They may seem to be the most mismatched couple imaginable—her, pragmatic and capable; him, the physical manifestation of chaos—but they *were* true mates. He could only hope that he and Diana could form such a strong, deep bond.

"We're both so relieved," his father continued. "We worry about you, you know."

Callum frowned, because he *hadn't* known. "But I'm the one you never have to worry about."

"That's why we worry about you the most," his father said, cryptically. His voice brightened, taking on the enthusiastic, helpful tones that always preceded an absolutely *terrible* idea. "Now, let's plan your strategy. First things first. Does your lady-to-be like vintage World War II airplanes?"

"No," he said, in his most curt and discouraging tone.

It didn't work. It never had.

"Then this will be a lot harder for you than it was for me," his father informed him. "Although also, quite a lot cheaper. Have you got a pen and paper ready? Okay, so here's what you're going to need:

six dozen roses, as many strings of fairy lights as you can lay your hands on, some gardening shears, a length of ribbon, a small alpaca—"

"*Thank you,* Chase," his mother's voice said. From the sounds of things, she was bodily wrestling her phone away from her mate. "I think Callum will be fine on his own."

"I just want to help," his father protested in the background, slightly muffled. "I don't want him to make the same mistakes that I did."

"I know, my love. But honestly, I think that's highly unlikely." His mother addressed him again. "You weren't so daft as to propose to her the moment you met, at least, were you Callum?"

This didn't seem to be a good moment to admit that he'd skipped over that whole step and gone straight to 'have a baby together.'

"No," he said, cautiously. "But there are some…complications."

One complication, really. One adorable, delightful complication that he wouldn't have changed for all the world, no matter how difficult she made things.

"There always are, love," his mother said gently. "Just don't overthink things. Trust your heart. And trust *her.*"

"I do. I will." He cleared his throat. "But I do need your help, actually."

"I *told* you so," his father called triumphantly. "So, like I was saying, you take the alpaca, and you—*ack!*"

The call was voice-only, but even without video Callum was certain that his mother was now literally sitting on top of his father.

"Of course, we'll be happy to help," his mother said, raising her voice over the muffled, incoherent protests coming from somewhere beneath her. "Anything you need. We're always here for you. We're family."

"That's what I need help with, actually. I don't have Connor or Conleth's phone numbers."

Absolute silence. Even his dad seemed to have stilled.

When his mother spoke again, she sounded cautious, as if she thought she'd misheard. "You *want* to contact your brothers?"

Want wasn't exactly the word. "It's…necessary. They have to find out about this from me."

"Oh." His mother sounded suspiciously snuffly, like she was on the verge of tears again. "Oh, Callum. That'll mean so much to them. It means so much to *me*, that you're reaching out to them like this. They do miss you, you know."

Missed having a straight man for their endless juvenile pranks, perhaps. Callum grimaced, but didn't correct his mother's misunderstanding. He knew the estrangement between himself and his brothers upset her.

He pulled out his ever-present notebook and pencil. "Their numbers?"

His mother rattled them off, clearly without having to look them up. "Though you probably won't be able to get hold of Connor for a few days. He's jumping a late fire in Alaska at the moment, so he'll be out of contact. If you leave a message, though, I'm sure he'll get back to you the moment he's back in civilization."

"Thanks." That suited him perfectly. He needed all the time he could get, to think and plan. "I'll do that. I have to go now."

"Will you be coming home for a visit now that fire season is over?" his mother said, sounding wistful. "I'd love to meet your mate."

"I do want you to meet—" he caught himself just before he said *them*. "Ah, her. But there are…a few things I need to take care of first, before that can happen."

"I understand. Complications." She sighed. "I'm glad you've got Rory and the rest of the gang there with you, at least, even if I can't be there. Promise me you'll let them help?"

"They already are."

"Good. Just remember you aren't alone." Her voice softened. "Love you, Callum."

"Love you too. And I'll let you know as soon as anything changes."

He hung up, before his father could grab the phone and start babbling about alpacas again. He stared at the two names and phone numbers he'd scribbled down.

He felt a bit like Schrodinger, contemplating a metaphorical box containing a cat that could be either dead or alive (at school, the analogy had completely baffled him until he'd finally realized that other people needed to *open the box* to determine the state of the cat). At the moment, he could still be Beth's father. But once he made these phone calls…

He took a deep breath, steeling himself, and started with the easier one. As his mother had predicted, Connor's phone went straight to voicemail. He left a brief, curt message: *It's Callum. Call me as soon as you can. It's important.*

That left the other one.

Given how early it was in the morning, he'd somewhat expected to have to leave a voicemail on Conleth's phone too. But to his surprise, his brother picked up on the second ring.

"Conleth Tiernach-West, Tiernach Enterprises," his brother said, crisp and professional. *He* clearly wasn't in bed.

"It's me."

This, apparently, wasn't enough.

"I'm sorry, who?" Conleth sounded distracted. He could hear the rapid *clickclickclick* of a keyboard in the background. "Who is this?"

"Callum." For the sake of clarity, he added, "Your brother."

"*Callum?*" Conleth's typing ceased abruptly. His voice sharpened, taking on a raw edge of alarm. "What's wrong? Is someone hurt? Mom? Dad?"

Why did everyone act like him calling was some kind of national emergency? "Nothing's wrong. Can we go to video?"

He could practically *hear* Conleth's eyebrows raising. "Why? Forgotten what you look like?"

Despite the mockery, the screen flickered, showing him his brother. As usual, he was sleek and sharp in a dark, tailored business suit, with a red-gold silk tie that perfectly matched his hair. The wide window behind him showed a gray, misty view of the London skyline, the early dawn light turning the city into a pencil sketch of itself.

Although he'd been braced for it, the familiar brief stab of envy went through him at Conleth's effortlessly elegant, sophisticated appearance. They might technically have exactly the same face, but Conleth always made it look better.

"You're at the office already?" Callum said, a little surprised.

Conleth wrinkled his nose. "There's always some bullshit crisis requiring my attention. Sometimes I think the whole business connives to generate drama just to keep me chained to my desk." He hunched forward, evidently peering at his own phone screen. A crease appeared between his brows. "Where are you, a cave? Is *that* why you're calling? I mean, I can pull some strings and scramble a helicopter and a SWAT team if you've fallen down a well or something, but I warn you, I'm never going to let you live this down."

"I'm *fine*," he said, through gritted teeth. "I'm at my base. In Montana."

"I do know where you live, you know." Conleth leaned back in his leather executive chair, idly swiveling back and forth. "So why *are* you calling in the middle of your night? Just because you were missing me?"

"No," he said, emphatically. "I have news. I met my mate."

All traces of mockery fled Conleth's face. He'd never before seen his brother look so entirely nonplussed.

"Uhh...congratulations," Conleth said, sounding like he expected some kind of trap. "And you're telling me this why, exactly?"

"Mom. You know she'd like us to be closer."

It was, after all, the truth. Just not the *whole* truth.

You keep telling yourself that, his pegasus murmured.

Ignoring his unhelpful inner beast, he tapped at his phone screen. "Her name's Diana Whitehawk. Here. I'm sending you a picture."

His heart thudded at the *swoosh* of the file transferring from his phone to Conleth's. He'd sent Conleth the second photo he'd taken of Diana—the one that didn't include Beth. He focused on his brother's face, watching for any sign of reaction.

Conleth's eyes flickered over the photo. His expression didn't change in the slightest. "She's very pretty. I'm happy for you."

He let out the breath he'd been holding. It wasn't Conleth.

Thank God. It was going to be hard enough to explain things to

Diana as it was. If he'd had to reveal that Beth's *actual* biological father was the sophisticated billionaire who'd twice beaten out actual princes to be named 'England's Most Eligible Bachelor' by three different gossip magazines…well, he might as well have given up and booked Diana and Beth's plane tickets to London now.

"Thanks," he said. "Bye."

"Wait!" Conleth jerked upright, reaching out as if to physically grab him through the phone screen to stop him from hanging up. "Is that really the only reason you called?"

He paused with his thumb over the 'End call' button. "Yes. Why?"

"Well…" Conleth dropped his hand, looking uncharacteristically awkward. "You know. I thought maybe you wanted to talk about the last time we saw each other face-to-face."

His new-found relief lurched. *That* had been the ill-fated bachelor auction, of course. How had Conleth known? Had his own expression given something away?

He masked his alarm with his best withering, stony-faced stare. "Not really. Why? Something you need to tell me?"

Conleth fidgeted with some papers scattered across his desk. "Just…look, did you know Connor ended up having to take your place?"

"I heard something about that," he said, cautiously. "But I thought it might have been you."

"Hell no. Even Connor couldn't talk me into that one. He only convinced me to get involved in the first place because…never mind." Conleth shook his head. "Look, the point is, you *won*, okay? Connor bitched about it for months. So for once in your life, can you please just let it go? How long are you going to keep holding this stupid grudge?"

You have no idea. "Goodbye, Conleth."

This time, he managed to hang up before his brother could interrupt. He switched his phone off before dropping it back into his pocket, feeling like he'd spent two hours running up Thunder Mountain with a double-loaded pack. Phones were *exhausting.*

He closed his eyes for a moment, losing himself in the small, soothing energies of the nocturnal creatures going about their private business all around. He'd always preferred the base at night, when the distracting glare of human lives dimmed into dreams. He could think better.

And thinking was exactly what he needed to do.

So. It's me or Connor.

Either way, it was clear that Diana had fallen for Connor's charm. He couldn't blame her for that, even though it made him want to punch Connor in the face even more than usual. *Everyone* liked Connor. He was wild, funny, charismatic…

And totally unsuitable to be a father.

Which…gave him the faintest glimmering outline of a plan.

He flipped over to a fresh page in his notebook, and started to make a list.

CHAPTER 11

Miracle of miracles, for once Beth slept through the entire night. Diana awoke at the positively luxurious hour of six o'clock in the morning, to find Beth just starting to stir at her side. Soft golden light winked through the crack in the curtain. She yawned, stretching—and immediately there was a quiet tap on the door.

"May I come in?" Callum's voice said from the other side. "I have coffee."

She hesitated, self-conscious. She always looked terrible in the morning. Then again, it wasn't like she was trying to seduce Callum.

More's the pity, whispered some part of her that definitely wasn't Gertrude.

Diana shook away the silly thought. She sat up, pulling the sheet over her bare legs. "If you have coffee, you can definitely come in."

He entered, carefully balancing a tray. Beth shrieked in excitement, crawling over to him at top speed. Diana's heart thudded in alarm, but Callum deftly side-stepped Beth's grab at him, still holding the tray perfectly level. He set it down on the bedside table, then scooped up the baby.

"Hello," he said softly, gazing into her eyes.

Beth gurgled, beamed, and, with an unmistakable loud, triumphant noise, filled her diaper.

"Oh dear," Diana said, as the smell permeated the small room. She tugged her t-shirt down over her panties as best she could, preparing to get up. "Sorry about that. I'll change her."

Callum shook his head. He tucked the giggling Beth under his arm like a football, squatting down to reach for a towel. "I'll do it. You have your coffee."

"Are you sure?" Diana said anxiously, as he spread the towel on the floor.

"Yes." His sweet, hesitant smile briefly lit up his face. "It's definitely my turn, after all."

He laid Beth down on the his impromptu changing mat, arranging a diaper, wipes, and a plastic bag around her. For a moment he studied the scene, with the air of a man preparing to perform complex brain surgery. Then, a little gingerly, he unfastened the snaps at the bottom of Beth's romper.

He'll get it wrong. He won't wipe her properly. He doesn't know what he's doing. You should take over.

Diana forced herself to keep her mouth shut, despite Gertrude's fretting. No one had taught *her* how to change a diaper, after all. Callum was a grown-ass man. He could work it out.

He flashed her a rather wry look, wrestling one-handed with Beth, who had decided this was the ideal moment for a spot of morning yoga. "Thanks."

"For what?"

"Not saying anything."

"Well, I reckon if you can put out forest fires, you can handle a baby."

He let out a breath of near-silent laughter. "Fires are easy. *This* is hard. Don't forget your coffee."

Leaving Callum to his epic battle, she investigated the tray. There was a battered thermos full of pitch-black coffee, along with a tin mug, a scratched spoon, a handful of tiny creamer pots, and some packets of sugar. Despite the well-worn appearance of the implements, the whole thing was laid out as carefully as room service at a fancy hotel—packets fanned, spoon peeking out of a folded paper napkin, creamers neatly stacked. He'd even put a tiny spray of wildflowers next to the mug.

She shook her head in amazement. "You did all this for me? This early?"

"It's not early for hotshots. Crew gets up at five, most days." He was trying to stuff Beth back into her romper, while she did her best rendition of the Hokey-Pokey. "Er. Is there a trick to this?"

"I usually distract her with a toy." Smothering a smile, Diana dangled the coffee spoon over Beth's head. "Hey, baby, look at this."

Beth made a grab for the spoon, giving Callum time to finally finish clothing her. He sat back, a little out of breath, looking down at his daughter with the pride of someone who had just ascended Mount Everest…and then muttered a swearword.

Diana giggled. "Hey, for a first attempt, it was pretty amazing." With the deftness of long practice, she undid the crooked snaps, fastening them correctly. "I once managed to put her romper on upside-down. She looked like a little baby seal, flapping her footie-flippers, with her feet sticking out the arm-sleeves at the bottom. Took me an embarrassingly long time to work out what on earth I'd done wrong."

"I'll get better." He stood up, gingerly holding the plastic bag with the dirty diaper in it. "I'll go throw this out. Do you like chocolate chips in your pancakes?"

"Yes," Diana said automatically, and then blinked. "Wait, what?"

"Breakfast." Apparently he felt that this was all the explanation necessary. He nodded down at Beth, who was now enthusiastically banging the spoon on the floor. "Can she eat pancakes?"

"She'd eat gravel if you put chocolate chips in it."

His heart-melting smile flashed again. "I'll be back soon. Don't go anywhere."

He slipped out the door without waiting for a response, closing it softly behind him. Beth squawked. She crawled over to it, plopped down onto her bottom, and screwed up her face in preparation for a wail.

"Oh no. He's coming right back, baby. Don't do that." Diana hastily snatched up the napkin and draped it over her head. "Look! Where's Mommy? Peek-a-boo!"

Beth cast her a look of deep and withering scorn. Clearly peek-a-boo was a game for *babies*. Then again, it had never really held her interest. Even when she'd been four months old, she'd always seemed to know exactly where Mommy was.

"How about a cuddle?" Diana picked her up, trying to settle her on her lap. "Some milk? No?"

Even boob was no consolation for lack of Daddy, apparently. Beth firmly pushed away Diana's attempts to feed her, kicking her in the stomach. Her face was turning an ominous shade of tomato, heralding an incipient tantrum.

Then, suddenly, she stopped thrashing. Her head swiveled, turning toward the door. For no apparent reason, she giggled.

"What is it, baby?" Puzzled, Diana listened, but couldn't hear anything that might have attracted Beth's attention. "Are you seeing ghosts again?"

Sometimes she genuinely wondered if Beth *could* see ghosts. Or at least, whether she had abnormally sharp hearing. She often seemed to be paying attention to something that Diana couldn't perceive herself.

Perhaps Beth had heard Callum coming back. Shifting her daughter to one arm, she went to the door, opening it. She took a step out into the common room—and her foot bumped something soft.

A dead rat! She bit back a yelp, jerking back—and then realized that the limp thing was bright blue, which made it unlikely to be a real animal.

A little gingerly, she picked it up. It was fuzzy and floppy and had clearly been well-loved. It was missing an ear, but she was pretty certain that at some point it had been a stuffed rabbit.

Callum must have left it out for Beth to play with. From the well-worn look of the bunny, it must have been a treasured childhood toy.

Sweet that he still takes it with him wherever he goes. A bit strange, but sweet.

It probably reminded him of home, she decided. He'd mentioned that he had family back in England. It had to be tough, being apart from them for half the year.

"Buhbuhbuhbuh!" Beth pronounced, stretching out her arms in demand.

"That's right, sweetie. Bunny." Diana gave the toy a quick once-over. It seemed safe. The eyes and nose were embroidered on rather than plastic, so Beth couldn't chew them off. Setting Beth down, she gave her the toy. "You like Bunny? You want to play with him while Mommy has her coffee?"

"Buhbuhbuh!" Beth seized the rabbit, squeezing it with all her strength. It made a loud, unexpected *squeak!*, which Beth clearly found to be the most hilarious thing ever.

Who puts a squeaker in a baby's teddy? Someone who didn't have children, Diana could only assume. Still, at least it was keeping Beth amused. Trying to ignore the persistent *squeaksqueaksqueakSQUEAK-squeak* as Beth practiced the Heimlich maneuver on poor Bunny, she went back to her coffee.

Drawing back the curtain, she gazed out as she sipped her steaming mug. Callum's cabin was set right at the edge of the hotshot base, a little way off from the other buildings. Her window faced downslope, giving her a spectacular view out over the surrounding forest. A faint haze hung over everything, as the autumn sun slowly burned off the morning dew. Mountains shimmered on the horizon, looking like they had been painted in watercolor.

The peaceful surroundings warmed her soul as much as the coffee warmed her body. As a kid, she'd often gone on long camping trips with her parents. That had stopped after her mom had passed away, though. Her dad had always claimed that he just enjoyed the comforts of modern life too much to want to sleep in a tent, but she'd always suspected that actually the wilderness reminded him too much of what he'd lost.

As an adult, she'd always gone out hiking whenever she could, but that had all come to an end with Beth's arrival. This was the closest she'd gotten to nature for a long time. Something inside her seemed to uncurl, stretching out like a flower unfurling to greet the sun.

A flash of movement at the edge of the forest caught her eye. Something was picking its way through the undergrowth, pale coat glimmering in the mottled shafts of sunlight.

A deer? A white deer? She held very still, though her heart beat harder in excitement. White animals held special meaning to Lakota, like they did to many other tribes. To see a white deer on her first morning here felt like a sign—an affirmation that she was on the right path.

She could sorely use a bit of reassurance on that point. She held her breath, silently entreating the deer to step forward just a little bit more, so she could see it properly.

As if it had heard her, it picked its way out of the forest, placing every hoof as delicately as a dancer. It was small—bigger than a fawn, but still with the adorable gangliness of youth. Its coat was pure white, without a single blemish. Against the gold and greens of the forest, it shone like a star.

It turned its head, seeming to meet her eyes through the window. It pricked up its small, pointed ears.

It wasn't a deer.

Diana stared. She rubbed her eyes, and looked again.

The young unicorn continued to gaze calmly back.

It couldn't be a trick of perspective. It was looking right at her, clearly showing that it only had a single, perfectly straight horn, directly in the center of its forehead. Its body wasn't entirely deer-like either. A slight breeze rippled its long, silky mane, and tugged at the feathery fur around its fetlocks. It wasn't a goat, or a miniature pony, or some other mundane creature.

It was a unicorn.

The sound of the cabin's door opening made her jump, spilling coffee across her hand. Across the clearing, the creature leaped back into the forest in a single graceful bound, disappearing from view as if it had never existed at all.

"Breakfast," Callum announced, entering. He paused, looking at her more closely. "Something wrong?"

There was no way she could tell him what she'd seen. Especially when she couldn't believe it herself. She grabbed a napkin, dabbing at the coffee she'd spilled. "I, um, was just looking at the view. I thought I saw, uh, an animal. Moving in the woods."

Callum cocked his head a little to one side, like he was listening to something. "A white deer?"

She twitched guiltily. "What makes you say that?"

"A herd of them lives on Thunder Mountain. They're very tame. Hang around the base a lot." He was still studying her. His eyebrows drew together. "*Did* you see a white deer?"

You can't really have seen a unicorn. You're going crazy. You hit your head yesterday and now you're seeing things and if you tell anybody they'll take Beth away—

"Yes," she said firmly. "Yes. That must be what it was."

He drew in a breath as though about to say something, then let it out again unused. He turned to put his tray down—and paused.

"Ah." He stared at Beth, who was waving Bunny about by one leg. "Has that, er, been in her mouth?"

Beth answered this question by stuffing the toy's entire butt into her beaming face.

"Well, it has *now*," Diana sighed over the *squeaksqueaksqueak* as Beth gnawed on the rabbit. "Is that a problem?"

"Er." Callum winced as he watched his daughter brutalize the toy. "Well. It probably should have been washed first."

"Sorry. I found it outside the door. I assumed you'd left it for her."

"Not me. That belongs to...one of my colleagues. He must have thought she'd like to play with it."

"Oh." Diana didn't much like the thought of someone sneaking into the cabin softly enough that she hadn't noticed, but at least the firefighter had clearly meant well. "That was kind of him."

"Yes," Callum said, rather darkly. He shook his head, turning back to his tray. "I brought breakfast. I didn't know what you'd like, so I made everything."

He wasn't kidding. As well as the promised chocolate-chip pancakes, there was a plate piled high with crispy bacon and three sorts of eggs; a bowl of cornflakes and another of porridge; a towering stack of toast surrounded by a thicket of jars and bottles. Diana didn't think she'd would even have been able to *lift* the tray, let alone carry it all the way across the base.

"This is incredible. Thank you. Though I couldn't possibly eat all that."

Her stomach chose that moment to loudly announce that it was perfectly willing to try.

Callum's mouth twitched up. "It's for us all to share. But don't hold back. I can always make more."

He took a small saucer piled with miniature pancakes from the tray, and sat down cross-legged on the floor. Detecting trace amounts of chocolate with the sensitivity of a bloodhound, Beth abandoned Bunny to make a bee-line for his lap. Callum sat her on his knee, handing her baby-sized bites of pancake.

Diana hunted through the crowded bottles in search of syrup. There were condiments on the tray that she didn't even recognize, let alone know whether she wanted to put them on her breakfast.

She picked one up, examining the hand-written label. "What's Dragonbreath?"

"Hot sauce. Joe makes it." Callum broke off baby-sized bits of pancake, handing them one at a time to Beth. "He insisted I bring some for you. Don't try it."

"Thanks for the warning." She put the bottle back, picking up a squat black jar. "What about Marmite?"

"Food of the gods," Callum said, with a perfectly straight face.

She unscrewed the lid, took a sniff, and quickly recapped it again. "Which gods? Cthulhu and Hades?"

Callum made another of those voiceless laughs. "Maybe you have to have grown up with it. Blaise brings it over from England."

"That's where most of the squad is from, right? I can tell from the accents."

He nodded, handing Beth another piece of pancake. "City called

Brighton, on the south coast. Our parents are best friends, so we all grew up together. I'm actually Irish, though. Not English. Very different."

"I'll have to take your word for it. I've never been out of the States." Finding the maple syrup at last, she liberally doused her pancakes. "So does that mean Beth is Irish too, by descent?"

"Yes. If we register the birth there, she can claim citizenship when she's older, if she wants."

"American, Lakota, Irish." Diana paused to savor a heavenly mouthful of sweet, fluffy, chocolatey pancake goodness. "I'm glad that she's been blessed with such a rich heritage. It's good to belong to more than one world."

"Yes." Callum hesitated for a second, as though tempted to add something more, then shook his head a little. "I don't know anything about Lakota culture. I'll have to learn."

"Well, I have whole stacks of books and papers if you're serious about that. You'd be doing me a favor, actually." She sighed, thinking of all the boxes cluttering up her small apartment. "I've been meaning to get rid of all that stuff."

He glanced up at her. "Why?"

"It's just in the way. Now that Beth's more active, she needs more space. And it's not like I need all my old research materials now. I was doing a doctorate in Lakota storytelling traditions, you see. But then..." She gestured at Beth in explanation.

His eyebrows drew down. "Do you *want* to finish your thesis?"

"Well...yes. But it's not—"

"Then you should," he interrupted. He released another piece of pancake into Beth's demanding hands. "We'll work it out."

He said it so simply, as if it was no big deal. As though she should just take it as a given that he would be around to help now, in whatever way she needed...

"Why are you being so nice to me?" she blurted out.

Callum paused, pancake dangling from his fingers. Beth squawked impatiently, making grabby motions, her hands outstretched like hungry starfish.

"You said it yourself." Callum gave Beth the pancake, then nodded down at her. "We're permanently bound together."

"Yes, but that doesn't explain all, all *this*." Diana waved round at the ridiculously lavish breakfast, the cabin that he'd so carefully prepared, Callum himself. "You're Beth's father. I'm really glad that you're taking that seriously, but honestly, you don't have to wait on *me* hand and foot. I'm just her mother, not a princess."

"No," Callum agreed. The corner of his mouth hooked up, just a little. "You're a goddess."

Diana huffed in exasperation, despite the way her insides melted at that devastating almost-smile. "I'm serious, Callum. I meant what I said yesterday. You don't have to pander to me out of fear that I'll keep Beth away if you don't."

His smile flickered out. "Do you really think that's the only reason I'd want to do things for you?"

"Well, it's the one that makes most sense. We only met yesterday, yet you seem eager to upend your entire life."

Beth had finished the pancake, and was now patting her hands happily in the remaining puddle of syrup. Callum caught her wrists before she could start rubbing her palms across her head. He reached for a wet wipe.

He kept his eyes on Beth, cleaning each of her fingers with infinite care. "She upended your entire life, didn't she?"

"Yes, but...that's different."

Callum finished Beth's first hand, and started on the next. "Don't see how."

"I *chose* to have her. It was my decision, and I took it, and I don't regret that. You didn't get that choice. I've sprung all this on you without warning." She chased the last bit of pancake around her plate, and eyed up the bacon, wondering if it would be greedy to help herself to some. "You're taking it so well that it's honestly starting to give me the heebie-jeebies. Maybe it's just my anxiety disorder, but I can't help worrying about what's really going through your head."

Callum put Beth on the floor, getting up. Without being asked, he forked a generous helping of bacon and eggs onto her plate. He didn't sit down again. Instead, he started collecting up the used breakfast things, stacking them neatly on the tray.

"Do you believe in fate?" he said abruptly, out of nowhere.

The words rang an echo in her memory. "You asked me that before."

He flashed her a brief, strangely startled glance. "Did I?"

"Before the auction. Remember?"

He shook his head slightly. "I...don't recall that. What did you say?"

She struggled to remember herself. "I'm not sure I said anything. I thought it was kind of a weird question to ask someone you'd just met."

His intent gaze searched her face. "What about now?"

To be the subject of such utter focus was unnerving. She scooped up a forkful of her breakfast as an excuse to avoid his eyes. The scrambled eggs were light as buttery clouds, perfectly complimented by the smoky, salty bacon. Hot damn, the man could cook.

She forced her attention away from the food and back onto his question. "I still think it's weird, to be honest. Why do you keep asking, anyway? Do *you* believe in fate?"

He fidgeted with the bottles and jars on the tray, arranging them into rigidly straight lines.

"I believe that some things happen for a reason," he said at last. He jerked his chin in the direction of Beth, who was once again playing with Bunny. "Like her. I think...I think we were meant to come together in this way."

His words sent an odd shiver through her. Something at the very center of her soul seemed to resonate to them, whispering *yes*, even as the rest of her mind shrieked that the whole thing was crazy.

He spoke before she'd had a chance to work out how to respond, or even how she *wanted* to respond. "I called my parents last night. I told them about you."

Her heart twisted with a bittersweet pang. She was delighted that Beth at least had one set of living grandparents, of course...but it only sharpened her sorrow that her own parents would never know their granddaughter.

She forced a smile to cover her conflicted emotions. "I hope you didn't tell them *every* detail about how we met."

That wry half-smile tugged at his mouth once more. "No fear of that."

"Great. I don't want them thinking the mother of their granddaughter is a *total* floozy." She ate another mouthful of eggs, trying to look casual. "So what did they say?"

His smile widened, adding a spike of pure lust to her emotional cocktail. "My father thinks I should propose to you immediately. Possibly with an alpaca."

She choked on her eggs, and had to spend an unladylike moment coughing. Callum passed her a glass of water, and waited patiently.

"Thanks," she gasped, when she was no longer in danger of having the world's most embarrassing obituary. "Um. I guess your parents are really old-fashioned, huh?"

Callum's eyebrows rose. "Alpacas are traditional?"

"No! I meant—the other thing. A shotgun wedding."

"No shotguns would be involved." He grimaced a little. "Ideally no alpacas, either, but I can't promise that. Once my father's set on an idea, there's no stopping him."

She started to reply, and then paused, staring at him. "Wait. *You* think we should get married? Just because we have a baby together?"

The amusement lurking in his eyes vanished. She'd never seen him look so utterly serious. Her ovaries ripped off their clothes shrieking *Take us now!*

"No," he said. "Not just for that reason."

Her mouth hung open. She realized that she was still holding a forkful of eggs, frozen in mid-air. She put it down again untasted, appetite suddenly chased away by butterflies.

"I don't understand," she said, because she *couldn't* be understanding him correctly. "What are you trying to say?"

"Gubuhdababababa," suggested Beth. She was tugging at Callum's pants, trying to haul herself up. She managed to get most of the way to her feet, tottered for an instant, and sat down hard on her butt.

Callum swooped down as her bottom lip started to tremble. He put his hands under her arms, lifting her back to her feet. Beth's threatened tears instantly turned to a delighted chuckle. She flexed her legs happily, Callum taking most of her weight like a human baby bouncer.

"You said we have to be honest with each other if this is going to work." Callum's head was bent over Beth, hiding his face. His arms stayed rock-steady regardless of how Beth yanked against them. "So I want to be clear on one thing. I want you. I want to be with you. Not just as Beth's father. I want to be your lover. Your partner."

He looked up at her at last. His eyes were utterly certain. "Your husband."

Her mouth had gone dry. She swallowed, hard. "But you barely know me."

"I have loved you from the first moment we met," he said, simply.

"That—that's—" She shook her head, suddenly wondering if she was still asleep, and this was all a dream. "I'm sorry, and I'm not trying to tell you how you feel, but I don't believe in love at first sight. Not the sort of love that lasts, at least. I think you can only really love someone when you truly know them. That takes more than eyes meeting across a crowded room."

Callum's gaze was as steady as his arms. "I think you can know at a single glance that you want to spend the rest of your life getting to know someone."

Diana opened her mouth—to say what, she had no idea—but Callum shook his head, forestalling her.

"I'm not expecting you to feel the same way," he said. He looked down at Beth again, whose legs were starting to wobble. He eased her back down onto her bottom. "I just wanted you to know that's how *I* feel. So we're clear. Do you want to take a shower?"

A shower sounded distinctly appealing. Ideally a very, very cold one. She needed to get away from Callum's brain-melting sex aura long enough to think, without her traitor hormones hollering *Proven fertile stud! Claim that excellent genetic material ASAP!* at her.

"Yes," she said faintly. "A shower sounds like a good idea."

"I'll watch Beth." He picked up the baby, settling her on his hip.

"Don't worry, we won't leave the cabin." He hesitated, clearing his throat. "If you want to keep the door to the bathroom open so you can keep us in sight, I'll…I'll *try* not to look. No promises. Sorry."

Well, she *had* asked him to be honest. And she was touched that he'd remembered her anxiety over Beth leaving her sight.

"It's okay," she said. "I trust you."

It was, she realized, true. She *did* trust Callum. Gertrude didn't raise a single peep at the prospect of him looking after Beth solo for a short time. She still didn't know what to make of him, or his self-admitted infatuation with her, but…she trusted him.

"Why don't you take her for a little walk?" she said. "Some fresh air would be good for her."

Callum treated her to a flash of that brilliant, dazzling smile. She pushed down a mad urge to accept his insane proposal on the spot, alpacas and all.

"Thank you," he said. He started to take Beth out of the bedroom, then paused, glancing at her over his shoulder. "There's something else you should know."

Oh God. At this point, Diana was fully prepared for him to tell her that he was actually a werewolf. "What?"

"There's one way I'm like my father." He still had that teasing smile, but his eyes darkened, filled with unmistakable heat. "Once I'm set on something, I don't give up."

And she was left wondering if she even wanted him to.

CHAPTER 12

So far, his plan was going perfectly.

Callum set Beth down on the soft meadow grass outside his cabin. She was immediately entranced by the long, waving stalks, seizing a double handful in her fat little fists. Since she didn't seem inclined to stuff the grass into her mouth—possibly due to already being full of pancake—Callum let her explore.

He sat down next to her, pulling out his notebook. Thanks to his pegasus senses, he didn't need to be physically looking at Beth in order to keep an eye on her. He flipped past his already-completed list items (*Breakfast* ran to three pages of sub-items, all neatly crossed off), finding his place.

Serve breakfast
    Feed Beth
    Clean Beth
    Attempt to not be a total idiot
    Declare undying love to Diana

Clean up breakfast things

~

He crossed off the first three items, then dithered over the fourth. He didn't think he'd been a *total* idiot, but then again, he had inadvertently started babbling about alpacas. He ended up circling that line, drawing three arrows pointing to it for emphasis. It was more an ongoing life goal than a to-do item, anyway.

He ticked off *Declare undying love to Diana* with a bold, confident stroke. *That* had gone better than he'd expected. It wasn't the sort of thing that was easy to work into normal conversation, but she'd given him the perfect opening. And she hadn't immediately grabbed Beth and run screaming from his cabin. All in all, he was giving himself an A+++ on that front.

He had a few days of grace, before Connor was back in contact and he would be able to finally confirm which one of them was the father. He had to use every single precious minute to show Diana that *he* was the right man to be Beth's father, regardless of her actual biological parentage.

And then, when he *did* finally reveal the truth to her—whatever it was—she would pick him.

He hoped.

He quickly skimmed his itinerary for the rest of the day. Normally his daily routine when they were at base was consistent enough that he didn't need a list—it was one of the things he liked best about the job—but today was different. There was a lot to be done to prepare the base for the winter months: clean all the gym equipment, inventory the supply room, check and lock up all the cabins, oil and wrap tools for storage…

He could sense the crew moving around, going about their assigned tasks. Everyone was working briskly, eager to finish as soon as possible. Once Buck gave the all-clear, most of the Thunder Mountain hotshots would be collecting their final paychecks and scattering, going wherever they went off-season. Only A-squad and Buck would be left behind.

Good. He was looking forward to having fewer lives around. It would make it easier to concentrate on Diana, and winning her heart.

Beth had lost interest in the grass, and was now digging her fingers into the dirt instead. She scooped up a handful, mouth opening ominously. Hastily shoving his notepad back into his pocket, he intercepted her.

"Sorry. Not chocolate flavored." He brushed off her palms, then offered her his own hands. "Want to practice walking some more?"

She seized his fingers in a surprisingly strong grip. With his help, she could get herself up, but she didn't seem to know what to do from there. He could practically feel the frustration welling up inside her.

"It's okay," he told her, easing her back to a sitting position. "You'll get it."

From the way Beth screwed up her face, she wanted to get it *now*. She drummed her heels against the ground as if trying to kick gravity in the face.

She gave voice to her feelings with a heart-felt, angry, "Abadababada*da!*"

Whatever she'd been trying to say, she clearly felt strongly about it. And from the way she sucked in her breath, she was preparing to launch into a long, loud speech on the topic. He didn't want Diana to hear and start worrying that she'd made a mistake, trusting him to look after Beth solo. He cast around for a distraction.

"Look!" He pointed into the trees. "Squirrels!"

There *were* a pair of squirrels chasing each other around a pine tree at the edge of the woods. But, as Beth's head snapped round, he belatedly realized that she wouldn't possibly be able to see them. *He* couldn't see them. Not with his eyes, anyway.

He braced himself for a betrayed wail—but Beth clapped her hands. She let out a delighted belly-laugh, as though he'd just whipped out a full three-ring circus for her entertainment. Her gaze perfectly tracked the squirrels, despite the foliage hiding them from view.

She could sense them. *She could sense them.*

His pegasus flicked its tail in mild exasperation. *Of course she can. She is our foal.*

He squatted down to Beth's level, studying her face. She returned his stare guilelessly, her green eyes clear and innocent. Was her own pegasus looking back at him, from the hidden depths of her soul? Was *that* how she had seemed to recognize him as her father at first sight?

Acting on impulse, he reached out to her telepathically, as he would to another mythic shifter. *Hello?*

She blinked. "Babadadada?"

He could feel the faintest, haziest touch against his own mind, soft as butterfly wings. No words—just pure emotion, shining on his soul like summer sunlight.

Recognition. Delight.

Simple, uncomplicated joy.

Emotion choked his throat. She *was* a shifter. She was a pegasus, like him. And she knew him.

She loved him.

Ours, his own pegasus whispered. It came forward—not to shift, just stepping further out of his shadowed soul, into the light of Beth's awareness. It stretched out its neck, reaching out to nuzzle her. *Hello, little one.*

Beth's eyes widened. He could feel her attention running over his inner animal, like she was stroking it with her little fingers. It tickled, but he held still, not wanting to do anything to break that delicate communion.

"That's right," he said, the barest breath. "That's me. You have one too. Inside. Part of you."

Beth cocked her head to one side, barely-there eyebrows drawing down. Her rosebud mouth pursed. She looked even more determined than she had when she'd been attempting to stand up.

"Ba!" she announced in triumphant tones, and shifted.

It happened so fast, he didn't have time to stop her. Not that he would have had the faintest idea *how* to stop her. One second, Beth was sitting in the grass, cute and adorable and completely human.

And the next second, she was cute and adorable and a pegasus.

WHAT DID YOU DO? he roared at his inner animal, as Beth fluttered her tiny wings experimentally.

Nothing! His stallion pranced, looking distinctly proud. *She did that all by herself! How clever our foal is!*

Diana, of course, picked that moment to come out of the shower.

He could sense her moving around, heading back into her bedroom. Her bedroom, with the window that looked out over this meadow. If she glanced out...

He flung himself between Beth and the cabin, squaring his shoulders to try to block her from view as much as possible. Mythic shifters could make themselves invisible to ordinary humans...but it didn't work on close family members.

This was *not* how he wanted Diana to find out about the existence of shifters.

Make her change back! he shouted at his pegasus. *Quickly!*

His pegasus snorted, tail swishing. *If she wants to change back, she'll have to do it herself. But why would she want to? Look how magnificent she is!*

Beth also seemed to be pleased with her achievement. She was a deep chestnut red, similar to his own pegasus, though her mane and tail were black. Long black socks marked her legs, like she'd been dipped into ink. Her wings were mottled in unusual shades of red, black, and white. He'd never seen a pegasus with such striking coloring.

Beth dipped her soft muzzle to nose curiously at her own tiny hooves, as though trying to work out what they were. Tentatively, she pushed herself up onto all four legs. Her knees wobbled, but she stayed upright.

Oh no. He spread his arms wider, wishing that he was wearing his firefighting jacket, or possibly a cape.

"Beth," he said desperately. "Please don't do that. Please lie back down."

Beth took a single, tentative step. And another. And another—

He whirled, lunging for her. *"Beth!"*

Too late.

With a delighted flick of her tail, Beth skipped just out of reach of his grasping fingers. He fell flat on his face, hard enough to knock the breath out of his lungs. Beth took the opportunity to bound away, growing more confident with every leap.

So strong! Callum's pegasus enthused. *So swift!*

He widened the mental channel, flinging out a desperate, indiscriminate plea. *HELP!*

Startled responses from his squad pelted into his mind like a barrage of snowballs. There were too many of them for him to be able to distinguish individual words, but they all carried the same fundamental meaning—*we're coming!*

Rory's mental roar cut through the overlapping babble. *Callum! What's wrong?*

Beth, he sent back, scrambling to his feet. She was already out of eyesight, skipping happily into the forest. *She shifted—she's running—Diana's going to come out here any second! I need help!*

Blaise, Joe, go stall Diana, Rory ordered, dropping instantly into command mode. *Fenrir, find Beth, cut her off if you can. Callum, don't panic. We're on our way.*

He was already charging into the woods after Beth. He could sense the squad dropping what they were doing, scrambling to come to his assistance.

He flung his awareness wider, searching for any hint of threat. What if Beth ran into a bear? What if she tripped and hurt herself? What if Lupa's hellhounds were still lurking, in that mysterious place outside his awareness, just waiting for an opportunity to pounce?

A new life *did* flare into being in front of Beth—but it was only Fenrir. Beth's random, zig-zagging run came to an abrupt stop.

Don't scare her! he flung into the hellhound's mind.

Don't think *can* scare this one,* Fenrir sent back, sounding both impressed and amused. *Peace, Shadowhorse. Cub is safe.*

He saw that with his own eyes a second later. Beth had come to a spraddle-legged halt, leaning against Fenrir's black side, apparently having exhausted her energy. Her flanks heaved, but she looked distinctly smug.

Fenrir's broad pink tongue smoothed Beth's tangled mane in long, soothing strokes. *There, clever cub. Back with pack now. All very proud of you.*

"Speak for yourself," Callum managed to gasp out. Sheer relief hit him like a mallet to the forehead. He sat down hard, putting his head between his knees. "My life just flashed before my eyes. Fenrir, you're my hero. I forgive you for sharing your rabbit chew toy with Beth."

Beth staggered over to him, apparently having more trouble coordinating her new legs at low speed. Her soft muzzle nudged his hair. She let out a brief, worried-sounding snort.

"I'm okay, baby." He patted her in reassurance, stroking her folded wings. Like all young pegasi, she had soft, short feathers rather than being downy like a baby bird. "And I'm not mad. You just scared me. A lot."

Fenrir's tongue lolled out in a canine grin. *Least she didn't fly away, Shadowhorse.*

One of Beth's ears tilted in the hellhound's direction. Her head turned, looking up at the sky speculatively.

Callum grabbed her as she started to spread her wings. "Please don't go giving her any ideas."

Beth wriggled on his lap. He tightened his grip, hugging her. He didn't think she would *actually* be able to fly—her full set of primary feathers wouldn't come in for years. Then again, he hadn't thought she'd be able to shift, either. He'd first shifted sometime around his second birthday, and *that* had been considered precocious enough.

He sensed more lives converging on their location. Rory, Seren and Wystan emerged from the undergrowth, in various degrees of dishevelment. Wystan immediately dropped to his knees next to him, reaching out to Beth. With a nod of thanks, Callum loosened his grip so that the paramedic could check Beth for any scratches or bumps she might have sustained during her brief escapade.

Rory muttered a swearword, staring down at Beth. He was shirtless and barefoot, a towel barely clinging to his hips. He must have been in the shower when Callum's mental scream had hit him.

"Now there's a complication we could do without," he said, shaking water out of his eyes. "How the hell did she manage to shift so young?"

Callum shrugged as best he could with an armful of distinctly disgruntled baby pegasus. "She *really* wanted to be able to walk."

"Well, she hasn't come to any harm from the experience," Wystan said, finishing his examination. "So now all we have to do is persuade her to shift back. Somehow."

"Quickly," Callum added. "Before Diana starts to wonder where we are."

"Do not fret overmuch on that account. Joe is with her. He's extremely good at being a distraction." Seren tilted her head, eyes unfocusing as she communed with her mate. "He says he can keep her occupied for some time. Though he may have to tell her the…apple story?" She looked round at them, frowning. "What is the apple story?"

Callum winced. "We need to get Beth to shift back *fast*."

He set Beth back on her hooves in front of him, fixing her with a stern look. She eyed him suspiciously, as though she could tell he wanted to put an end to her fun. She didn't look the slightest bit ready to shift back into a baby.

"You need to turn back now, Beth." He tried to send her a mental image of Diana. "Mommy can't see you like this. She wouldn't understand."

Beth's wings fluttered indecisively. She pranced a little, as if to say: *But look! Walking!*

"I know. I'll run with you later, I promise. But right now we need to go back to Mommy." He kept flooding her with encouraging thoughts, more emotional impressions than images—Diana's warmth, the softness of her hands, the way she smelled of home. "Mommy misses you. Let's go back to her now, okay?"

With a soft *pop!*, Beth shrank down into a human baby once more, balanced on her hands and knees. Callum caught her up before she could topple over. She snuggled happily against his chest, clearly worn out by her brief adventure.

"Well, that's step one accomplished." Rory ran a hand through his tousled blond hair, blowing out his breath. "Now how are we going to stop her from doing it *again*?"

CHAPTER 13

Diana fingered the braided red cord tied around Beth's ankle. "I'm still worried that she might be able to get it off and swallow it."

"I tied it securely. It can't slip off." Callum demonstrated, tugging at the anklet. It fit closely against Beth's skin; not tight enough to dig in, but snug enough that it couldn't go anywhere. "Please, let her keep it on? I wore one like this too, for a while, though I was a little older at the time. It's something of a family tradition."

Diana rubbed her finger over the soft, flat braid again. It *was* a beautiful thing—just red string, but knotted and tied in an intricate, intriguing pattern. And she liked Beth wearing something that Callum had made for her with his own two hands. It felt like a way for Beth to be carrying her father's love and protection wherever she went.

"Okay," she conceded. "As long as it doesn't bother her."

At the moment, nothing short of a nuclear explosion looked like it would bother Beth. She lay sprawled on the mattress, arms and legs outflung in total abandon. She'd spent the day crawling around the hotshot base, getting underfoot despite Diana's best efforts to contain her.

Fortunately, no one had seemed to mind. Even Superintendent

Buck, for all his growls and scowls, had succumbed to Beth's charms. Diana had found him carrying her about in the crook of one arm while he barked orders at his crew. He'd *claimed* he'd just picked her up so that Callum could get on with his work, but Diana had noticed Buck hadn't been in a hurry to hand Beth back.

Now, having received a full day of worship from her adoring fan club, Beth had completely crashed. Diana drew the sheet up over her, making sure it was tucked in securely. With a last kiss on her daughter's forehead, she tiptoed out of the bedroom.

She went out onto the front steps, leaving the cabin door cracked open behind her so that she would be able to hear if Beth woke up. Evening was falling, painting the mountains in gorgeous shades of violet and deep blue.

Callum produced a steaming mug out of nowhere, handing it to her. She sipped, tasting the tang of peppermint. He'd even remembered her favorite tea.

"Thank you." She sat down on the steps, cupping her hands around the warm mug. There was just starting to be a distinct chill in the air. "So, what does it mean? The red string thing. You said it was a family tradition."

Without being asked, Callum draped a soft woolen blanket over her shoulders. He sat down next to her, leaning his elbows on his knees. He didn't answer for a moment, staring up at the darkening sky.

"It's based on an Irish custom," he said at last. "To protect babies from the fae folk. Fairies don't like the color red, according to our stories. So mothers would tie bits of red string to their babies' cradles. To stop them from being stolen away in the night, and replaced with an uncanny changeling child."

"You tied it to Beth herself, though."

"Well, she doesn't have a cradle." His brow furrowed. "Which reminds me, I forgot to order a cot today. You can't keep sleeping on the floor with her. I have to make a note."

He evidently meant that literally, as he pulled a small notebook out of his back pocket. She caught a glimpse of pages and pages filled with dense, neat handwriting as he flipped through it.

"Wow," she said, a little startled. "You're certainly organized."

She'd meant it as a compliment, but he shot her a brief, furtive glance, cupping the notebook in his hand. He looked more like he'd been caught with porn rather than a planner.

"I—just like to have a list." He scribbled a brief note, and made the book disappear again. "There. I won't forget now. If you think of anything else she needs to be comfortable, just let me know."

"Thanks. I'll pay you back, of course."

He shook his head. "She's my daughter. Anything she needs, I'll get her. Or you."

That was edging too close to a topic that she wasn't entirely sure she was ready to address yet. After his startling declaration of love that morning, he'd stuck strictly to sensible, practical matters ever since. But she'd felt his unspoken feelings following her around all day, like a very polite elephant.

She retreated back to safer ground. "So, once Beth *does* have a cot, will you put the red string on that instead of round her ankle?"

"No." He hesitated, looking at her side-long. "I want it to keep her safe when she's awake, not just when she's asleep. I'm sorry. I know that sounds ridiculous. Talking about fairies like I believe in them."

"*Do* you believe in them?"

He was silent for a long, long time. Just when she'd decided he wasn't going to answer the question, he spoke at last.

"I believe there's a world most people don't even know exists. I believe that there are things that walk among us, invisible to human eyes. Powers. Creatures. Some fair. Some dangerous. Some both."

His voice was deep and solemn. It seemed to echo in her bones, in the center of her chest. The skin on her arms prickled under the blanket.

"I believe that Beth needs to be protected from that world," Callum went on. He stared out into the forest, his face in profile to her. "At least until she's old enough to know its risks. I gave her the anklet to keep it out of her reach for now, the same way that I would put a child-lock on a knife drawer. To keep her safe."

He turned toward her at last. His mouth curved in a wry, self-deprecating smile, though the rest of his face was still utterly serious.

"And now you must think I'm crazy," he said.

"No." Her mouth had gone dry. She couldn't tear herself away from those green, green eyes. "No, I don't think that."

His eyes darkened further, drawing her in. She felt that if she leaned forward, she would fall through them, into that other world. A place of mystery, and magic, and stars.

She broke away, taking a sip from her mug to cover her flustered confusion. "I believe in things that other people find weird too. Lakota stories, our rituals...they aren't just quaint, interesting traditions to me. They're real. I learned not to talk about that too, growing up."

He nodded, slowly. "Most people don't believe what they can't see for themselves."

"Well, my mother raised me to know better than that."

"My parents too." He hesitated, still studying her intently. "Diana, I have to tell you something. Something that happened today. With Beth."

Even though she knew, *knew*, that Beth was perfectly well and sleeping soundly, her heart still seized with sudden terror. All the air left her lungs. A hundred horrific possibilities seared through her mind—

"Diana!" Callum's hand closed over hers, bringing her back to herself. "It's all right. She's safe. She's well. Breathe."

She did so, a great, gasping breath that probably sounded like a dying walrus. She fought back against the iron fist constricting her chest. Slowly, she managed to regain her mental balance.

"I-I'm sorry," she got out at last. "I couldn't, couldn't take my meds today. Lost them in the fire. M-makes me more vulnerable to panic attacks."

"I should have asked if you needed any prescriptions replaced." Callum was still gripping her hand. His palm was rough, hardened by manual work. She could feel the strength in his fingers. "I'm sorry. I'll fly down to town first thing in the morning."

She managed a shaky laugh. "Fly? I didn't think we were *that* far from civilization."

Callum's fingers twitched on her own. "Figure of speech. Can you wait that long? If not, I'll take you to the ER. Right now."

"No, no. It's okay." She *was* okay now, her pulse starting to slow as the surge of adrenaline ebbed away. "I'm fine, really. Sometimes things just hit me hard, and I need a moment to handle them. What were you saying about Beth?"

Did he hesitate, for the barest fraction of a second? "She…she managed to slip out of my sight today, while you were having your shower. Not for long. Maybe half a minute. But it was the longest thirty seconds of my life."

He looked so sickened by the memory, she couldn't feel anything other than sympathy. She squeezed his hand in reassurance. "She's done the same to me, a few times. I know what it feels like."

"I've seen a wildfire bearing down on me, consuming whole trees in an instant. I've been on the third floor of a burning building when it started to collapse. I've seen—other things." His expression was haunted; his mouth a flat, grim line. "But I've never felt terror like I did today."

"She's okay, though. Nothing happened." She could feel the tension in his arm. She rubbed the palm of his hand with her thumb in small, soothing circles. "Thank you for being honest with me."

He was still looking like he wanted her to beat him with a stick for his sin. "I should have told you earlier."

"You didn't have to tell me at all. But you did."

The corner of his mouth twitched up, very slightly. "You're setting the bar very low for me there. You should demand higher standards."

"I have high standards," she protested, nettled. "I want Beth to have the best of everything."

He studied her face, a thoughtful expression stealing across his own. "Yes. You do. But not yourself."

"What?"

"You're so devoted to her." He spoke slowly, as if working the thought out one word at a time. "You're totally dedicated to her needs. But that doesn't leave any space for *you*. What you need. What you want."

"I just want Beth to be happy. That's all I need."

His voice roughened, taking on a slight, growling edge that sent a delicious shiver down her spine. "Is it?"

That intense, focused look was back in his eyes, leaving no doubt what he meant. The clear heat in his gaze shot through her, tingling in every nerve. She was suddenly powerfully, exhilaratingly alive. It had been so long since she had been aware of her body like that—not as a mother, but as a woman.

"Callum…" She was still holding his hand. She knew she should let go, but somehow she couldn't bring herself to pull away. "I don't think this is a good idea."

He said nothing. He just looked at her, as though she was the only woman in the world. As though nothing else mattered.

But that wasn't right. Something else *did* matter.

Someone else.

She drew her hand away from his at last, feeling oddly cold without that small point of contact. She tugged the blanket closer round her shoulders.

"Beth," she said firmly. "We have to think of what's best for her. If we got together, and then it didn't work out…it could make it harder for us to be good co-parents."

"What if it did work out?" His voice still held that hint of feral hunger. "Wouldn't that make things easier?"

Her body yearned to feel his warmth again. She stood up before she could do something stupid.

"It's too risky," she said. "We barely know each other. We can't let ourselves get carried away. Not yet."

He nodded, slowly, not seeming at all dismayed by this rejection. His mouth curled in a slow, pleased smile.

"Not yet," he said. "But you *do* want me."

Oh God yes! screamed every part of her body, some specific parts louder than others. That wicked, knowing smile slammed into her resolve like a battering ram.

"It's getting late. Beth will be up early. I need to get some rest if I'm not going to be a zombie in the morning." She took a step back, away from temptation, fumbling for the door. "Goodnight, Callum."

"Goodnight." He made no move to follow her, but she could feel the heat of his gaze, still watching her. "And Diana?"

She didn't dare look back at him, out of fear that all her clothes might spontaneously fall off. "Yes?"

His voice curled round her like an embrace. "Dream of what you want."

And, despite her best efforts, she did.

CHAPTER 14

Blaise turned a box over in her hands, squinting down at it. "What in the name of all that's unholy is a nasal aspirator?"

"It's for cleaning snot out of your baby's nose," Diana replied absently, scanning the superstore's shelves for baby shampoo. "You stick one end in their nostril, and suck on the other end."

"With your *mouth?*" Blaise stared for an instant, then laughed. "Okay, I admit it, you got me good there. Seriously, what's it for?"

"That really *is* what it's for. Read the back of the packet."

Blaise did so. Her mouth made a perfect 'o' of pure horror.

"You can put it back, though," Diana added. "I could never make those things work. Beth had a bad cold a few months back, and I ended up…well, maybe I'd better not tell you. Don't want to put you off your custard donut later."

They'd made the hour-long trip from the hotshot base to go shopping at the nearest out-of-town big box store. Beautiful as Thunder Mountain was, Diana was enjoying the change of scenery. With Blaise and Edith for company, it felt like a girls' day out.

Blaise dropped the nasal aspirator back onto the shelf with a shudder. "Every time I think babies can't get any more gross, you manage to surprise me. It's a miracle the human race didn't die out in the Stone Age."

Diana grinned at her. "The cuteness makes up for all the assorted bodily fluids. Most of the time."

"Definitely," Edith said, gazing down at Beth. Beth beamed back, as best she could around Bunny, who was as usual stuffed into her mouth. "I could put up with a fountain of diarrhea and projectile vomiting for cheeks this chubby."

Over the past few days with the crew, Diana had noticed that Edith seized any excuse to have a cuddle with Beth. The capable, strong firefighter was definitely broody.

She normally wouldn't raise the topic, in case it was a sensitive issue, but she'd grown close enough to Edith that she decided to risk asking. And Edith had told her flat-out that she preferred it when people spoke their minds rather than tried to drop hints. "Have you thought about having a baby of your own?"

Edith rocked on the balls of her feet in a short, repetitive motion. Her autistic body language wasn't hard to read, once you got over expecting her to express her emotions like neurotypical people. Diana could tell from Edith's subtle stimming that she was feeling a little shy, but still wanted to talk about this.

"I've been thinking about it a lot," Edith confessed. "Especially since meeting Beth. And I know Rory wants to have kids. He comes from a big family, you see. He often talks about how much he loved growing up with all his brothers and sisters."

"I wish I'd had siblings." Diana sighed wistfully. "I mean, I had a happy childhood, don't get me wrong…but it must be nice, having someone close to your age who'll always be there for you. Sometimes I worry about Beth being an only child."

Blaise waggled her eyebrows suggestively. "Well, I can think of someone who'd be *more* than eager to help you out on that front."

Diana's face heated. It wasn't the first such sly remark she'd heard from Callum's friends. He'd clearly told them about his feelings for her.

Or maybe they'd just been able to guess from his actions. He hadn't been shy about demonstrating his affection. Not that he was pestering her or anything. He was always just…there. With a sandwich, or a cup of coffee, or an offer to take Beth for a walk for an hour so that she could have a nap.

And with that devastating slight, subtle smile that never failed to make her toes curl. And those green, hungry eyes that made her feel seen in the best sort of way. Not to mention those broad, muscled shoulders…

Diana put the brakes on *that* train of thought before it could reach Destination: Very Very Bad (But Oh So Good). She cleared her throat, hoping that her blush wasn't *too* visible.

"I think Rory would be a great dad," she told Edith. "And you'd make a fantastic mother. Just look how much Beth adores you."

"I love her too. And I'm really grateful to you for letting me help take care of her. It's helped my confidence a lot." Edith was avoiding eye contact, but that was just her way. Diana knew that she meant every word. "I was worried that…well, nobody's quite sure how the genetics work for autism. There's a good chance that our baby would be like Rory. Neurotypical, I mean. As well as a—"

Edith seemed to catch herself, clamping her mouth shut as though to catch a word before it escaped. It wasn't the first time she'd stumbled like that. And she wasn't the only one on the crew who sometimes seemed to be censoring themselves. Sometimes Diana couldn't help feel that there was some big secret that everyone else knew, and was conspiring to hide from her.

Shut up, Gertrude, she told herself firmly. It was just her anxiety talking. She's seen enough of the crew to trust that they were good people. And she *was* a newcomer, an interloper. She couldn't expect them to include her in everything.

"Anyway," Edith went on, after that brief, peculiar pause. "I was worried that I might not be able to relate to my own baby. Or them to me. And if they *were* autistic, maybe that would make Rory feel left out. Though when I told him that he just laughed and said he'd love it if our kids took after me."

"So would I," Blaise put in. "A whole pack of mini-Rorys would be *insufferable*. Just imagine it. Little blond kids following you around like your own personal Scout group, itching for any opportunity to be helpful."

Diana smothered a giggle at the mental image. Rory *was* somewhat overprotective of Edith. He clearly trusted her skills and competence at work, but he still leaped on any chance to open a stuck jar or carry something heavy for her. Diana was certain he would have carried *Edith* around on a cushion, if she'd let him.

"No matter who they take after, your child is going to be their own person," she said to Edith. "The older Beth gets, the more I appreciate that fact. I mean, when she was first born, she was a tiny pink blob who basically slept, nursed and pooped. I still loved her from the moment I first saw her, but…" She searched for the right words to explain it. "That was because she was my daughter, not because she was *her*. Now, as I get to know her personality, I love her even more. Because she *is* a real, amazing, entire person. It doesn't matter how different to me she might turn out to be."

Edith gave her an embarrassingly admiring look. "Beth's really lucky to have you as a mom, you know."

Diana could feel her face going pink again. She wasn't used to praise. "Well. Your kids will be lucky to have *you*, if you do decide to go for it."

Edith bit her lip, her eyes darting around. "I do really want to. But…I love my job too. And I can't fight fires with a baby strapped into my backpack."

Diana, who'd been ready to leap in with further words of encouragement, felt her stomach drop. Of course, Edith would have to give up her career if she wanted to become a mother. Just like she'd had to give up her own academic aspirations when she'd decided to have Beth.

Blaise, however, snorted loudly. "So you take a year off to have the baby, and then Rory takes the next year off, and you keep alternating. You both get to work *and* look after your sprog. What's the problem?"

Diana blinked, taken aback by the proposal. Rory was the squad leader, after all. She'd assumed he had further career ambitions. "Would Rory be happy with that?"

"Are you kidding me? He'd love being a stay-at-home dad every other summer. Probably start an Instagram account and be constantly posting sickening photos with hashtag 'bestlife'" Blaise perked up, her habitual cynicism falling away. "Edith! *You* could be our squad boss, the years that Rory isn't here! Like a job share sort of thing!"

Edith's eyes widened. "You really think Buck would let us do that?"

"Now *you've* got to be kidding me. You know he's been grooming you for promotion, right? I'm pretty sure he was hoping that you'd apply for the C-squad boss position at the beginning of this year."

Edith shook her head. "I wouldn't want to leave A-squad."

"I know, and I think Buck knew that too, so he didn't want to say anything to you directly in case it put you in an awkward spot. But he was extra-grumpy when he was posting the job ad."

"Oh!" Edith bounced on her toes—and then abruptly stilled, her rising excitement draining away. "Oh. But we can't. Rory can't take any time away from A-squad."

"Sure he can," Blaise started.

"He *can't*," Edith interrupted. She hardly ever looked people in the face, but now she fixed Blaise with a pointed stare. "Not at the moment. With…everything that's happened. And that's still going on."

Blaise opened her mouth, paused, and grimaced. "You have a point."

"What do you mean?" Diana asked, looking between them.

The two firefighters exchanged yet another of those odd, irritatingly opaque glances.

"Lupa," Blaise said. "And her gang. They're still out there. Rory wouldn't leave the rest of us to face her without him."

Diana shivered. Thanks to her self-calming rituals and her refilled prescription, she'd managed to avoid obsessing over the attack on her and Beth *too* much. But it was like a black, gaping hole in her mind that she had to keep consciously walking around, lest it swallow her up entirely.

"Has there been any news on that front?" she asked. "Have the police found any leads?"

Blaise shook her head. "Not yet. But there are some, uh, special agents on the case now. If anyone can track Lupa down, they will."

"Special agents? You mean the FBI?"

"Not exactly. Related agency, though. They're experts in this sort of thing." Blaise gave her a light, friendly punch on the arm. Sometimes it was very obvious that she'd spent her childhood hanging out with boys. "Anyway, don't worry. You can count on us to keep you and Beth safe until the bad guys are all behind bars."

Diana forced a smile in return. "I just hope that's soon."

Even as she said it, she was uncomfortably aware that the words weren't *entirely* true. Not that she *wanted* to be the target of a criminal arson gang, of course…but she couldn't deny that she liked staying at the hotshot base.

She liked the peace and quiet of the woods, being surrounded by nature. She liked hanging out with the squad, laughing at their banter. She liked waking up to find Callum already there, holding out her morning coffee…

It was like an enforced vacation from real life. Once Lupa and her goons had been caught, it would all come to an end. She'd have to face all the things she'd been avoiding thinking about.

Like Callum.

Blaise was watching her with an uncomfortably knowing way, as though Diana's inner thoughts were scrolling across her forehead. "Have you and Callum talked about what you're going to do after Lupa's no longer a threat?"

"Not really," she admitted. "I mean, he's very clear that he wants to be as hands-on a father as he can, but we haven't sat down and worked out all the practicalities of that. I don't think Callum's ready to talk about it yet, and I don't want to push him too fast. This is all still very new to him."

"Mmm." Blaise's dark brown eyes still held that thoughtful, reserved look. "If you wait for him to speak first, you're likely to be waiting a long, long time. Tell me to butt out if this is none of my business, but I think you *should* push Callum. With a bulldozer, if necessary. There are some things that you really, really need to talk about."

"I know." Diana sighed, thinking of the mountain of admin that they had to thrash out between them. "I really want to get on and register him as Beth's father officially, but I have to make sure he understands all the legal and financial implications of that. And then there's the visitation rights, and how we're going to handle any disagreements on Beth's care, and—"

"All important," Blaise interrupted. "But not what I meant." She bit her lip, looking uncharacteristically hesitant. "Look, has Callum talked at all about his family?"

"Of course. He's told me a lot about his parents, especially his mom." Diana smiled, thinking of Callum's obvious pride in his mother's many achievements. "I can't wait for Beth to meet them."

"Mmm," Blaise said again, sounding distinctly noncommittal. "And what about his brothers?"

"Brothers?" Diana stared at her, taken aback. "Callum has *brothers*?"

Although, now that Blaise mentioned it, she *did* dimly recall Callum saying something about a brother…not in the last few days, but way back during that drunken, reckless night at the charity auction.

It had been when she'd run into him at the elevator, and offered to help him back to his hotel room. During the long ride up, she'd succumbed to temptation and hurled herself at him. All the time they'd been making out, he'd kept mumbling about his brother…

She tried to remember what he'd said, but it was lost in a vague haze of tequila. At the time, she'd been far too focused on getting his mouth on hers to pay much attention to the words coming out of it.

Diana wanted to quiz Blaise further, but Callum picked that moment to appear at the end of the store aisle with a heavily-laden shopping cart. Joe was at his side, carrying a basket of his own. The huge black man beamed the moment he caught sight of them all, waving one hand in greeting.

"Bros! Look what I found!" Joe bounced up like an overexcited

Labrador who'd just uncovered the *best stick ever*. He thrust out his hand to display a tiny pink garment. "Isn't it perfect?"

Diana examined the vest. It was very small, and very, very pink. Purple sparkly lettering across the front proudly declared *When I grow up, I want to be just like Mommy!*

"It's, um, really cute," she said to Joe. "But this is newborn size. I wouldn't even be able to get it over Beth's head."

"Oh, it's not for *her*," Joe assured her. "It's for me."

"Joe," Edith said. "I really don't think it's going to fit you."

Blaise nudged her. "I think he means for his hypothetical kid. His very, *very* hypothetical kid. You'd better not be planning to leave that on Seren's pillow, Joe. Not unless you've worked out a way that *you* can push something the size of a watermelon out of your most private orifice."

"I wish I could," Joe said mournfully. "Why hasn't science come up with a way for guys to carry babies yet?"

"Probably because a lot of scientists are men," Diana said. "Blaise is right, Joe. Don't you dare pressure poor Seren into anything before she's ready."

"Of course not," Joe said, sounding indignant. He put the garment into his shopping basket, next to a copy of *What to Expect When You're Expecting*. "I'm not going to show her any of this stuff. I just want to be prepared."

Blaise eyed him, with a look of sudden suspicion. "Something you aren't telling us, Joe?"

Joe let out a heavy sigh. "Sadly not. And believe me, I've been looking."

"Looking for what?" Diana asked, baffled by the exchange.

"Auspicious omens," Joe said, without a trace of self-consciousness. "I kind of dabble in fortune-telling. No hints of babies in my future yet." He shook his basket, regaining his usual cheer. "But when there are, I'll be ready!"

Diana glanced again at the screamingly pink vest. "What if you have a boy?"

"That's why I'm getting unisex clothes," Joe said, with complete sincerity. "Did you guys find everything you needed?"

"I thought I had," Diana said, displaying her own basket. She nodded in the direction of Callum's cart. "What on earth is all that stuff? I thought we were just picking up a few essentials."

Callum looked into his cart, then back at her, poker-faced. "These are essentials."

Diana poked through his finds. "A nightlight with built-in music streaming service and seventy configurable soothing light patterns is essential?"

The faintest trace of embarrassment crept across his features. "*Most* of them are essential. I...may have gotten a little distracted from the list."

"More than a little. Baby Einstein sensory blocks? Aromatherapy massage oils? A ..." She frowned at a brush set she'd just pulled out of the pile. "Wait a sec. Isn't this for grooming pets?"

Callum plucked the brushes out of her hand, hiding them again under his stash. "It's for, uh, Fenrir. Is there anything in here you really aren't happy about me getting for Beth?"

Diana fished a brand-new, top-of-the-line e-reader out from the baby stuff. "Well, this is definitely a bit advanced for her."

A small smile curved his lips. "That one's for you. You said yesterday you missed reading."

"I said I missed having *time* for reading," Diana corrected him.

He shrugged a shoulder at her. "I'm off work for five months. That should give you time to catch up on your books."

"That's very sweet of you." She firmly set the gadget down on the nearest shelf. "But I can't accept this."

Callum promptly reclaimed the e-reader. With a bland expression, he tucked it under one arm.

"*Callum.*" Diana tugged futilely at his iron-hard bicep. "I'm serious. You can't buy me that."

"Twenty dollars on Callum," announced Blaise, leaning against a display of diapers and looking like she wished she had popcorn.

Joe held up his hands. "No way I'm taking that bet."

I will," Edith said. "My money's on Diana."

Diana was fully prepared to win that bet for Edith, but she didn't get the chance. Before she could wrestle Callum for the e-reader, his cellphone rang. Keeping a wary eye on her, as though he suspected *she'd* somehow called him as a distraction, he answered.

"Rory?" Callum said into the phone. He listened for a moment—and then his expression went set and hard, all playfulness gone in an instant. "Right. On our way."

"What is it?" Diana said, apprehension tightening her throat. "Bad news?"

"No. Good." Despite his words, Callum looked grim as death. "Remember the man who attacked you?"

As if she could forget. "The police found out his identity?"

"More than that. We have to go down to the station." Callum took Beth from Edith, holding her protectively in his arms. "They caught him."

CHAPTER 15

Diana stared through the one-way mirror, her face pale. She hugged Beth closer, shielding her with her own body, even though there was no way the line-up could see her through the obscuring glass. "Yes. That's him. Number five."

Callum had only caught a single, fleeting glimpse of the man's face during their brief fight, but he nodded too, confirming Diana's identification. To his pegasus senses, the fifth man in the line-up smoldered like the embers of a forest fire. He was definitely the hellhound who had attacked Diana.

The police officer in charge of the identity parade spoke briefly into a radio, murmuring orders to her colleagues on the other side of the glass. They cut the fifth man out of the lineup. The bearded man glowered over his shoulder as they led him away in handcuffs. Even though the hellhound couldn't see them through the one-way glass, the smoldering rage in his eyes made Callum's pegasus bare its teeth, ears flat.

He put an arm around Diana protectively, drawing her closer to his side. His pegasus was on high alert, ready just beneath the surface of his skin. He was so close to shifting that his bones ached. His awareness flicked constantly over the surroundings, touching every life, looking for any sign of a trap.

He struggled to focus on the police officer. "You said you picked him up for vagrancy?"

"Yep," she said absently, still busy filling in paperwork on her clipboard. "Found him passed out in an alleyway, reeking of cheap spirits. Was just going to throw him in the drunk tank to cool off, but then the computer matched his picture against the photofit for your case. He must have the brains of a bag of hammers. My favorite sort of criminal."

It certainly seemed careless. *Too* careless.

"Has he been cuffed the whole time he's been in custody?" he asked the police officer, wondering why the man hadn't simply shifted and used his hellhound power to phase out of jail.

"Every second. Even before he woke up. By special order on his file. The Feds warned us this guy was dangerous."

That would explain why the man hadn't managed to escape. Hellhounds, like mythic shifters, could take their clothes with them when they shifted—but it didn't work on items they hadn't put on willingly. Since a hellhound's wrist was substantially bigger in animal form, handcuffs would prevent the man from shifting. The anklet Callum had put on Beth worked the same way—although in her case the knotted cord was more of a light deterrent rather than an unbreakable restriction.

The police woman scrawled her signature at the bottom of her form and tore it off. "I'll be happy to hand him over to the Feds' tender care. Just got some procedure to go through before they can cart him off. Ms. Whitehawk, I need to go over your previous statement again with you, if you don't mind."

Diana wrapped her arms around herself, but nodded. "Anything if it will get that man off the streets and into prison, where he belongs."

The police woman gave her a warm smile before turning to Callum. "Mr. Tiernach-West, the agents investigating this case want to have a word with you. Something about the wider investigation."

Callum had been expecting this. Pushing down his instinct to stay with his mate and child, he released Diana. She couldn't be present during this conversation.

"Will you be all right?" he asked her. "I'll try not to be too long."

"I'll be fine." She lifted her chin bravely, though her face was still pale. "You go talk to the Feds. I'll see you later."

He desperately wanted to press a reassuring kiss to her set, determined mouth. He wished he could reassure her, promise her that he would protect her no matter what, but the siren blare of lives made it impossible to think of the right words. He had too many secrets, and in his distracted state it would be too easy to let one slip.

All he could do was give her an awkward nod, and let a police officer lead him away. With every step, he felt like an elastic cord was tugging on his heart, trying to pull him back.

The police officer guided him to a small, plain room. There was a suspiciously large mirror on the wall. Callum took the seat the officer indicated. He couldn't help noticing that there were steel loops on the arms where handcuffs could be attached.

The police officer caught him looking, and gave him a sympathetic grimace over his shoulder as he left. "Sorry, sir. The Feds insisted on using our most secure interview room. They're on their way now."

Callum didn't need the officer to tell him that. He could sense two bright lives approaching, gleaming like precious jewels amidst all the mundane humans. There was something curiously familiar about those glittering energies...

The door opened again. To be more accurate, it slammed back on its hinges with a defining *crash* as a tiny red-haired woman burst through it like a fireball.

"Callum!" She hurled herself bodily at him, nearly knocking him off his chair. "So this is where you've been hiding! Come here, beanpole!"

He found himself seized in an enthusiastic embrace. It wasn't entirely the greeting he'd been expecting from a Shifter Affairs agent.

"Min-Seo?" he said, startled out of his distraction.

"Surprise!" She stepped back, still holding his shoulders. "Wow, you've certainly filled out. Not such a scrawny kid anymore, huh?"

"You haven't changed." The Korean fox shifter still barely topped five feet, and three inches of that was high, bright-red ponytail. Even in her tailored black government suit, she looked exactly like the teenager she'd been when he'd last seen her.

The gumiho wrinkled her nose at him. "OK, don't rub it in, beanpole. Remember I could always trounce you in combat class at school."

"Only because you bite," rumbled a deep voice.

A man made a rather more sedate entrance into the room than Min-Seo, mainly because he had to turn sideways and duck in order to fit through the doorway. Callum hoped that *he* wouldn't decide to hug him in greeting.

"Shan," he said, pushing Min-Seo off and standing up. His inner pegasus stamped a hoof, head lowering warily. "It's been a long time."

The Qiong Qi—a rare Chinese winged tiger shifter—dipped his head in acknowledgement. He didn't offer his hand.

"Last I heard, you were working for East Sussex Fire and Rescue as a structural firefighter," Min-Seo said. "What are you doing out here?"

"Change of career," Callum said shortly, not wanting to get into *that* brief, unpleasant part of his life. "I'm a hotshot now."

"Well, if we'd known you were so close, we would have dropped by sooner." Min-Seo poked him in the chest. "And we *would* have known, if *someone* hadn't missed the class reunion last summer."

"Fire season. I was working. Sorry."

He genuinely *was* sorry. His years as a boarding student at Shifting Sands Academy had been some of the happiest of his life. Mainly due to the fact that his brothers hadn't been there. It was good to see two of his fellow alumni again, even if one of them *was* Shan.

"Well, we'll have to catch up properly later." Min-Seo hopped up onto the table, swinging her legs like a schoolgirl. "When *we're* not working. Shan, you wanna go fetch our special guest?"

The winged tiger shifter nodded and squeezed his vast bulk back out the door. Callum stared after him for a second, then back at Min-Seo. "You actually work with him?"

"Shan? Oh, he's a sweetheart once you get to know him." Min-Seo pulled a bright pink lollypop out of her suit jacket, unwrapping it. She popped the candy into her mouth, speaking round the stick. "And us monsters have to stick together. Listen, I need your help with the interrogation. I can't influence emotions that aren't there, and this asshole is too dumb and too full of himself to be scared of me or Shan. You, though, might be a different matter."

"I want to help in any way I can. But you know I'm not good at talking."

She grinned at him around the lollipop stick, for a moment looking as feral as her fox form. "Just follow my lead. Like the good old days, huh?"

Callum wanted to ask how in the world Min-Seo (and *Shan*, of all people) had ended up working for the Federal Bureau of Shifter Affairs, but there wasn't time. Shan came back into the room, dragging the hellhound after him. With efficient, practiced motions, Shan chained the man to the interrogation chair.

The hellhound caught sight of Callum, and his face darkened. "*You.* This is all your fault, you asswipe!"

"Interesting," Min-Seo murmured around her lollipop. She pulled it out in order to treat the cuffed hellhound to a bright, cheerful smile. "Hi again! Have you had a change of heart yet? It would save everyone a lot of time and effort if you'd just tell us what you know of your own free will."

"You don't scare me, bitch." The hellhound sneered at Min-Seo and Shan alike. "You or your pet kitty-cat. I know Shifter Affairs agents ain't allowed to rough up suspects. You so much as lay a finger on me and you'll be in big trouble."

"True." Min-Seo pointed at Callum with her lollipop. "But *he's* not bound by any of those pesky rules"

The hellhound eyed him, bravado flickering a little. Callum stood up straighter, attempting to look intimidating. He felt ridiculous.

He tried to harm our mate and foal. His pegasus reared, muscles bunching. *Kick his head from his shoulders! Snatch him up and drop him from a great height! Trample him flat and grind his bones into the ground!*

Suddenly he didn't feel quite so silly after all.

The hellhound visibly blanched, shrinking back in his chains. Min-Seo raised an eyebrow, glancing at Callum.

"Huh. Barely had to lean on him at all," she murmured to him. She turned back to the prisoner. "So, are you going to talk, or are me and Shan going to leave you alone with my friend in this nice, very soundproof room while we go enjoy a very *long* coffee break?"

The hellhound swallowed nervously. "You—you wouldn't."

"Let's go, Shan," Min-Seo said. "I have a sudden hankering to check out that donut place waaaaay on the other side of town."

"Wait!" The hellhound was sweating now. Callum didn't think he was *that* intimidating, so Min-Seo must be using her gumiho ability to enhance emotions, increasing the hellhound's fear into full-blown terror. "Don't leave me alone with him! I'll talk!"

"Delighted to hear it," Min-Seo said to the hellhound. "Let's start with something easy. What's your name?"

The hellhound was still eying Callum as though afraid he might lunge for his throat at any moment. "Gerulf."

Min-Seo cocked an eyebrow at Shan, who shook his head slightly. "Nice try, 'Gerulf.' That's not the name on your birth certificate, is it?"

"It's my pack name," the hellhound growled. "And it's all you're getting."

Callum's hands fisted. It was all he could do to keep his pegasus in check. "No. It isn't. Tell us your real name. *Now.*"

The hellhound made a strangled whimper, cringing away from him. "Maurice! Maurice Grundy!"

Shan nodded. "Truth."

Min-Seo sucked on her lollipop. "Yeah, I would have tried to get away with 'Gerulf' too. Why are you here, Maurice?"

"L-Lupa. The bitch kicked me out of the pack." In contrast to his earlier bravado, Maurice—or Gerulf—now seemed positively eager to spill his guts. He jerked his chin in Callum's direction. "Because of *him.*"

"Because I stopped you from abducting my mate and child?" Callum asked.

Maurice shook his head. "Because I went after them in the first place. Lupa flipped her lid when I reported back. Said we don't ever touch families. Especially kids."

"Truth," Shan said, his dark eyebrows rising very slightly.

Min-Seo rolled her lollipop over her tongue in a thoughtful sort of way. "Hmm. If your boss was so pissed off, why didn't she just kill you, Maurice? *I* certainly would have."

Maurice's lip curled in a sneer. "Because she's soft. Prances around with her nose in the air, acting like she's oh-so-tough, but she's just a little girl. No balls. Never lets anyone have any fun. We're *hellhounds*, not lapdogs. Most she ever lets us do is scare stray campers out of random-ass bits of forest, and we're not even allowed to have some sport with one or two that no-one would ever miss."

"All true," Shan said, brow furrowing.

"Ah," Min-Seo murmured, as though a puzzle piece had just clicked into place. She cast a glance at Callum. "That fit with what you know of Lupa?"

Callum opened his mouth to say no…and hesitated. True, Lupa *had* attempted to kidnap Joe and sacrifice him to a demon earlier in the summer. She'd very nearly been successful. She'd started at least one wildfire, too, in order to ambush the squad.

But…she'd ambushed them with poisoned darts that stopped them from being able to shift. The hellhound alpha *could* have chosen something a lot more lethal. And although she'd started the wildfire close to a town, she hadn't jumped the crew until they'd finished containing it. Nobody had gotten hurt. There hadn't even been any property damage.

"I don't think she kills if she can avoid it," he said slowly. "But she *is* willing to kill. If there's no other way to achieve her goal. What *is* her goal, Maurice?"

The hellhound shrugged sullenly. "All I know is that she's obsessed with that damn big bird. That's the only thing she summons the whole pack to hunt. Fucking bitch. Getting my tail fried with lightning isn't my idea of a good time."

"Hmm." Min-Seo finished her lollipop with a last *crunch,* like a fox biting through a chicken bone. "And how long have you worked for Lupa?"

"Dunno exactly. Two, three years, maybe."

"Truth," Shan confirmed.

"A long time to spend somewhere you don't fit in," Callum said. He knew *that* all too well. It was about the length of time he'd been a structural firefighter back in Brighton, before joining the Thunder Mountain Hotshots.

Maurice fidgeted, his gaze sliding away. "A hellhound needs a pack. Didn't have anywhere else to go."

"Truth," Shan rumbled.

Min-Seo leaned back on her hands, regarding the hellhound thoughtfully. "If Lupa's so weak, how come she's pack alpha?"

"Most of 'em are losers that she bit and turned herself, so she's got them pussy-whipped. Plus she's got that damn wendigo wrapped around her little finger." Maurice scowled, his face twisting. "He's her enforcer. Anyone says boo to her, he kicks their ass six ways to hell. If she actually fought for herself, like a *proper* alpha, I'd've challenged her myself."

"Suuuuure," Min-Seo said, drawing out the word sarcastically. "Shan?"

Shan see-sawed one hand back and forth. "Mixed. He's more frightened of Lupa than he's admitting. But it's true he doesn't respect her."

"Well, well, well." Min-Seo treated Maurice to a megawatt smile. "I'm beginning to think it might be your lucky day after all, Mo—can I call you Mo?"

From the slack, idiotic smile spreading across the hellhound's face, Min-Seo was leaning on an entirely different emotion now. "You can call me whatever you like, sweet tits."

"You have no idea how close to death you just came," Min-Seo muttered.

"Truth," Shan noted, eyes gleaming.

"Shut up." Min-Seo returned her attention to Maurice, adopting a breathless, girlish tone. "Mo, you seem to be a practical kind of man. And I do like a practical man. Maybe we can strike a bargain?"

Maurice nodded eagerly. "Sure. Sure. I like bargains."

"Why don't you let us take care of Lupa for you?" Min-Seo's voice was honey-sweet, but her eyes were sharp as knives. "We do all the hard work, you walk out of here with a slap on the wrist, back to a pack that's suddenly in need of fresh, dynamic new leadership…win-win all round. All you have to do is tell us where to find her."

"Oh." Maurice's face fell. "I don't know. No one in the pack knows where she lives, except maybe her wendigo. She just summons us wherever and whenever she needs us."

The corner of Shan's mouth twisted downward. "Truth."

"Of course, because when do we ever get an easy job?" Min-Seo sighed, rubbing her forehead. "I'm nearly tapped out. Take him away for now, Shan."

"Do you believe him?" Callum asked Min-Seo in a low voice as Shan frog-marched the hellhound out again.

"Well, this could still all be a spectacularly ill-considered and complicated way to get you to relax your guard, but I wouldn't put money on it." Min-Seo searched through her suit pockets as she spoke. "Damn it, I'm out of candy. This is at least a three-lollipop case."

Min-Seo's abilities had always left her drained afterward, and in need of sugar. Fortunately, one of the first things you learned as a hotshot was to always have a high-calorie snack to hand. Callum usually carried protein bars around, but he'd recently switched to peanut M&Ms after Diana had mentioned that they were her favorite candy. He fished a packet out of his jacket pocket, tossing it to Min-Seo.

"You are an angel. Technically a horse angel, I guess, given the wings and all." Min-Seo ripped open the candy. "Anyway, returning to our friend Maurice. Honestly? I think he's telling the truth."

Callum let out his breath. "You really think Lupa won't go after Beth?"

"Well, our unpleasant friend in handcuffs notwithstanding, it's a rare shifter who can lift a finger against a kid. Our inner animals are a lot stronger than a human conscience on that particular topic. And if Lupa *was* that sort of monster, it's unlikely she would have been able to hide it for as long as Maurice has been in her pack."

Min-Seo flicked an M&M into her mouth, crunching thoughtfully for a moment before continuing. "And I don't see any reason why she would have *tried* to hide it. With pack members like our delightful Mo, it would've been a helluva lot easier to let them indulge their darker desires than to keep them on a tight leash, like she seems to have done."

Callum had to trust Min-Seo's expertise on such matters. He'd never been able to figure out what made normal people tick, let alone criminal masterminds. Thankfully, wildfires didn't have motivations.

"What about Diana, though?" he asked. "Even if Lupa's moral code won't let her touch Beth, she could still go after my mate."

Min-Seo pursed her lips. "I'm not going to say there's *no* risk, but... Lupa would be acting out of character. I've spent a lot of time going over her file. She's missed a *lot* of opportunities to grab a human hostage or two, if that was her style. I mean, if *I* was going after you guys, I'd've picked off at least Wystan's mate Candice by now. Or gone a bit wider, and started kidnapping members of Edith or Seren's families to use as leverage. Lupa is either not as smart as me, or a whole lot nicer."

"Probably both."

Min-Seo flashed her fox-sharp grin at him. "You say the sweetest things, beanpole. Anyway, leave this to me. Shan and I are *very* good at uncovering secrets. Especially ones people don't know they know. No matter why Lupa cut Maurice loose, she's gonna regret it real soon. I might need you to fly around a bit for us though, once we've narrowed down some search areas." She wiggled her fingers by her forehead. "You know, do your pegasus thing. That okay?"

"Of course. Fire season is over. I'm at your disposal."

"Watch out. I'll make an agent out of you yet." Min-Seo tipped the remaining M&Ms into her mouth, cheeks bulging like a chipmunk hoarding nuts. "In the meantime, you can tell your mate that it's my professional opinion that she can relax a bit. Not that she should drop her guard entirely, but she doesn't need to stay locked in a panic room with a loaded shotgun in hand."

It was good news. Great news. The best news. He was thrilled.

What he said was, "Oh."

Min-Seo cocked her head. "You seem to have badly mispronounced 'Yay!' there. Don't tell me you *want* your mate to be in imminent danger of kidnapping?"

"No! No, of course not." Callum really *was* relieved that the danger to Diana and Beth wasn't as great as they'd first feared. "It's just…this means she doesn't have to keep living with me. The hotshot base isn't the ideal place for a baby. She'll want to take Beth somewhere else. Probably back to L.A."

"Ah." Min-Seo's bright, sharp eyes skewered him. "So you haven't told her she's your mate yet."

Callum drew in a deep breath, and let it out again slowly. "There's a lot I haven't told her."

"That you're scared to tell her."

It wasn't a question. Min-Seo never needed to ask about anyone's emotional state, thanks to her gift. He nodded anyway.

Min-Seo gave him a long, considering look. "Do you want some help with that?"

There was a reason they'd become friends at school. She'd been able to calm him, take away some of his raging frustration with his too-sensitive pegasus, make him more confident. And in return, he simply hadn't shunned her, as most of the other students had.

Callum had never been frightened of her manipulative power. She couldn't help her nature, any more than he could help his. And if she ever *had* used her ability on him without his consent…well, she couldn't create an emotion that didn't already exist. He had to have liked her, at least a little, right from the start.

Her influence never lasted long…but maybe it would be long enough. "Please."

Min-Seo hopped off the table. She stretched up on her toes, beckoning to him in a brief, imperious motion. Callum bent down to her level.

She kissed his cheek. As she did so, something seemed to lighten in his chest. The worries that he'd been locked up in his heart faded away. He felt…clearer. More certain. Calm.

His pegasus shook itself all over, as though a rainstorm had finally stopped. *That's better.*

"For old times' sake," Min-Seo murmured in his ear. She kissed his cheek again, though this time there was no magic in it. "Now go talk to your mate."

"Yes." Callum straightened, setting his shoulders. "It's time."

CHAPTER 16

Diana hesitated in the door of the cabin, having second thoughts. "Are you *sure* you'll be okay?"

"We're going to be more than okay." Joe beamed, hoisting Beth up onto his shoulder. "We're going to have the best time ever, aren't we, sprat?"

Beth chortled, delighted by her new, lofty position. She'd always loved being up high. She grabbed hold of Joe's curly blue-black hair, tugging with all her strength. Joe winced, but his grin didn't waver in the slightest.

"Do not fear, Diana." Seren was flicking through pages of paper covered in dense, neat handwriting. "Callum has left us instructions for any eventuality. Very, ah, thorough instructions."

Diana gave the room one last check. Callum had transformed the space since she'd first arrived. From the soft, brightly-patterned rug on the floor to the cute pegasus mobile dangling over the brand-new cot, every inch was dedicated to Beth's comfort. Diana had to concede that Beth had everything she could possibly need (and some, like the ridiculous nightlight, that she definitely didn't).

Nonetheless, she hesitated. "Maybe this isn't a good idea. I should cancel. I'm sure Callum will understand."

"Callum needs to speak with you alone." Seren shooed her out the door as though she was an indecisive cat. "Without distractions."

"And Cal *volunteering* to talk is rarer than unicorns," Joe put in from over Seren's shoulder. "A lot rarer, actually. Seize the opportunity with both hands." He winked. "I have a feeling that you won't regret it."

Seren handed Diana her coat. "He has a way of knowing these things, unlikely as it may sound. Trust him. Trust us both. And trust that Callum has a very good reason for this request."

Diana was fairly sure she knew what that reason was. With her attacker safely in police custody and special agents pursuing Lupa, there was no longer any need for her to stay with the Thunder Mountain Hotshots. Callum must want to talk about what she would do now.

And she had no doubt what he *wanted* her to do.

He'd been even quieter than usual after their visit to the police station. But she didn't need words to know that his feelings hadn't changed. He shouted them with every glance, every door held open for her, every cup of coffee he brought her. He wanted to be more than co-parents.

Diana couldn't deny that she wanted him too. She'd hoped that close proximity, the drudgery of daily life, would have made her immune to Callum's blazing sex appeal. Unfortunately, the opposite seemed to have happened. Whenever she caught sight of him, she was dizzied with lust. Even when he was doing something as mundane as vacuuming. Maybe *especially* when he was doing something as mundane as vacuuming.

She thrust aside the terribly distracting memory of Callum leaning over a little, jeans taut across his ass, sleeves rolled up, gravely pushing the vacuum back and forth with the total, absolute attention that he gave to everything he did. Joe and Seren were right. She and Callum *did* need to talk.

"I won't be far away," Diana said. "Callum promised we'd only go for a short hike. If anything's the slightest bit wrong, if you're unsure about *anything*, call me and I'll come right back."

"Nothing's going to go wrong," Joe said with his usual sunny, unshakeable confidence. "I've read all about babies. I'm fully prepared. This is going to be *awesome*."

Seren's eyes danced, her mouth pressing into a thin line as if struggling to hold back laughter. She took Diana's arm, drawing her away from the cabin.

"Sometimes Joe needs to be hit over the head by reality," she murmured into Diana's ear. "I have no doubt that he will look after your daughter diligently, but I would not mind him being just a *little* relieved to hand her back. I entreat you. Go. And I would consider it a great favor if you did not hasten to return."

Diana smothered a giggle. "Well, when you put it like that...okay. But you *will* call me if Beth gets upset, won't you?"

Seren gave her an odd, old-fashioned bow, one fist pressed over her heart. "On my honor, I swear it."

Diana had seen Seren practicing actual sword-fighting drills every dawn. Evidently the solemn, serious woman was *really* into historical re-enactment. Sometimes she seemed to have stepped out of some long-vanished medieval kingdom.

Still, no matter Seren's quirks, she was definitely responsible. She more than made up for what Joe might lack in common sense.

Giving Seren a last wave—and smothering a last surge of anxiety—she crossed the meadow behind the cabin. Callum was already waiting for her at the edge of the forest. He was wearing jeans and a t-shirt rather than his firefighter gear, but his bulky pack was strapped to his back.

"Hi," Diana said. She nodded at his backpack. "What's all that? I thought we were going on a short hike, not an overnight trip."

"Supplies," he said enigmatically. "All set?"

"Yep." Diana lifted a foot to display her borrowed boots. "Luckily Edith has the same size feet as me, even though we're wildly different in every other dimension."

His gaze ran over her with slow, obvious appreciation. "I like your dimensions."

She was dressed in cargo pants and an oversized flannel shirt, and he was *still* looking at her like she was some kind of sex goddess. He'd said that he wanted to take her into the woods just to talk…but that clearly wasn't all that was on his mind.

Or hers.

It was hard to remember all the reasons why it would be a bad idea to get involved with Callum when he was standing right there in front of her. With his autumnal hair and green, green eyes, he looked like part of the forest itself; a primal spirit, mysterious and wild, tempting her down a path from which there was no return.

Diana cleared her throat, tearing her eyes away from him. "Shall we go? Er…wherever we're going?"

Callum twitched as though he too was having to snap himself out of some kind of trance. "Yes. This way. Tell me if you get tired."

His legs were much longer than hers, but he set a slow, easy pace. Diana had no trouble keeping up with him despite the rugged terrain.

Callum kept glancing back to check up on her, but he didn't seem to want to talk yet. Although she was agog to find out what he was thinking, Diana found herself relaxing into the silence.

The forest was beautiful, speaking to her soul. Gradually, all her worries faded away. Even Gertrude fell still in her mind. There was only the simple, enjoyable rhythm of walking, the soft calls of birds, the clean air in her lungs.

And Callum.

In the stillness of the forest, his own habitual stillness fell away. He seemed more at ease in his own body out here; the set of his shoulders looser, his expression less guarded. His heavy-soled firefighter boots didn't make the slightest sound on the dense leaf litter.

It was as if he'd been born in the wilderness. Every step, every turn of his head, every movement he made had the unselfconscious grace of an animal.

This was where he belonged, Diana realized. The forest was his soul's true home.

Just as it was hers.

It was easy, so easy, to fall into step with him. Callum pointed things out as they walked; not with words, but with a glance, a nod, the barest gesture.

A sleek, sinuous marten, running along a branch. A trio of mule deer picking their way through the woods with the grace of ballerinas. A roosting pygmy owl, nearly invisible in the crevice of a lightning-split tree, its yellow eyes blinking open as they passed by.

Callum cocked his head, apparently listening to something that she couldn't hear herself. Still without speaking a word, he touched her elbow, motioning her to follow him off the path. Diana stumbled a little, her foot catching on a fallen branch, and he caught her hand. He steadied her, eyebrows lifting a fraction in inquiry: *All right?*

She nodded. Somehow, out here, it seemed the most natural thing in the world to be touching him. She didn't let go.

Hand-in-hand, he drew her further into the woods. A squeeze of his fingers, and Diana knew to crouch down next to him behind the cover of a tangled bush. He put a finger across her lips—the tiny contact sent heat rushing through her—then motioned her to look out.

Diana did so, and her breath caught. They were at the edge of a small clearing. The ground dropped sharply away on the other side, making a break in the forest and giving a stunning view of the valley below. She hadn't realized how high they'd climbed.

But the majestic landscape wasn't what made her heart thump harder in awe.

A pair of moose grazed in the waving grass, not far away. She'd never seen one outside of a zoo, never truly appreciated how *big* they were. Yet for all their incredible bulk, they moved like ghosts. They could have been aliens, or spirits; beautiful and strange visitors from another world.

The male lifted his huge head, looking straight at them. His spreading antlers were wider than Diana's outstretched arms, yet with Callum at her side she didn't feel a trace of fear.

The bull regarded them for a moment with deep, enigmatic eyes, then snorted. He nosed at his mate, gently chivvying her further away. Silently, gracefully, they drifted into the trees, and were gone.

Callum caught her eye. His mouth quirked in that small, wry, heart-melting smile.

"I'll pretend that I planned that," he said, drawing her back up to her feet.

Diana hugged him, on pure impulse, heart too full for words. He froze for an instant, muscles rigid under her palms. She could feel the hammer-beat of his heart.

Then, hesitantly, his arms enfolded her. And it was *right*, it was home, it was where she was meant to be.

She couldn't believe she'd been so stupid. Not to hug him—but that it had taken her so *long* to hug him. To realize that all her fears had just been Gertrude talking. Now, surrounded by his warmth, breathing in his scent, she knew that Callum had been right.

This *was* fate. If they hadn't met as they had, if Beth hadn't brought them together and bound them…maybe her fear would always have held her back. Made her keep her distance, not wanting to risk her heart.

"Callum," she started. "I—"

"Wait." Gently, reluctantly, Callum stepped out of the embrace, moving beyond her reach. "We need to talk first."

Her hormones were of the opinion that they really, really needed to kiss. That all-too-brief contact with his hard, intoxicating body had every inch of her own begging for more.

But he was right. And fortunately—or possibly sadly—she was good at pushing down her own desires. Diana took a step back, even though what she really wanted to do was tackle him to the soft grass and make up for lost time.

"Okay," Diana said. She attempted a sultry smile, hoping that it looked inviting and not like she'd had a stroke. "As long as we can do some more *not* talking afterward."

Oh God. She was the worst flirt ever.

From the look in Callum's eyes, he took her meaning though. His shoulders tensed, hands flexing. The sheer, overpowering need in his heated gaze had her reconsidering whether it was *really* necessary for them to discuss practicalities before pleasure.

"Yes." His throat worked. "If…if you still want to."

Callum turned away with a sharp, jerky movement, as though having to physically stop himself from sweeping her into his arms again. He shrugged off his backpack and knelt down next to it.

"I brought a picnic," he said, taking a blanket from his pack and spreading it out. "You must be hungry after the hike."

Diana could think of much more interesting things they could do on top of that blanket, but the hike *had* left her ravenous. She didn't want her stomach making embarrassing gurgling sounds in the middle of a romantic moment.

She sat down next to Callum, helping him to unpack the picnic. This, it turned out, took some time. He'd brought a *lot* of food. Pastrami sandwiches, melon fruit salad, peanut M&Ms…

Diana suddenly realized that every single item was something that he knew she liked. Even the mint-double-stuff-Oreos, which she was certain she'd only looked at longingly when they'd been out shopping with the squad. He really *had* been paying attention.

And he's got a guilty conscience.

That was definitely a Gertrude thought. Diana tried to shake off the unfair suspicion. The carefully-chosen food was just a typical sweet, romantic, Callum gesture. It didn't mean he was trying to butter her up before dropping a bomb on her.

Of course, it would have been a lot easier to ignore Gertrude if Callum hadn't *looked* like he was about to drop a bomb on her. He seemed to be avoiding her eyes, fussing with the containers and cutlery with even more than his usual fastidiousness. Although he insisted that she fill her plate, she noticed that he barely touched his own food.

Anxiety swamped appetite. Diana put down her sandwich, unable to bear the tension any longer. "You said you wanted to talk."

Callum's jaw tightened. He picked up a cookie; crumbled one edge of it; dropped it again. "Yes."

She waited.

He let out an explosive breath, like a diver coming up for air. "I'm not good at this."

"Talking?"

Callum's chin jerked in a slight, unhappy nod. "Never been good at finding the right words. And I'm terrified of getting this wrong."

A pang of sympathy went through her. She knew what *that* felt like. He was so obviously miserable, she couldn't help wanting to reassure him, even though her own throat was tight with growing anxiety.

"Well, if it's any consolation, at least you have a lot of other talents." Diana gestured at the lavish spread. "You're definitely good at picnics, for a start."

His tight, guarded expression relaxed, just a fraction. "Not really. I'm just good at making lists. And working through them."

"I've noticed that." She'd caught a few glimpses of him consulting his small black notebook over the past few days, although he'd always hidden it again as soon as he realized she was looking. "I'm pretty sure you're the most organized person I've ever met."

"I have to be." Callum hesitated, then went on, every word coming slower and slower. "Otherwise I lose focus. I...get distracted very easily. It's...it's part of what I need to tell you. What I should have told you earlier. Something you need to know about me."

This was his deep, dark secret? That he struggled with his own mental issues?

Suddenly it all made perfect sense. His silences, his weird evasions, the way he hid his coping strategies...he'd been ashamed, afraid that his illness might make him less of a man in her eyes. Maybe Callum had even been scared that she would think it made him unfit to look after Beth.

No wonder Callum had been so desperate to prove himself, so reluctant to talk. He'd wanted to show that he could be a good father, a good partner, before he trusted her with his secret.

"Callum." Diana took his hand, trying to show with the touch how much she understood, how this only made her care for him even more. "Are you trying to tell me that you have ADHD?"

"No!"

Diana rocked back on her heels, startled by his sudden vehemence. She'd never heard him raise his voice before. Callum must have seen her shock, because he grimaced, rubbing his free hand across his face.

"Sorry," he said. "Sore point. My brothers *do* have ADHD. Severely. My dad too, probably, though he's always refused a formal diagnosis. But I'm not like them."

Has Callum told you about his brothers? Blaise had asked her. Was this the reason why? Had Blaise been trying to hint that Callum might have an undiagnosed issue, one that he refused to admit to himself?

"It's just a brain chemistry imbalance," Diana said. "There's nothing shameful about it."

"I'm *not* like them," he said, in tones of utter finality. "I don't have ADHD."

Diana had to admit, she'd never met anyone *less* hyperactive than Callum in her entire life. Still, the defensive set of his shoulders had her wondering…

This wasn't the moment to push him, though. "Okay. You know yourself better than I do, after all. So what *are* you trying to tell me?"

His throat worked. "I'm a pegasus."

"Uh," Diana said, when he didn't go on. "You're a what?"

"A pegasus."

She hadn't misheard him after all.

"I'm sorry." She could only assume it was a slang term for something, or maybe the name of a club. "I don't know what that is."

"A winged horse," Callum said, as if this would help. "Like in Greek mythology."

"No! I didn't mean…I know what a pegasus is. You're saying you're an actual winged horse?"

"Yes. Well, sometimes. I turn into one."

Well, he's definitely right about one thing. He doesn't have ADHD.

Though, not being a psychologist, Diana didn't know what he *could* have. Dissociative disorder? Schizophrenia? A very odd psychosis?

"Have you ever talked to anyone about this?" she asked, cautiously.

Callum gave her a rather wry look, his mouth curving. "I'm not crazy."

"I'm, uh, glad that you trusted me enough to share this, then. But I really think you need to talk to someone else too. A professional. Someone who can help—"

"No," he interrupted, his crooked smile hooking up even further. "I mean literally, I'm not crazy. I don't need help. I really do turn into a pegasus. I'll show you."

Callum stood up, stepped backward, and—vanished.

And in his place, there was, indeed, a pegasus.

Now you're having hallucinations. Or you're in a coma and this is all a dream. Or he drugged the food, or...or...

Diana's flailing mind stuttered to a halt, unable to come up with a convincing excuse that would explain the evidence right in front of her. He was *there*, furry and four-legged and feathered.

Callum's long head turned, watching her from one solemn eye. It was a horse's eye, deep brown and alien...and yet somehow it was *his* eye, Callum looking out at her from behind that dark, horizontal pupil.

He snorted, softly, his breath ruffling her hair. She could smell him; the clean, earthy, wild scent of an animal.

Hesitantly, she touched a finger to the nearest pale, gleaming hoof. It was solid. It was real.

He was real.

A shimmer ran over his body, as if she was looking at him through heat haze. He blurred, shrank, and was Callum again.

No—he was a *man* again. The pegasus had been him too.

"You turn into a pegasus," Diana said, faintly.

Callum nodded. He didn't say a word. He just stood there, looking like he thought she was about to pull out a gun and shoot him.

"You turn into a *pegasus*," Diana repeated. She scrambled to her feet, grabbing for his hands. *"You turn into a pegasus!"*

Callum did not seem to have been expecting this reaction. He swiveled at the center of her circle, looking totally nonplussed, while she whooped and cackled and hopped around him.

"You aren't angry?" he said, as though people who were furious with him *always* tried to cajole him into an impromptu dance.

"Angry?" Releasing him, she spun round in circles, arms flung wide, incredulous delight too great to contain. "The world is full of wonders and more magic than I ever imagined, and you think I might be *angry?*"

"Er...yes?" Callum seemed honestly baffled. "I've been keeping it a secret from you, after all."

"Of course you have. You couldn't trust just anyone with this. You had to make sure I wasn't going to, to sell you to a zoo or stuff you as a trophy or something." Diana clapped her hands in glee as something occurred to her. "Oh! Are there more people like you? More shapeshifters?"

"Shifters. We call ourselves shifters. Yes. Lots. The rest of the squad, for a start."

"You're *all* pegasuses?" Should that be pegasi? She was too excited for linguistics. "Because actually, that would explain a lot."

He shook his head. "Rory is a griffin. Joe is a sea dragon. Seren's a shark. Wystan's a unicorn. Fenrir..." he hesitated, eying her. "Fenrir is a shifter too, though he can't take human form. He may look like a dog, but he's really a man."

"Fenrir is a *person?*" And to think she'd treated him like a dangerous beast. She was going to owe the poor dog—man—*shifter*—a big apology. "And Edith? Blaise?"

A smile tugged at his mouth. "Also people."

"*Callum.*" She poked him playfully in the middle of his chest, glad that the worry was starting to ebb from his expression. "You know what I mean. Are they shifters too?"

"Edith is human. Blaise..." Callum hesitated again. "Blaise can shift, but she chooses not to. She doesn't like people talking about it. And...there's one other person you should know about."

Who could he mean? She mentally ran through the Thunder Mountain Hotshots, and realized that it was obvious.

"I *knew* it," she crowed, triumphant. "I *knew* there was something strange about Buck. Let me guess. Is he a grizzly bear?"

"Ah, no. Buck is human too." Callum set his feet, bracing himself as though he was expecting a punch in the gut. "But Beth is like me. A pegasus."

"Beth?" The world tilted, spun. "*Our* Beth?"

"I'm sorry." His hands closed over her shoulders, steadying her. "I'm so sorry—"

"*Sorry?* Our little girl is, is magic, and she's going to be able to fly, and, and...why on earth would you be *sorry?*"

"Because it's not all good." A shadow crossed his face. "Remember what I told you earlier, about getting distracted easily? That's part of being a pegasus. We can sense living creatures, detect their location and nature. That's how I knew that the moose were in this meadow."

Diana furrowed her brow, not seeing the problem. "How is that a bad thing?"

"For most pegasi, it isn't. They can turn off their power. But I can't." He made a brief gesture, indicating the general surroundings. "Everything's always shouting at me, in my head. It makes things...difficult."

"Oh, Callum." She laid a hand on his forearm. "You're scared that Beth might have inherited the same problem?"

His jaw tightened. "I hope she hasn't. But there's a small possibility. And...there's a substantial risk that she'll have ADHD, given my family background."

"If she does, then we'll get her whatever help she needs," Diana said firmly. "And if she has issues with her powers, then *you'll* be able to help her. She's lucky to have you, Callum. *I'm* lucky to have you. You're even more amazing than I thought."

Callum blinked at her for a second—then, without warning, pulled her into a tight embrace. Diana pressed against him, glorying in the hard strength of his body, the heat of his skin, the possessive way his fingers twined through her hair.

"You," he murmured, "are the most incredible woman in the world."

"Says the man who literally turns into an *actual pegasus.*" Her breath caught, a sudden mad hope blooming in her chest. "Is...is it something that you can share? With a bite or something, like werewolves in movies?"

He shook his head, his cheek rubbing against the top of her head. "Some shifters can. Not my type though. You have to be born with it."

"Oh," she said, trying to conceal her disappointment. "Well, I'm glad that Beth is magic, at least. And that I came to find you. I would have had a heart attack if I'd walked into her room one day to find a baby pegasus in her cot. Or will she only be able to transform when she's older?"

"She can shift now." A hint of pride showed in his tone. "She's very precocious. That's the real reason I put the string on her ankle. To stop her from shifting and running off."

Now Diana was *really* glad that she'd decided to bring Beth to meet Callum. "Is that what happened the other day? When you told me you'd lost sight of her for a minute?"

"Yes. I'm sorry I didn't tell you the truth."

Diana leaned back in his arms to fix him with a mock glare. "Stop apologizing, Callum."

Callum brushed a stray lock of her hair back, tucking it behind her ear. His fingers lingered on her cheek, cupping her face. "I wish I didn't have to."

"You *don't* have to."

"I do." He took a deep breath, his jaw setting. "Because there's more."

CHAPTER 17

This was it. The moment that Callum had been dreading.

The moment that he was going to wipe out all that shining, happy trust in her face. The moment the warmth in her eyes would turn to disgust, betrayal, hatred...

But he owed her the truth. The whole truth.

He steeled himself. "I think you should sit down for this."

She gave him a look. "You just told me that you turn into a pegasus, and *now* you think I should sit down?"

Nonetheless, Diana obediently sank to the grass, sitting cross-legged. He sat down too, facing her.

His pegasus stamped a hoof. *Too far away. Touch her! Hold her! Our mate wants us!*

But she wouldn't. Not after she knew the truth.

"Diana..." Callum stalled. His mind was too full, with his increasingly-insistent pegasus, with his mate's intoxicating proximity, with every life on the mountain. There wasn't room for words.

He shook his head, struggling to focus. "Do you mind if I check my list?"

Diana patted his knee. "You do whatever you need to do, Callum. I'm not going anywhere."

It was strange not to have to hide his habit. Callum pulled out his notebook, feeling oddly naked, and flicked to the right page.

Picnic
Tell Diana about:
Shifters (will probably have to shift as proof)
Beth being a pegasus
True mates
Doubt over Beth's biological father

The rest of the page was blank. He hadn't been able to plan past that final, apocalyptic item.

Callum ran a finger down the list, stopping on *True mates.* Of course, he had to explain that first. Otherwise Diana wouldn't understand why he'd recognized her on sight at the car crash, even though they might not have met before.

He tucked the notebook back into his pocket. "I need to tell you about true mates."

"True mates?" Diana looked a bit perplexed. "You mean soulmates? Like, there being one person in all the world who's your perfect match? Someone you're bound to by fate?"

Well, that had been easier than he'd expected. "Yes. Exactly. You're mine."

Diana stared at him.

Good, his pegasus said. *Now kiss her.*

Even for his inner beast, that was unhelpful.

Callum gritted his teeth against the surge of need sweeping through his blood. The memory of Diana's lush body pressed against his own was burned into his skin. He clenched his fists, forcing himself to stay still, and waited.

"Er," Diana said at last. "Let me make sure we're on the same page here. You're saying that soulmates are real, and I'm…yours?"

"Yes." When she continued to stare at him, he added, "Shifters recognize their true mates on sight. That's why I—"

And then his arms were abruptly full of the most gorgeous woman in the world, as Diana launched herself at him.

Caught completely off-guard, he went straight over backward, his shoulders slamming into the ground. Diana's soft thighs straddled him. She pinned him down, and for a split-second he honestly thought that she was attacking him in fury.

Then her mouth found his.

All other thought fled. There was only Diana, the heat of her, the softness of her, the taste of her. He gripped the back of her head, pulling her even closer. She matched his urgency, tongue tangling with his, fierce and triumphant. She claimed him as though she too had been waiting her whole life for this.

"Diana," he gasped. "Mine. My mate."

"Yes," she murmured, never breaking the desperate kiss. "Yes."

Yes, his pegasus echoed. *At last. Now.*

Callum could no more have fought the instinct surging through him than he could have commanded his heart to stop beating. Diana was here, and he was hers, and she was *his*. Nothing else mattered.

He rolled, reversing their positions. Her thighs gripped his sides, wonderfully soft, wonderfully strong. The feel of her body underneath his was glorious. Maddening. He needed more.

Diana fisted her hands in his shirt, tugging in wordless command. He ripped it off, and caught his breath at the touch of her palms on his bare back. She was fire, she was life, she was everything.

He had to touch her in return. He propped himself up just far enough to tear open the buttons of her shirt. She wriggled eagerly, helping him to strip away her bra. The first incredible brush of her hard nipples against his chest very nearly had him coming in his pants there and then.

"Wait," he growled. He backed away from her, struggling for control. "Wait. I want to see you."

Diana shook back her tangled hair and sat up. A blush rose across her throat. Her arms wrapped around her middle. He could see her trying to suck in her stomach.

She smiled, but it looked forced. "If you want. But I haven't exactly improved."

How could she say that? Every inch of her was soft and enticing. Her breasts hung full and ripe, large dark nipples begging to be worshipped. His hands ached to explore the contours of her belly, the lush curves of her hips. He burned to discover the places that would make her gasp, bite her lip, moan his name.

"You're perfect." He took her wrists, gently forcing her to move her arms aside. "You're my goddess."

For some reason, that made Diana laugh. She lay back again, allowing him to explore her incredible body.

Her breasts were a dream, impossibly soft. He teased her nipples to hard peaks, relishing the way she gasped and caught her breath. She was gloriously responsive, telling him without words exactly what pleased her. Where to bite harder, feeling her shudder; when to torment her with butterfly-light licks, her hands fisting in his hair.

He worked his way lower, delighting in every inch. He found the silvery scar that ran across her stomach, and traced it with kisses. He would never have words sufficient to express his awe and wonder at the miracle she had made, the life she had brought into the world. But he could show her, silently. Telling her his feelings with his hands, his mouth, his whole body.

She squirmed delightfully as he pressed his mouth to her soft hip. He worked at the buttons of her pants, tugging them down. Fierce satisfaction surged through him as he discovered that she was even more sensitive here, the lightest touch making her moan.

The crease of her inner thigh. Her soft, dark curls. Her salt-sweet taste.

"Oh God." Diana's hips bucked, her legs spreading as far as they could with her pants still hobbling her. "Callum, whatever you do, *don't stop.*"

Callum had absolutely no intention of that. He was going to stay here forever, discovering her body, drawing out those delicious, helpless cries.

Diana, it seemed, had other ideas. He'd only brought her to one shuddering, intoxicating climax when she pounded a fist against his shoulder.

"Clothes," she ordered. "Off. Now."

She was his mate. Whatever she wanted, he had to provide.

Once he'd stripped every last item from her incredible body, he had to pause again. Not for control this time—though he was so hard it hurt—but just in sheer awestruck appreciation. Splayed out on the green grass, Diana was a work of art. He could stare at her for hours.

She folded her arms behind her head, arching her back, and Callum abruptly reconsidered. He needed to be inside her, *now*. He struggled with his own clothes, hands clumsy on his belt.

"Oh yes," Diana purred. Her eyes were dark with desire, hungry and possessive. Her legs fell open in invitation. "Callum. Yes."

He fitted himself to her, claiming her mouth once more. His straining cock parted her wet folds—not entering, not yet, *not yet*—and they both gasped.

"Callum," Diana groaned. "Please. Now!"

Her hips jerked. She rubbed herself against his hardness, hot and wet, and it was all he could do not to plunge straight into her. He pulled away a little, clenching his teeth until his jaw ached, arms shaking with the effort of holding back.

"Diana," he gritted out. "I want to mate you."

Her fingernails dug into his sides. "Yes. *Yes.*"

"You don't—" She ground against him again, and he bit back a curse. "You don't understand. Not just sex. More. A joining of souls. Permanent."

She stilled underneath him, her dark eyes searching his face. "You mean magic?"

"Yes. Magic. We'll be bound together. Always."

Diana's hands came up, stroking through his hair, holding his head. She pulled him down to her lips. He felt her smile.

"Callum," she whispered. "We already are."

Her hips moved once more, and this time there was no holding back. He slid into her, deep and hard, and it was better than good, better than dreams, better than anything he could ever have imagined.

She embraced him, strong and silky and wet. For once, the rest of the world fell away. There was only Diana. He lost himself, lost everything but her, thrusting in total abandon. She urged him on, shuddering around him, taking all of him and demanding more.

"Callum!" Diana shrieked, her body arcing underneath him, tightening around him one final time. *"Callum!"*

He let out a feral snarl, all human language gone. He emptied himself into her in white-hot pulses. And as ecstasy blasted through him, he felt her join him there too; her soul, bright and breathtaking, striking through him like lightning.

Claiming him forever.

CHAPTER 18

Maurice jerked at the handcuffs again. Fresh blood trickled down his wrists. The steel links didn't budge.

He let out a long, heartfelt string of swearwords, which didn't help relieve his feelings at all. Maurice slumped against the wall, gritting his teeth, waiting for the pain to recede enough for him to try again.

He *had* to break these damned cuffs. Once the Shifter Affairs spooks took him away, his chances of escape would drop to a big fat zero. His next prison would be a lot more secure than this mere human holding cell, with its pathetic concrete walls and steel bars.

If he could shift, he could phase and walk straight out of here, and there wouldn't be a thing anyone could do to stop him. Not even that creepy Asian bitch with her mind tricks, or her hulking kitty bodyguard.

Maurice tried to shift again, but his inner hellhound backed away, refusing to come out. *Can't. Too tight.*

"We don't have a choice, you dumb dog," Maurice said under his breath. "Come on, it's just a bit of steel. Shift it with us!"

Can't, his hellhound whined. *Not ours. Not part of us. Don't like it.*

"You're gonna like shifter prison a fuckton less," Maurice growled. "We *have* to get out of here."

Maurice cursed the damn firefighter again for somehow forcing him to give his real name. Once the spooks started combing through his record, it was only a matter of time before they joined up the dots with some old, unsolved cases. If he didn't get out of here fast, he could kiss his freedom goodbye forever. *If* he was lucky, and the judge was feeling lenient.

If not...

Maurice set his jaw, and grimly started yanking at the cuffs again.

I can help you.

Maurice paused. "Well, why didn't you say so earlier, you stupid mutt?"

His inner animal flattened its ears uneasily. *That wasn't me.*

No. The foreign voice slithered through his head. *It was me.*

His hellhound growled, fur raising. The hair on the back of Maurice's neck prickled too. He shot to his feet, raising his shackled hands defensively.

"Who's there?" he snarled.

A friend.

Maurice pressed his back into the corner of his cell, swiveling his head. He couldn't see much of the corridor beyond his barred door, but he couldn't smell anyone. As far as he could tell, he was alone.

He swallowed, trying to hide his growing unease. "If this is another of your freaky mind tricks, you fox-faced bitch--"

Soft laughter curled through his head. *No. I am not the agent you fear so deliciously. I am your salvation. Your prayers have been heard, faithful hound. The queen has sent me in answer.*

Something about that hissing, amused voice made him press back harder into the corner. Still, he wasn't in a position to be picky.

"I don't know what the fuck you're yakking about," he said. "And I don't care, as long as you can get me out of this cell. But first I want to see who I'm talking to."

Very well.

Something scurried out of the shadows, in the corridor beyond his cell. Something small and gray and fluffy, with eyes like red sparks. At first glance, it looked like a squirrel…but no squirrel had fangs that sharp and pointed.

And no squirrel had small, curving horns jutting from its forehead.

Maurice recoiled. You didn't spend as long as he had in Lupa's pack without learning what *those* meant. There was a demon curled up in the squirrel's body, its true nature twisting the rodent's form into something closer to its real shape.

"You're one of them," he said uneasily. "Lupa's…pets."

The animal twitched its whiskers, looking amused. *Not a pet. Oh, very much not a pet. But you should be less concerned about what I am, and more about what I can give you.*

It sat up. Gripped between those jagged, not-at-all rodent-like fangs was a small, shiny key.

Maurice hurled himself against the cell door, revulsion forgotten. "Give me that!"

The demon skipped away, easily evading his grasp. *Not yet. Not until we have a bargain.*

Maurice cast a wary glance at the security camera blinking in one corner of his cell. He crouched down, blocking the demon from view. "Did Lupa send you?"

No. The queen Herself. The demon flicked an ear. *She is uncertain of Her scion's loyalty, after recent events. Lupa grows less obedient. The queen does not think that she will do what must be done. You, however, are not so tender-hearted. You are the tool we need.*

Maurice still had no idea who this so-called queen was, but he didn't much care. "Fine. Whatever you want, I'm your man. I'll do anything. No problem."

You accept this bargain willingly? You will carry out the queen's will without question? You will give your soul to Her service?

No, Maurice's inner hellhound said suddenly. He felt it tugging at him, like a needy dog latching its teeth into its owner's sleeve. *No!*

Maurice kicked his animal to the back of his mind, ignoring its whimpers. "Yes. Whatever. Long live her Majesty, whoever the fuck she is. Now give me the damn key!"

Hold out your hand first. To seal the deal.

Maurice started to do so...and then hesitated. Lupa kept her demon-things out of sight of the pack most of the time, but he'd seen her feeding one once. Seen the mangy, mutated squirrel sink its fangs into a bound, struggling wolf; seen the light fade from the squirrel's eyes, and the wolf's light up with an evil red glow...

"You ain't gonna bite me, are you?" he said warily.

No. The demon's lips wrinkled back from its fangs. It sounded surly now. *I am hungry, but my queen has other plans for you. I swear in Her name that I will not harm you.*

Maurice hesitated, but he was shit out of options. Reluctantly, he put his hand through the bars.

The demon bared its teeth again, and Maurice instinctively jerked back—but the creature only bit its own paw. Blood welled from the wound, black and strange. It smelled wrong, like ditchwater and rot.

Maurice's skin crawled as the demon crawled over the back of his hand. The smear of blood it left behind shimmered and twisted into some kind of symbol, all on its own.

There, the demon said, sitting back on its haunches. *You are Hers now.*

Maurice tried to wipe the blood off on his pants, but the symbol stayed put. It looked like a curled snake with horns. Well, it wasn't the worst tattoo he'd ever gotten.

"Okay, you did your thing, I swore my oath, we're all good," he said, privately resolving to run as fast and far away as he could the instant he was out of here. "Hand over the fucking key!"

The demon flicked its head, opening its jaws. Maurice dove after the key as it skidded into the cell.

He almost had the handcuffs unlocked when he felt claws scrabbling at his pants. He yelped, trying to kick the demon off.

Peace, new cousin. I swore I would not bite you. The squirrel scurried up his back. *I am merely hitching a ride.*

Maurice shuddered, but let the thing perch on his shoulder. He could kill it later. Right now he had to get out of here.

Dropping to all fours, he shifted. The world blurred into gray shadows as he stepped *sideways*, into that weird wherever-it-was that his hellhound could take him. Maurice had never cared how his hellhound power worked, as long as it could get him out of a sticky situation.

He sprang forward. In *this* place, the wall was no obstacle. He passed through it as easily as jumping through smoke, and kept running. Distance worked differently, here. In mere minutes, he'd left the town behind.

Keep running, his hellhound urged him. The stupid beast cowered in his head, shivering like a beaten puppy. *Don't shift back, not ever. Stay here, where we're safe.*

No, said a different voice. The demon's tail tightened around his throat. It was still on him, clinging to the back of his neck. Maurice felt the warning prick of its claws. *That's far enough. Turn back into a man, so you can listen.*

Maurice dropped out of hellspace, and straightened back up on two legs. Quick as a flash, he snatched the demon off his neck, flinging the writhing creature away. "I got what I wanted. What the fuck makes you think I need to listen to you now?"

Something moved in his mind.

Maurice froze, every muscle in his body locking up in sheer terror, as that alien presence shoved his whimpering hellhound aside. He didn't see anything, but he could *feel* something hanging over him, cold and inescapable. He could feel it opening vast, burning eyes.

Something huge, and old, and very, very hungry.

Not to me. The demon struggled back to its feet, baring its fangs at him in a sneer. *To Her.*

CHAPTER 19

Diana lay with her head resting on Callum's chest, his arm warm around her. Despite the chill autumnal breeze, she wasn't the slightest bit cold. She felt like she was floating in a hot bath, every part of her simultaneously heavy with exhaustion and weightless with bliss.

Mine, she thought wonderingly, listening to the slow, steady beat of Callum's heart. She could *feel* it, inside her own chest, warming her from within. *My mate.*

A satisfied, distinctly masculine chuckle floated through her mind, without her ears being involved in any way. *Yes.*

Diana lifted her head to stare at him. "Was that you?"

Callum's lips curved. They didn't move further, but she heard his voice clearly inside her head. *Hello.*

"Wow," she whispered. "Can I do that too?"

He chuckled again, out loud this time, and rolled over to press a long, lingering kiss to her mouth. *Yes. Try.*

She tried to focus her thoughts, which was terribly difficult when his tongue was doing such wonderful things. *HELLO MORE FUCK MORE RIGHT NOW YOUR COCK YES PLEASE FUCK ME HARD NOW*

Callum burst out laughing.

Diana covered her face, laughing too despite her mortification. "This may take a bit of practice."

He kissed her again, one hand sliding up. "You didn't mean all that?"

"Well..." She gasped as his fingertip circled her nipple. Reluctantly, she caught his hand, moving it away. "Whatever my subconscious thinks, we should probably get going. We can't leave Beth with Joe and Seren *too* long, and it's a long hike back."

His green eyes gleamed. "But a very short flight."

An embarrassing squeak escaped her as she realized what he meant. "You'd let me *ride* you?"

His expression turned rather wicked. "Of course. But I thought you wanted to get back."

"Callum!" She slapped his rock-hard chest. "Right, just for that, you're getting a tickling."

Diana attempted to make good her threat, but Callum twisted away, inhumanly fast. He pinned her wrists to the ground, laughing even harder despite her failure.

"No fair." She pouted at him, though a thrill went through her at the way he'd so effortlessly immobilized her. "Are all shifters as strong as you?"

"If I say yes, will you be less impressed?"

"Callum, you turn into a *flying horse*. Believe me, nothing is going to make me less impressed by you."

He chuckled, releasing her. "I'm about average for a shifter."

Diana cast a meaningful glance downward. "There's nothing average about you."

Callum kissed her again. "Or you."

His cock was becoming increasingly above-average again, she noted. With a sigh of regret, she tore herself away, casting around for her discarded clothes.

"We really should be getting back." She picked up her bra. "If we've finished everything on your list?"

Diana had meant it as a joke, but the lingering laughter in Callum's face vanished instantly. A strange, icy sensation closed around her heart.

"Callum?" It wasn't her own anxiety she was feeling—she knew what *that* was like. With a jolt of shock, she realized that she was feeling *his* emotions, down that strange new bond between them. "What's wrong?"

He rolled upright, abruptly, reaching for his own clothes. "You're right. We should go."

"*Callum.*" Her sense of him had gone weirdly cloudy, like he'd retreated into a fog bank. "You can't just pretend everything's okay. Not to me. I'm your mate."

Callum kept his back to her. He pulled his shirt over his head. "I shouldn't have done this."

"Done what?" Diana's stomach dropped. "You mean mate with me?"

He nodded, every muscle tense. "Not yet. Not before…before you knew everything."

There was *more*?

Callum's shoulders dropped in a sigh. He turned around at last, doing up his jeans. His expression was cold and shuttered again, but now she could sense the deep turmoil behind that stony facade.

"I didn't want to tell you this until…until there was a connection between us," Callum said, sounding like he was having to force out every word. "I didn't mean it to go this far. I just thought…I needed…I wanted to make sure you wouldn't leave me when you found out."

It was more than his dread knotting Diana's stomach now. Whatever it was Callum had to say, it was clearly serious.

Pulling up her pants, she went over to him. He flinched a little as she reached out. Before, that would have made her back off, but now, with the mate bond binding their hearts together, she knew better.

It wasn't that he didn't want her. He felt he wasn't *worthy* of her. Deep, crushing shame shadowed his soul.

"Callum," Diana said, taking his hands. "Just tell me. I'm not going anywhere. We're soulmates. And even if you think we shouldn't have mated until I knew everything, we were *already* bound together, by Beth. That's a connection even stronger than magic."

She'd thought that would reassure him, but she might as well have taken a dagger and plunged it into his chest. Callum's face never changed, but Diana could sense how every word ripped through his heart.

"Diana." Callum's voice was hoarse, raw with pain. He let go of her hands. "I...I..."

A loud, shrill ringing sound interrupted him. Diana abruptly found herself behind a wall of feathers, Callum's glossy red flank crowding her protectively.

"Um." She pointed at his backpack. "I think that's your phone."

The pegasus blurred back into Callum. Looking a little sheepish, he bent to retrieve the vibrating device, holding it up to his ear. "Callum Tiernach-West."

Callum listened for a moment. His face went even grimmer. His free hand clenched into a fist, knuckles white.

"Understood," he said. "I'll be there as soon as I can."

Diana's heart thumped in fear as he lowered the phone again. "Was that Joe? Is something wrong with Beth?"

"No. Min-Seo." Callum was already gathering up the remains of their forgotten picnic, shoving everything carelessly into his pack. "I need to take you back to the base. Right away. You have to stay there. The squad will protect you while I'm gone."

"Gone? Gone where? Protect me from what?"

Callum swung the pack onto his back, tightening the straps. All the angst she'd sensed in him previously was gone. His soul burned with dangerous, focused purpose.

"Maurice," he said. "He's escaped."

CHAPTER 20

Seren met them just outside the cabin. For once, the usually composed, calm woman looked less than totally serene.

"Thank the Sea," Seren said. Little wisps of hair had escaped her tight, cornrow braids, and her gray eyes were distinctly frazzled. "You're back."

Diana slid off Callum's broad furry back. Even her worry about the escaped Maurice hadn't been able to *totally* overshadow the sheer wonder of soaring through the sky, carried on her pegasus's flame-red wings.

Now, with her feet back on the ground, all her anxieties crashed down on her like a landslide. Callum hadn't told the rest of the crew about Maurice's escape yet—there hadn't been time. So why was Seren so relieved to see them?

"What's happened?" Diana asked, her heart like ice in her chest. "Where's Beth?"

"My apologies. I did not mean to alarm you. I assure you, Beth is fine. More than fine." Seren pushed back her braids, still looking rather wild-eyed despite her reassuring words. "Joe has been having a wonderful time with her."

Diana started breathing again. "Ah. Sorry about that."

Callum, who'd just shifted back to human form, gave her a very puzzled look.

Diana patted his arm. "Explain later. Don't worry, Seren. I'll ask Joe to babysit next time she's got a tooth coming through and is snotty and grumpy. That'll put him off."

Seren shook her head. "You misunderstand me. Beth was an utter delight until a few hours ago, when she was so obviously tired that we tried to put her down for a nap. This made her incandescently furious. Which apparently significantly upset her digestion. At both ends."

Diana winced, able to picture this all too well. "Oh. And you got stuck with the clean-up?"

Seren had the haunted, thousand-yard stare of a veteran soldier returning from the front lines. "No."

"Well, I have to say, I'm disappointed in Joe. I expected better of him than to hand her back the moment—" Diana's brain caught up with her ears. "No? What do you mean, no?"

Seren gestured toward the cabin. "Perhaps it will be easier to show than explain."

Completely baffled, Diana followed Seren through the door. Inside, it was dim and peaceful. All the curtains were drawn, and a soft, deep lullaby filled the air. Gentle, ever-shifting pastel colors played across the bedroom, cast by the ridiculous nightlight.

Joe was pacing up and down in patient, even steps. Beth sprawled bonelessly across the firefighter's shoulder, deeply asleep, dribbling snot and spit in a wide damp patch across his shirt.

The soft music stopped as Joe caught sight of them, and Diana realized it had been him, humming. He put a finger to his lips, never stopping his slow rocking motion.

"Hi," Joe whispered. "Don't worry, her temperature is normal. She was just over-tired and ran out of cope. Poor little sprat."

Diana glanced at Seren. She was staring at her partner—her mate, Diana realized—with a sort of dazed, drunken expression. She looked like she'd just come home and found Jason Momoa waiting for her in her bath. With Channing Tatum.

Diana smothered a grin as she realized just how thoroughly Seren's plan had backfired on her. "Thanks, Joe. I'll take her now."

Joe made no move to relinquish his burden. "But she might wake up. She's only been asleep for an hour or so. I'm happy to keep rocking her."

"Joe." Seren's tongue ran over her lips. "Give Beth back to Diana and come with me. *Now*."

"But—" Joe broke off as he looked at his mate. He grinned suddenly, turquoise eyes lighting up with an unmistakable masculine heat. "Yes ma'am."

The instant Joe handed Beth over, Seren seized his shirt. Diana could practically *feel* the lust steaming off Seren as she dragged Joe away. Diana could only hope that the pair would make it as far as their own cabin.

"I have to go too," Callum said, pitching his voice low so as not to wake Beth up. He hesitated, looking torn. "Min-Seo wants me to use my pegasus abilities to try to find Maurice. But if you'd rather I stayed—"

"No, go." Diana settled Beth down in her cot as she spoke. Beth stirred fretfully for a moment, then surrendered to sleep once more. "We'll be fine here. Will you tell the squad what's going on?"

"Already informed Rory." Callum made a gesture at his own forehead. "Telepathy. It's a mythic shifter thing."

"Okay, I've clearly still got a *lot* to learn about shifters."

And Callum, she thought with a shiver of unease. She still didn't know what he'd started to tell her…

"Diana." Callum's arms closed around her, drawing her close. "No more secrets. I promise. As soon as I get back, I'll tell you everything."

The sheer *rightness* of his touch made her nagging worry fade and vanish. She leaned into him, hugging him back, breathing in his warm, reassuring scent. The strange connection between them burned so brightly that she almost felt that she should be able to *see* it, like a rainbow running between their hearts.

"Be careful." Reluctantly, she released him. "Stay safe. And come back to me as soon as you can."

Callum cupped her face. He dipped his head down to press his lips to hers. The kiss was only brief, but she felt it all the way down to the tips of her toes.

"Always," he breathed.

∼

"Gotta say." Blaise leaned back against the wall, pushing her empty plate away. "It is *such* a relief to be able to talk freely at last. I'm so glad Callum finally told you about shifters."

Diana had barely touched her own dinner, even though she'd mainly been listening rather than talking. She was so stuffed full of new knowledge, there didn't seem to be room for food as well. Her head spun with everything that the squad had told her: Maurice's true nature, Lupa's pack, hellhounds and Thunderbirds and body-snatching demon snakes…

"I'm glad you told me about everything else," Diana said. "And also, to be totally honest, terrified."

"I know all this must be overwhelming, but you truly are safe with us," Wystan said. He cocked an eyebrow at Candice, placing one hand flat on the table, palm down. "A demonstration?"

Candice grinned. She picked up her fork, holding it like a dagger, and jabbed it full-force down at her husband's hand. An inch above his skin, it bounced off thin air, in a crackle of golden sparks.

Candice held up her now-bent fork. "Wystan's got this whole base shielded. Our ranch, too. Any enemy tries to set foot over the boundary, they'll get a big surprise."

Wystan grimaced, looking a touch embarrassed. "As did the mailman, before I learned how to tweak the wards to only keep out people with evil intentions. I had to persuade him we had a faulty buried electrical cable that kept shocking him. I think he's still reluctant to come up here."

"And the wards are just the last line of defense," Edith chirped brightly from her customary position tucked up under Rory's arm.

"Between Callum, Fenrir, and Seren, pretty much nothing can even get close to the base without us noticing. And of course, there are the unicorns."

"Of course," Diana echoed faintly.

It had been kind of a relief to learn that she hadn't been going crazy. She really *had* seen a unicorn on her first morning here. But it had also been quite a shock to discover that not only were there people who could turn into unicorns, there were also *actual unicorns*, living right here on Thunder Mountain.

"Feel free to yell," Buck suggested. The grumpy Superintendent's scowl was even darker than usual, for all that he was bouncing a delighted Beth up and down on his knee. "Let it all out. Trust me, you'll feel better for a bit of cussing and cursing. I know I did, when *I* found out about all this motherloving magic crap."

"You still yell," Blaise pointed out.

"I'm still pissed off about it all," Buck retorted. "I like my fairy tales to stay where they belong. In stories."

Something tickled the back of Diana's mind. "The creatures that you've been fighting, the ones that Lupa seems to be working with. You said that they look like serpents with horns? And the one that Lupa summoned, the one she was going to feed Joe to—she called it Unktehi?"

"Something like that," Rory replied. "You'd have to ask Joe or Seren. They were the only ones who were there."

Edith looked round, her brow creasing. "Where *are* Joe and Seren? They missed dinner."

"I think they're, um, resting after looking after Beth all day." Diana would put money on them being in bed, at least. "Anyway, I think I know what your demons actually are. Or at least, what my people would call them."

Wystan sat up straighter, scholarly interest sharpening his eyes. "Lakota legends?"

"Yes." Diana glanced at Buck. "You're Lakota too. You know the tales of the Wakinyan and Uncegila?"

A muscle tightened in Buck's jaw. "No. My sister Wanda was the one who sat at our grandma's feet, learning the old stories. Me, I was too busy playing football and trying to fit in with a bunch of dumb white boys, idiot that I was."

"Who's Wakinyan?" Edith asked, stumbling a little over the word.

"Not a who, a what. Thunder spirits. What you call Thunderbirds." Diana hesitated, biting her lip. "You have to understand, for me this is a little different than learning that dragons and unicorns and whatnot are real. I've always believed in the Wakinyan. I just...well, to put it in Christian terms, it's a bit like finding out Archangel Gabriel has been flying around the local woods starting wildfires with his flaming sword."

Blaise side-eyed Buck. "Probably shouldn't tell you that *someone* was trying to shoot the Thunderbird down, then."

Buck grunted. "You thought an angel had murdered your entire family, you'd be dusting off your shotgun and avoiding the local churches too. There's a reason I kept my mouth shut. If people *did* believe me, I didn't want this whole mountain crawling with would-be shamans."

"Heyoka," Diana corrected. "People touched by the Thunderbird are heyoka."

"What does that mean?" Blaise asked.

Diana struggled for an adequate translation. "Holy fools. Wise clowns. People who aren't bound by normal rules, by traditions or even their own past. Though that doesn't cover the whole concept by a long way. Anyway, people that the Wakinyan choose to speak to are...changed. Sometimes just for a little while. Sometimes forever."

"Well, the Thunderbird didn't talk to us," Rory said, frowning thoughtfully. "We've tried to communicate with it telepathically, but I never had any sense that it understood us on anything more than an emotional level."

Blaise arched an eyebrow. "Maybe we aren't foolish enough."

"Rarely has *that* seemed likely," Wystan murmured.

"What was the other thing you mentioned?" Rory asked Diana. "The Un—uh, whatever you said?"

"Uncegila. A great horned serpent. She had a consort, Unktehi, and together they spawned a ravenous brood, far more than the land could support. It's a big sin, in Lakota culture, to take more than you need."

"Should be in all cultures, really," Candice said. "We'd all be a lot better off if it were."

"Uncegila could have lived in peace with other beings if she'd stopped eating when she was full, stopped birthing more hungry mouths," Diana went on. "But instead she was greedy. She and her brood would have stripped the world bare, if not for the Wakinyan. They battled the horned serpents, with fire and lightning. They called out to brave, true heroes, summoning them to defend their tribes. Uncegila was driven out of the world, but many stories say she still lurks with her few remaining children in the cold, wet places under the earth. Forever hungry, never sated. Waiting to emerge and feast once more."

Rory let out a low whistle. "And now we have a Thunderbird flying around starting fires. And horned serpents coming out of the earth."

"Guess that makes us the heroes." Buck looked less than thrilled at the prospect. "Yippee-kai-motherloving-yay."

Edith was wide-eyed. "Do the stories talk about the horned serpents being able to possess people?"

Diana hesitated, thinking it over. "Not exactly. Though the bite of one of Uncegila's children was supposed to kill instantly. And Uncegila herself was said to be able to kill with a look. And not just the people she gazed upon, but all their family and kin too."

"Now there's a cheery thought." Blaise grimaced. "Let's hope that part's been exaggerated in the retelling."

"Stories do change and grow," Diana said. "Just like all living things. My mom used to tell me bedtime stories of the Wakinyan and their battles with Uncegila, when I was very small. It's one of my earliest memories, listening to her voice in the dark, safe in her arms…"

She had to stop and swallow the lump in her throat. The squad just waited, in gentle, understanding silence. Beth, oblivious to the moment, banged a spoon on the table.

"Anyway," Diana said, when she could continue. "My mom's versions of the stories were a little different from others that I heard later, when I was researching my thesis. My mother said that Uncegila was so hungry, mere flesh and blood didn't satisfy her. She began to devour creature's spirits, not just their bodies, and she taught her brood to do the same. That was what made her different from others of her kind, the horned serpents who lived peacefully in the rivers and lakes. What made her into a monster."

Rory let out his breath. "I think we're going to need to hear every story you know about the horned serpents and the Thunderbirds. And I am now *very* glad that Callum finally came clean with you. I just wish he'd told you everything earlier."

Diana hesitated, looking round at them all; Callum's colleagues, his friends, the people he'd called his family. "Callum...Callum said there's still something he hasn't told me. Something important."

Everyone but Buck immediately avoided her eyes. From the way the Superintendent's bristling brows drew down, he'd both noticed the sudden shiftiness of the shifters, and was as much in the dark as she was.

"All right, you motherloving collection of walking throw rugs," Buck growled. "Someone want to tell me why you're all looking like you know where the body is buried?"

Before anyone could respond, Beth screwed up her face, went a strained red color, and produced a conversation-ending smell.

"Saved by the stink," Candice said, waving a hand in front of her face.

"For now," Buck held Beth out at arms-length as though she was suddenly radioactive. "Don't think we aren't returning to this topic. When I can draw breath without gagging."

"I'll take her," Diana said, rescuing the Superintendent. "Sorry about this."

"Shit happens," Blaise said with a grin. "In this case, literally."

Diana started to leave, then paused, looking back at the group.

"Listen, I know you're all Callum's best friends. And you don't want to betray him. I'm not going to ask you to blab his secret. Just tell me one thing. In your opinion, is it really as bad as he seems to think?"

"No," Rory said, his deep voice firm and certain. "It isn't."

"Well, it wouldn't have been," Blaise added. "If he hadn't been so stupid as to try to hide it in the first place. Now...well, not gonna lie. He deserves a good smack round his thick head. But don't go *too* hard on him, okay? He beats himself up enough as it is."

"Please don't hurt him," Edith said, looking anxious. "He made one bad decision, it's true. But he did it because he loves you, and was terrified that you wouldn't love him back. Just remember that you're true mates. Always, no matter what."

Reassured, Diana nodded. "I will. Thank you. All of you."

Carrying Beth—and trying not to breathe too deeply—Diana headed for the toilets next to the gym. There was no built-in changing unit, of course, but Callum had managed to squeeze a small folding table into the room, with diapers and wipes always laid out and waiting.

Diana put Beth down, wrestled her out of her romper...and discovered a serious containment breach. She searched the changing table, but not even Callum had thought to leave spare clothes down here.

"Oh, poo," Diana muttered, which was all too apt. "I wish *I* had telepathy. I could really do with someone fetching a clean romper."

She started cleaning Beth up as best she could, while Beth kicked and complained. "I know, I know it's cold and you don't like it, baby. Let Mommy sort you out, and then I'll...wrap you in my shirt or something to run you back to the cabin. Just hold still for me. I'm working as fast as I can."

Beth suddenly stopped kicking, as though she'd understood Diana's words. Her head swiveled, eyes fixing on the door.

"Ba!" Beth announced, stretching out her arms eagerly, just as a quiet, polite cough came from the other side of the door.

"It's not locked!" Diana called out, wondering if somehow she *had* managed to send a telepathic message to the squad without realizing. "Come in!"

The door stayed closed. The deep, sharp *huff!* noise came again, sounding like an animal snorting. It was followed by a soft scratching sound, coming from the lower edge of the door.

Keeping one hand on Beth, Diana managed to lean far enough to reach the door handle. Opening it, she discovered an empty corridor...and one of Beth's rompers, dropped in a heap just outside the bathroom.

Diana hooked the romper with her foot, dragging it close enough to pick up. It was very slightly damp on one sleeve, as though someone had been carrying it in their mouth.

"Fenrir?" Diana said. "It's okay, you don't have to hide from me anymore. Please come out."

A pause—and then the air shimmered. The enormous black dog appeared out of nowhere, belly pressed submissively to the floor. His plumed tail swished in a hesitant, uncertain wag.

For a moment, her mind flashed back to when she'd been seven years old, cowering behind her mom as the feral dog pack closed in. Frozen in terror as her mom stepped forward, facing all those maddened eyes and snarling fangs, not even a stick in her hands...

Diana swallowed the old memory. Her mom hadn't been afraid of the dogs back then, and she didn't need to be afraid of Fenrir now. He was a *person*, not a dangerous animal. She could trust him, just like the rest of the crew.

"Thank you," she said to him, holding up the romper. "I really appreciate this."

Is just what pack does. Provide for cubs, and for denning bitches.

Diana jumped at the deep, growling voice. Fenrir's canine jaws never moved, but she could hear him in her head. It was a bit different to the way that she'd heard Callum—just words rather than a deep communion of souls.

"I can hear you," she blurted out.

Fenrir's tail wagged harder. *Sky Bitch is pack now.*

Diana blinked. "Uh...my name is Diana."

Fenrir cocked his head, looking slightly baffled, as though this was exactly what he'd said. *Yes. Sky Bitch.*

Okaaaaaay. From Fenrir's perfectly polite, respectful tone, Diana could only assume that he didn't mean the nickname as an insult. Making a mental note to ask Callum about this later, she started getting Beth dressed again.

"Have you been following me around all this time?" she asked Fenrir, remembering how he'd appeared out of thin air. The squad had told her that hellhounds could make themselves invisible.

Fenrir's ears drooped in guilty contrition. *Not spying. Stayed outside den. Just wanted to help guard pack's first cub.*

Diana scooped up a newly-fragrant Beth. Screwing up her courage, she squatted down so that she was eye-to-eye with Fenrir, Beth on her hip.

"Thank you," Diana said to the hellhound, meaning it. "I'm sorry I was rude to you earlier. Would you like to…"

She stalled, not quite sure what to say. He couldn't *hold* Beth, and it seemed rude to invite a person to sniff her daughter.

Beth solved this problem by reaching out to Fenrir with both chubby fists. He leaned closer to allow her to grab at the long, thick fur on his neck and chest.

"Babababa!" Beth crowed, yanking with all her strength.

Fenrir stayed perfectly still—apart from his tail. *That* was a blur of motion, a mad windscreen-wiper of delight.

"No, baby. Gentle." Diana caught Beth's hand as she tried to grab Fenrir's ear. "Gentle with the nice doggy—uh, hellhound."

Can test her teeth on me, Fenrir said tolerantly. He poked Beth's cheek with his broad, wet nose, making her giggle. *Is how cubs learn, grow strong. Or stronger, in Stormhorse's case. Swift paws already, this one.*

Stormhorse? Diana wanted to ask why Fenrir had called Beth that, but she suspected he would just give her another of those puzzled looks. She was starting to get the impression that Fenrir had a rather strange, alien way of seeing things. Which, she supposed, made sense, if he couldn't shift into human shape.

Fenrir pricked up his pointed ears, muzzle turning in the direction of the door. At the same time, Beth looked round as well. Her little mouth wrinkled in a frown.

She can *sense things,* Diana realized with a jolt. Beth clearly had the same ability to sense life-forms as Callum. *That* was why she'd so often seemed to be paying attention to nothing.

"What is it, baby?" Diana picked Beth up again, a shiver of anxiety making her hold her daughter close. "What can you sense?"

Stone Bitch, Fenrir said in her head. His tail wagged again.

"Diana?" Edith called from outside. "Are you in here?"

"Coming!" Hastily tossing the dirty diaper into the trash, Diana went to meet the firefighter. "What's up?"

Edith beamed at her. "Callum's back. He's with the others, in the mess hall. Didn't you sense him through the mate bond?"

"No." As far as she could tell, her sense of Callum hadn't changed. The mate bond was just a dim, warm glow in her heart, not nearly as bright as it had been before Callum had left. "Is that wrong? Am I supposed to be able to tell when he's close?"

"Well, I can with Rory, but we've been mated for a while. This is still very new for you. I'm sure there's no need to worry." Edith held out her hands. "Can I carry Beth for you? That way you'll be able to hug Callum properly when you see him."

"Uh, thanks." Diana passed Beth to Edith.

Diana followed Edith, Fenrir padding at her side. As they approached the mess hall, she could hear the squad's voices drifting from the open door. No-one *sounded* alarmed…and yet anxiety tightened its grip on her stomach. She couldn't help thinking about horned serpents, and what the squad had said about how they could possess people…

Callum went out after Maurice. And maybe we were wrong. Maybe all this time, Maurice was still working for Lupa. Maybe it was all to lure Callum out into a trap. Maybe that's not him in there at all…

"Shut up, Gertrude," Diana muttered.

She went into the mess hall--and froze.

"Oh hey, Diana!" Blaise waved at her, beaming. "Look who's back!"

The man in the middle of the group turned. He was wearing

Callum's clothes. He looked exactly like him. He even *stood* exactly like him, spine straight, shoulders set. Yet his controlled, blank expression cracked as he caught sight of her. His green eyes widened in surprise.

"You?" he said, in Callum's voice.

At her side, Fenrir growled, the fur lifting all along his spine.

"That's not Callum." With every atom of her being, every beat of her heart, Diana knew it to be true. *"That's not Callum!"*

CHAPTER 21

Wait, Callum's pegasus said suddenly. What was that?

Callum stretched out his wings, balancing on the wind to search the glimmering life-forms in the small town below. Looking for the hellhound amidst the clamor of other lives was hard, like sifting through a handful of sand for a single grain. Try as he might, he couldn't find anything that might have attracted his pegasus's attention.

I don't see anything, he said to his inner animal, silently.

Not down there. His pegasus turned in his soul, looking inward rather than peering out through their shared senses. *Something is wrong.*

A jolt of fear constricted his chest. Not *his* fear, but Diana's. Her distress flared down the mate bond in a silent scream.

Our mate! His pegasus reared, hooves flashing, ready to strike. *She calls us! GO!*

Callum was already wheeling round, breaking off his search. Thunder Mountain was a dim smudge on the horizon. Wind shrieked past his flattened ears as he put his full power into his wingbeats, racing for home.

Faster! FASTER! his pegasus urged him, as though he wasn't already straining every muscle and bone to breaking point. *She needs us, now!*

Callum reached down the mate bond, trying to contact Diana, but he was too far away. He stretched his senses to the limit, searching for the hotshot base, looking for any sign of an intruder. Had Maurice somehow slipped past the squad's defenses? Was Lupa attacking, with the full might of her pack?

Home came within his range at last. His awareness skipped over the lives present. Diana, Beth, Rory, Edith, Buck, Joe, Seren, Wystan, Candice, Blaise, Fenrir—

And one other.

He'd thought he was flying at his limit. He'd been wrong. Callum put on a new burst of speed, faster than a falcon, faster than he'd ever flown before.

And he knew that he was already too late.

He almost broke a leg on landing, he was going so fast. Only shifting to human form saved him from a catastrophic tumble. He rolled, absorbing the momentum, came up on his feet, and sprinted for the mess hall. Rory met him at the door, looking unsurprised by his sudden arrival.

"I thought you might turn up in a hurry." The griffin shifter's broad arm barred Callum's way. "We have a problem. Well, to be more accurate, you have a problem."

Callum's chest was on fire. He had to respond telepathically, too out of breath to form words. *Did Diana see him?*

"Oh, she did more than just see him." Despite the grim line of his jaw, a hint of amusement sparked in Rory's golden eyes. "She brained him over the head with a water jug."

Callum stared at the griffin shifter.

"She thought he was a demon wearing your skin," Rory explained. He quirked a tawny eyebrow. "To be fair, it was a logical conclusion. He had the rest of us fooled, but she knew on sight that he wasn't you, thanks to the mate bond."

Callum managed to suck in enough air to wheeze out, "Has he said anything yet?"

"Yes." Rory was now clearly battling to keep a straight face. "'Ow.' Diana knocked him out cold. He's only just come round. You're very lucky your mate has such a strong right arm."

Callum wasn't feeling very lucky just then.

"Callum!" Diana came barreling out of the mess hall, ducking round Rory. She flung herself into Callum's arms, seizing him in a rib-crushing embrace. An instant later, she shoved him away. Her emotions were a turbulent storm down the mate bond—relief, shock, outrage, confusion. "You have a *twin*?"

"No," he said, honestly. "I have two. My brothers and I are identical triplets."

"Why on earth didn't you *tell* me?" Diana's voice rose. "Is this your big secret? I could have *killed* the poor man! Oh God, he's Beth's uncle, and now he's going to hate me!"

All his chickens were coming home to roost, and they'd grown into velociraptors. Of all the ways for Diana to find this out…at that moment, he could have happily brained Connor himself, for turning up unannounced, at the worst possible time.

"Diana." He took her hands, though he suspected he should really be falling to his knees to grovel at her feet. "I'm sorry. I didn't mean for you to find out like this. I promise, I'll tell you everything. But first, I need to speak with my brother."

∼

Callum found Connor in the infirmary, holding an ice pack to his head. Despite the bruise swelling on his temple, Connor flashed his trademark wide, cocky grin the moment he saw Callum.

"Well, that backfired on me," Connor said ruefully. "Still, considering how many chainsaws and axes you guys have lying around the place, I'm grateful that the most lethal object to hand was a water jug."

"I'm not." Callum clenched his fists, forcing down an intense desire to seize his brother around the neck and throttle him. "What are you *doing* here?"

"Hey, you're the one who called me. I got your message. You said it was important, so…" Connor threw open his arms with a flourish, like a magician finishing a trick. "Here I am."

Callum pinched the bridge of his nose. Five seconds in Connor's presence, and he already had a headache.

"I didn't mean for you to come in person," he hissed. "Or *as* me. Where did you even get that?"

Connor looked down at the Thunder Mountain Hotshots t-shirt he was wearing. "Nicked it from the storeroom when I arrived. Couldn't resist. Also, this is all your fault. Would it kill you to mix up your wardrobe a bit? I mean, if you didn't make it so easy to impersonate you, I wouldn't be sitting here with a concussion. That lady has one hell of a right hook. Is she really your mate?"

"Yes," Callum ground out. "She is. Diana."

"Well, she's lovely. And very strong. And jumps to conclusions *way* too fast. Why the hell did she think I was a demon? I mean, it's not like she's never met me before."

"She doesn't *know* she met you before."

Connor's forehead creased. "What are you talking about? She bought me at that awesome charity auction. We spent a whole night together."

It was Connor.

It was Connor.

With tremendous effort, Callum stayed still, though he wanted to howl in anguish and rip his brother apart. "I know. But she doesn't. She thinks she bought *me*."

Connor blinked at him for a second. Then he whooped at the top of his lungs, punching both fists into the air in triumph.

"You've been pretending to be me!" Connor crowed. "I knew you'd come round eventually. Go on, do me now. I'll give you notes. Oh wow, we're going to have *so* much fun."

"That's not what I meant! Of course I haven't been aping you. I'm not a child."

A flash of true anger darkened Connor's face for an instant. "Oh, right, I forgot. You were born perfect, and you'd never lower yourself to my level. So what *do* you mean, bro? Remember to use words of one syllable and speak slowly, so I can understand."

Here it was. The moment he couldn't put off any longer.

Callum set his shoulders, and forced the words out. "Diana has no idea that she's met more than one of us. She saw me doing a TV interview, and thought that I was you. She came looking for me—you—and…and I never corrected her mistake."

Connor frowned. "Why not? And why did she come looking for me in the first place? Sure, we had a fun time, but that's all it was."

"Because…" Words dried in his throat. Callum couldn't say it out loud, he *couldn't*. "Look around."

Connor stared around at the blank walls, then back at him. "I don't get it."

"Not like that. With your pegasus."

Callum knew the instant Connor sensed Beth. His brother went absolutely still. For once, his face lost all traces of laughter.

"That baby," Connor whispered at last. "That's…*her* baby?"

"*My* baby," Callum snarled. "No matter what happened that evening, Diana is my mate, and Beth is my daughter, and I will *not* let you ruin this for me!"

For a moment, Connor just stared at him, frozen.

Then, very slowly, his grin returned, even wider and cockier than ever.

"Okay," Connor said. He reached for his back pocket. "Now I see why you called me. No wonder you're so mad. This must be killing you. Wait a sec."

Callum had been braced for Connor to…he wasn't quite sure what. Shout, or try to deny responsibility, or go for his throat. He hadn't been expecting Connor to pull out his phone, holding it up with the camera angled toward him.

"Okay." Connor nodded at him from behind the device. "I'm recording. Go ahead."

Callum stared from the phone to his idiot brother.

Connor waved one hand in a rolling, get-on-with-it gesture. "Come on. It's just two words. You can do it."

The only two words that Callum could think of at that moment were 'off' and 'fuck.' Not in that order.

"Thaaaaaank youuuu," Connor said, drawing out the words with over-exaggerated care.

A conversation with Connor was always an exciting voyage into previously uncharted realms of stupidity. This, however, was overly bizarre even for him.

"What are you thanking me for?" Callum asked.

Connor heaved a put-upon sigh, lowering his phone again. "Not me, dumbass. You. You're welcome, by the way."

Pure rage swept through him. Only a lifetime of controlling his impulses stopped him from punching Connor in his smug, smirking face.

"You," he got out, voice shaking with fury, "think I should *thank* you?"

"Well, yeah." Connor's smile faded, leaving him looking honestly bewildered, and a little hurt. "I mean, I'm the reason you met her the night of the bachelor auction, right? If I hadn't kept her entertained and laughing all evening, she would have been long gone by the time you sulked back to the hotel. And you wouldn't even have been in L.A. in the first place if I hadn't pulled that prank. So come on. Admit it. For once in my life, I didn't screw something up."

The world tilted around him.

Conleth hadn't recognized Diana. He couldn't be Beth's father.

Yet here was Connor—idiot Connor, who never knew when to stop, who always partied until he passed out—*and he didn't think he was Beth's father either.*

"Hang on," Connor said, a frown crossing his face. "If you met Diana all the way back then—and she's delightful, by the way, and you definitely need to do Gangnam Style as your wedding dance because she can drop some *sick* moves on the chorus—why are you only telling the family now?"

Before Callum could even think of forming a response, Connor's mercurial mood flipped back to wicked glee. He threw back his head, laughing out loud.

"Oh, shit," Connor gasped. "She ran off, didn't she? It's taken you this long to find her. Fuck, bro, just how bad in the sack *are* you?"

Diana had said that Connor had been drinking all that evening. When they'd been younger, Connor had frequently been found in some random field or alleyway after a night out. It wouldn't be the first time Connor had woken up somewhere, with no idea how he'd got there...

Connor didn't remember that evening. Just like he himself didn't remember what had happened. Connor had no idea that either of them might be Beth's father.

Callum's pegasus stamped a hoof. *Then we must tell him.*

"Hey." Connor was staring at him, his ever-shifting expression changing yet again, to something Callum had never before seen on his brother's face. He looked almost...concerned. "Are you okay? It was just a joke."

How many times had he heard *that* phrase from Connor's mouth? *It was just a joke, why are you so upset, I didn't mean it...*

All his life, Connor had impersonated him. Teased him. Tormented him, just by existing. By so effortlessly being a better version of him. One that people liked.

Connor *owed* him.

No! His pegasus flattened its ears. *We owe our mate the truth! We promised!*

"Come on. We're brothers," Connor wheedled. "For once, don't freeze me out. Tell me what happened."

Callum shoved his inner animal back down. Its advice had always been terrible.

And Beth deserved a better father than Connor.

"Yes," Callum said. "I will."

CHAPTER 22

"This is your big secret?" Diana didn't know whether she wanted to hug Callum or throttle him. Possibly both. "I mistook you for your *identical brother?*"

"You can't blame him for trying to keep it under his hat," Connor said cheerfully. "I mean, clearly you're going to be utterly devastated that your mate isn't the witty, handsome, unbelievably sexy dance-floor god that you thought he was. Instead you've got…" He swept a hand at Callum. "Well, that. Feel free to burst into tears. Handkerchief?"

"Connor," Callum growled.

Connor—who had indeed just produced an astonishing neon paisley handkerchief out of nowhere with a flourish—subsided, dropping his arm. "Just trying to be helpful, bro. No need to bite my head off."

Diana stared from one brother to the other. No matter how hard she tried, she couldn't spot a single physical difference between them. From their curling auburn hair to the slight cleft in their chins, they were absolutely identical.

And yet, completely different.

Now that Connor was no longer mimicking Callum's stiff, closed body language, she could see the man that she'd met at the bachelor auction. Connor lounged against the cabin wall, posing like a male model; cocky, casual, displaying his body like a dare. His expressive, mobile face showed every passing thought.

Diana shook her head, turning back to Callum. "Why didn't you just tell me?"

"I should have done," Callum said. "I'm sorry."

"Words I have literally never heard him say before in my life." Connor's face lit up. "If you're going to make him grovel, can I record it? For posterity?"

"*Connor.*"

"Just asking." Catching Diana's eye, Connor stage-whispered, "*Please* make him grovel. Cal never fucks anything up. This is a rare opportunity for him to practice apologizing."

Callum made a wordless noise somewhere between a snarl and a groan of despair.

"Right, right." Connor mimed zipping his mouth shut. "Shutting up now. Cross my heart. Not another word."

Diana rubbed her forehead. She cast her mind back over the bachelor auction, struggling to remember the latter part of the evening. This was difficult, given how much tequila she'd been knocking back.

"So when did you two switch round?" she asked.

"Last thing I remember was heading back to my room to get a shirt," Connor chirped up, apparently completely forgetting his solemn vow of silence a mere ten seconds after making it. "Next thing I remember, I was in my hotel room and the sun was *way* too bright. After that, it's all a bit of a blur of vomit and misery. Ah, good times."

A memory surfaced from the alcohol-drenched fog. She *did* remember Connor—or Stallion, as she'd thought of him then— complaining about the air conditioning, very late in the evening. He'd staggered off…and then, when he hadn't come back, she'd gone looking for him…

"Oh God." Diana covered her mouth as realization hit her. "Callum, it was you I ran into in the elevator, wasn't it? You were drunk too. I practically threw myself at you, we made out all the way…oh no, *that's* why you initially didn't let me into your hotel room! And then I turned around and barged back in anyway…oh *God*. Why didn't you tell me I'd made a mistake?"

"I knew you were my mate," Callum said. His words became slower, as if he was struggling to find each one. "From the moment our eyes met, I knew. In that moment, I loved you with all my heart. All my soul. And you…I thought that you recognized me in return. Not as my brother. As your mate."

Given what the crew had told her about shifters, she couldn't entirely blame Callum for succumbing to instinct when they'd first met. It must have been overwhelming, to have his one true mate suddenly leap out of nowhere and attempt to climb him like a tree. But still…

"You can't have thought that for long, though," she said. "So why didn't you tell me the truth when I found you again?"

Callum's gaze flicked to Connor. "I'd rather discuss that in private."

"What's the matter?" Connor said solicitously. "Is your pegasus playing up? Well, *I* might not be the special one with the extra-strong power, but I can still tell that there isn't anyone within earshot. So go ahead. No one's listening."

A muscle ticked in Callum's jaw. He continued to stare at his brother, pointedly.

Connor looked round behind him, and then down at himself. "Oh. Right. You mean me. You want me to leave now."

"If you don't mind," Diana said, wondering at Callum's strange rudeness. "I'm sorry, but I think I really need to talk to Callum alone for a bit. I'd love to catch up with you soon, though."

"As long as you aren't going to bludgeon me with tableware again," Connor said, flashing his easy smile. He hesitated, for the first time losing his air of cocky confidence. "But before I go, can I see—can I see my niece?"

"She's sleeping," Callum said curtly, before Diana could respond.

"Tomorrow, then?" There was something vulnerable in Connor's expression, like he genuinely thought she might refuse to let him see Beth at all. "Please?"

"Of course," Diana said, giving him a warm smile. "I can't wait for her to meet her uncle. One of her uncles. I'm so happy you're here."

Connor's face broke out into his widest grin yet. "You say that now. But I have to warn you, Conleth is the one who's going to be the good uncle. He'll remember all her birthdays and set up sensible investment accounts in her name. *I'm* going to be the *awful* uncle."

"No doubt," Callum muttered.

"I meant awful from your perspective. Beth is going to think I'm awesome." Connor threw Callum a mock glare before turning back to Diana. He placed a hand over his heart, as though swearing an oath. "As the awful uncle, it is my sacred right to introduce my niece to all the best things in life, way too young, and behind your back. Like ice cream. And Norwegian death metal. And puns."

Despite everything, Diana had to giggle. "Those are the best things in life?"

"Definitely," Connor said solemnly. "I'm pretty sure that's what Genghis Khan said. Or was it Conan? I always get those two confused. My history essays were legendary at school. All my homework, actually. Some of them became memes. I'll send you the link to the Buzzfeed article."

"Connor," Callum said yet again, in the tones of someone who was starting to think that a life sentence for homicide would be an acceptable price to pay.

Connor held up his hands in surrender. "Going, going. I know when I'm not wanted. I'll leave you guys to talk." He raised an eyebrow suggestively as he backed out, grin hooking up even further. "Or whatever you're really planning to do."

Callum shut the door in Connor's face.

Diana started to speak, but Callum made a slight, 'not yet' gesture. He stayed with one hand on the door, motionless, head cocked.

Finally, Callum's shoulders dropped in a sigh. He turned. "He's gone. At last."

"You didn't have to throw Connor out like that," Diana said. "He may be a little, er, extra, but he seems to mean well. I like him."

Callum's jaw clenched. "Yes. Everyone does."

His face was expressionless, revealing nothing. But Diana could sense his tense misery down the mate bond. He was wound tight as a clock-spring, nearly to the point of breaking.

"That's the reason, isn't it?" It was like finding the missing piece of a jigsaw. Now that she'd met Connor, she could see how he'd shaped Callum. "You were scared to tell me that you weren't him, because you thought I'd like him better than you."

Callum dropped his gaze, looking away. He started to pace in stiff, jerky steps, back and forth across the small room, as though he had to let out some of that coiled energy, or else explode.

"Everyone always liked them best," he said. "Connor and Conleth. The impulsive, reckless, charming ones, just like my father. The loveable rogues that got away with everything. And I was…the other one. The quiet one. The odd one. The one who didn't cause any trouble."

Some of her irritation with him bled away in the face of that old, deep hurt. "That sounds very hard for you. Being excluded like that. Always being different."

He shook his head in a sharp, slight motion. "I didn't mind that. I *wanted* to be the good one. I could see how my brothers drove our mother to distraction. At least I could make sure she didn't have to worry about me too."

"I'm sure she worried about you anyway," Diana said softly, thinking of how much she herself worried over Beth.

Callum paused mid-step, as though her words had struck a nerve. "I did my best. But it wasn't enough."

He shook himself, returning to his pacing. "In any event, Connor and Conleth were always coming up with mad, hare-brained schemes, always trying to get me to join in their stupid pranks. But I wouldn't. So I became the butt of every joke. I wouldn't laugh with them, so they made everyone laugh at me instead. You've already seen their favorite trick."

Diana remembered how the squad had been gathered round Connor, totally fooled… "Pretending to be you?"

"They got so good at it, they could deceive nearly anyone. Teachers. My friends. Even my own family, sometimes." Callum's mouth twisted.

"Other kids thought it was hilarious. Egged on by the approval, my brothers started to mimic me almost constantly. This was before they were diagnosed, so they had absolutely no impulse control. It got so bad, I eventually begged my parents to let me go to a different school. A boarding school, a special one, for shifters. A long way from home."

"That must have been very lonely."

Callum let out an ironic huff of laughter. "I loved it. I kept coming up with excuses why I had to stay over vacations as well."

"Did it ever get better? At home, I mean. You said that your brothers were diagnosed eventually, so I assume they got help. Didn't that help you too?"

"Not really. Though Conleth stopped imitating me, at least. He didn't *need* to. Once his ADHD was under control, he became effortlessly charming, effortlessly popular, everything I'm not..." Callum cut himself off, taking a breath. "Now he acts like I owe *him* an apology. Like I abandoned my family, rather than being driven away."

"And Connor?"

Callum snorted. "You've seen what he's like. He only takes his meds when he really has to. He loves playing the fool, making himself the center of attention. Pretending to be me is still his favorite joke. And people love it. People love him. Always."

Diana let out her breath, slowly. "I think I understand now why you didn't tell me any of this before."

Callum gave her a small, bitter smile that didn't reach his eyes. "Connor can be me better than *I* can. Why wouldn't you prefer him?"

"Callum." Diana went to him, slipping her hands round his waist, feeling the coiled energy in his taut muscles. "You know I love you, right?"

The words slipped out easily. It was only when Callum looked down at her, eyes wide and startled, that she realized it was the first time she'd said them to him.

"Sometimes...sometimes it's hard for me to believe." His voice was very quiet, just the barest breath. The deep vulnerability in his green eyes made her heart miss a beat. "That you'd settle for me."

Diana leaned her head against his chest, hugging him hard. "I'm not."

His arms closed around her. His fingers clenched desperately on her back as if he was afraid she might slip out of his grasp if he didn't hold onto her with his whole strength.

"I don't deserve you," Callum murmured into her hair.

"Well, I admit, you still have some apologizing to do." She leaned back to glare at him, though she couldn't entirely hide the smile that was tugging at her mouth. "I understand why you kept this from me from so long, but you do realize it was a really, *really* bone-headed move, right?"

He let out a long, pained sigh. "Yes. If it's any consolation, when I sensed Connor was with you, sheer terror took about five years off my life."

"That's no consolation at all!" Diana gave him a gentle mock-slap to the chest. "I need you to have a long, long life. With me."

Callum ducked his head, claiming her mouth. She pressed up into him, closing her eyes, surrendering to the sweet fire of his kiss.

"So," she murmured, when she could speak again. "About that apology. I believe groveling was suggested?"

Callum made a growling sound; part hunger, part irritation. "For once in his life, Connor was right about something. Never tell him I said that."

Diana laughed, then squeaked as he scooped her up in his arms as though she weighed nothing at all. The feel of his flexed muscles, hard as steel underneath her thighs, sent a fresh surge of heat through her body.

"What about Beth?" she said breathlessly, as Callum carried her into his bedroom.

"Sound asleep." Callum laid her down on the bed, immediately covering her with his hard, long body.

"But..." She gasped as his legs straddled hers, pinning her down. "She's right next door. She could wake up--"

Callum silenced her with another long, fierce kiss.

"Then you'll just have to keep quiet," he whispered, eventually. She felt him smile. "If you can."

This, it turned out, was very, very hard.

She'd thought he'd been taking his time earlier, in the meadow. But that had been a rushed quickie compared to *this* slow, exquisite torment.

He made love to her with a methodical patience that was all the sweeter because she could feel his all-consuming desire for her burning down the mate bond. There was no room for self-consciousness or doubt; not when she *knew*, with soul-deep certainty, how much he needed her. Wanted her.

Loved her.

Knowing how hard he was fighting to hold back made her bolder. She scratched her nails down his back, delighting in the shudder that went through him; licked the hollow of his throat, and felt him swallow a groan. She explored every hard plane and angle of his body, claiming every inch as her own. So much man, and all hers.

"Yes," he gasped. He pulled her to the edge of the bed, rolling off himself to sink to his knees between her spread thighs. "Yours. Always."

He bent his head, sweeping his tongue through her slick folds. Diana bit her lip, clenching her fists in the bedcovers with the effort of staying silent. She gripped his head with her thighs, relishing the play of muscles in his back, the delicious tension in his shoulders, his utter focus on her pleasure. Every circle of his tongue, every suck and lick, drove her higher and higher, until she was writhing helplessly—

Ecstasy shuddered through her. Callum never stopped, his mouth drawing out her orgasm longer than she'd ever thought possible. By the time he finally lifted his head, she was wrung out and trembling, flat on her back.

Callum crawled back onto the bed, muscles flexing. His green eyes gleamed like a hunting tiger's, predatory and hungry.

"Turn over," he growled. "All fours."

Diana wasn't entirely sure that she *could*, her limbs were so limp. But that rough, ragged edge in his voice made her core clench in need.

Despite the mind-blowing orgasm he'd just given her, she was suddenly aching to have him deep inside her.

She rolled over, bracing herself on hands and knees. His hot weight settled across her back; not bearing her down, but pressing enough to show how much bigger he was, how much stronger, how fiercely he was struggling for control. His mouth closed on the side of her neck, the soft place at the junction of her shoulder. He didn't bite down enough to hurt; just holding her in place in a show of dominance that made her gasp in desire.

"Oh yes." She thrust back, desperate for him, needing to be filled. "Please, Callum, please, now!"

He slid into her in a deep, fierce thrust. She clenched her jaw, clenched her eyes shut, fighting not to scream her pleasure. He filled her utterly, claimed her utterly.

Mine. His teeth were still clenched on her shoulder. But she heard him in her mind, in her soul, in every atom of her body. *Nobody can ever take you away now. Mine, my beautiful mate, all mine, Diana!*

Finally, *finally* he let go, pounding into her with animal abandon. Every powerful drive of his hips sent her mad. She thrust back, matching his rhythm, demanding more.

Callum let go of her neck at last, flinging back his head, his whole body arcing. She felt him coming, in a hot rush deep inside, making her clench around him in a final wave of blinding delight.

He collapsed down to his elbows on top of her, still being careful not to flatten her with his weight. Diana lay underneath him, panting, totally wrung out.

Callum rolled, taking her with him, until he was spooned round her. She relaxed into his warmth, his scent, the utter comfort of his presence.

His breath tickled her ear. "I love you."

"Love you too," she mumbled, sleep already dragging her down. "No more secrets, okay?"

"No more secrets." His voice followed her into dreams. "I promise."

CHAPTER 23

Connor collapsed down onto the bed with a sigh, throwing one arm across his eyes. It had been hard, laughing and joking with Rory and the rest of the gang all evening; listening to their stories, topping them with his own. All the while struggling to control himself, to not be *too* crazy.

To not cross that invisible line that would turn all the laughter to stares and scorn.

He wished he could have kept on being Callum for the evening. The challenge of mimicking his brother kept just enough of his mind occupied to let the rest of him be *still*. It was peaceful.

And people looked at him differently. Nobody laughed at Callum. They respected him. It was nice, being Callum.

But he couldn't be Callum. So he'd been himself, or as much of himself as he could allow himself to be, until he was about ready to gnaw through the walls to escape.

And now, finally, he was alone.

Bored now, his pegasus announced. *Let's go fight someone!*

Connor grimaced. The need to do something prickled under his skin, like an imminent shift. For a moment, he seriously contemplated flying out to find the nearest town. There had to be a bar around here *somewhere*.

Instead, he dug in his pocket for his phone. Still lying flat on his back in the borrowed cabin—and boy, these ground-pounders didn't know how good they had it, with *actual beds* and *actual blankets* and *private cabins*, he had to remember to rib Rory and Joe and Wystan mercilessly about it all tomorrow, but not Blaise, because she'd probably set fire to his underwear if he so much as hinted she might be getting soft—he dialed.

"I fucked up," he said, the instant the video call connected. Then, belatedly, he added, "Hi."

"Hello to you too, brother mine," Conleth said, rather dryly. "How is this news? Isn't shambolic chaos your natural state of affairs?"

"This time I've *really* fucked up. Massively. Balls deep." Connor waved his arms, trying to indicate the extent of his cock up, and then realized he'd just treated Conleth to a blurry, jerky shot of the room. He brought the phone back in front of his face again. "Seriously, it's really bad."

Conleth gave him a look. "Again: how is this news?"

"Wow, who pissed in your cornflakes this morning?" Connor frowned, something occurring to him. "Wait, is it morning in London? I always forget whether you're ahead or behind me."

"I'm *always* ahead of you, brother mine. But in this specific case, only by a few hours." Conleth turned his phone, showing Connor a brief view of skyscrapers. "I'm in New York."

Now that he was thinking about it, Conleth's life-force *did* feel a lot closer than normal. Connor had always been able to sense his brothers' locations, no matter how far away they were. It was a strange exception to the normal limits on his pegasus's power. It wasn't as impressive as Callum's extraordinary sensitivity…but at least it was *his*, something that neither of his more talented brothers could do.

"What are you doing in New York?" Connor asked, curiosity briefly distracting him from his own pity party.

"A bullshit business meeting that could just as easily have taken place over Skype and saved us all a lot of time, money, and environmental damage." Conleth scowled. "I swear, these investors make alpha lions look like team players. Sometimes I just sit here and daydream about kicking them all in their pompous entitled butts."

Connor shook his head. "You really need a change of career, you know."

"Not all of us can run into fires for a living." Conleth leaned forward, peering into his screen. "Where are you, anyway?"

"Montana. Callum's base. Did you know he met his mate?"

Conleth went oddly still. "Yes."

"That's how I fucked up." Connor let his head fall back onto the pillow with a thump. "I fucked her."

Conleth stared at him.

"Not *now*," Connor added quickly. "Obviously. I mean, ages ago. You remember that charity bachelor auction? The nice lady that you bribed to bid on me? The one you thought might be my mate?"

"Yes," Conleth said, his voice tight. "Wait, you slept with her?"

"I must have done." Connor started to run a hand through his hair, then stopped, wincing, as his fingers encountered the bruise on his temple. "To be honest, I don't remember. But it's the only thing that makes sense. Callum would never have let his mate go again if he'd really met her in the elevator that night. So it must have been me."

Conleth seemed to be lagging several sentences behind the conversation. "Callum said he met his mate in the elevator?"

"Yeah. Well, I said it first. Told him that since I couldn't remember anything from that night—which is true, by the way—it could have been *him* that she ran into and took to bed. It was the only way out of the whole mess. You would have been proud of me, thinking on my feet like that. Anyway, he went for it hook, line, and sinker. Recited the whole cock-and-bull story to his mate with a straight face, confident that I'd play along. Or, well, not play along, exactly. I'm pretty sure he thinks I actually believe it."

Connor had known Callum had a low opinion of his intelligence. It still hurt, somehow, to discover that it was *that* low.

Conleth was looking increasingly bewildered. "Why on earth

would Callum lie to his mate? And if he really *does* think that you slept with her, why hasn't he beaten you to a pulp? Or is that why you have a bruise on your forehead?"

"Oh, that wasn't Callum. That was his mate. Diana." Connor grinned, remembering how she'd charged him like some totally metal Viking goddess, brandishing her improvised weapon. "She's *awesome*. Also, don't ever pretend to be Callum around her. Unless you're wearing a helmet. And probably some kind of groin protection. Maybe a full suit of plate armor. Thought that would be hard to pull off, if you're meant to be Callum. I guess you might get away with it on Halloween. Or maybe not. Considering how he hated trick-or-treating as a kid, I can't really see him dressing up now. Hey, wouldn't be hilarious if he was forced to go to a costume party? We should try to work out a way to make that happen sometime."

Conleth massaged his forehead with his fingertips. "Connor, are you off your meds?"

"Of course I am. It's end of fire season. You know I only take them when I'm working. Otherwise I can't drink."

"Do me a favor and take the damn pills before you call me next time, okay?" Conleth dropped his hand with a sigh. "Or at least give me enough warning so that *I* can go off my meds too. It's a lot easier to have a conversation with you when I'm on the same wavelength."

"Sorry. Oh, fuck, I meant to swear you to secrecy before telling you any of this."

Connor was a fuck-up. He knew he was a fuck-up. He fucked up everything he touched, whether he was on meds or not (which was why he didn't take them. If he was going to fuck up anyway, he might as well enjoy it).

Beth needed someone who wasn't a fuck-up. Someone responsible. Someone who could do things right. Someone who could be a *real* father to her.

And if he only did one thing right in his entire life, it was going to be to make sure she had one.

"Listen," Connor said urgently. "Don't you ever let on to Callum that I know he's lying, okay? He hates me enough already, not that I can blame him for that. At least this way he might still speak to me once in a blue moon. And don't ever, *ever* breathe a word of this to his mate. As far as Diana knows, Callum's the father. She'll hit the roof if she ever finds out the truth. Promise you won't tell."

Conleth started to speak—and then stopped dead.

"Conleth?" Connor shook his phone, wondering if the video feed had frozen. "Hello? You still there?"

"Yes." His brother's face had gone white. "What do you mean, Callum's the father?"

CHAPTER 24

"Still no word from Connor?" Diana asked, looking concerned.

Callum shook his head, most of his attention occupied with stopping Beth from stuffing her face full of grass. Having discovered that it was tasty in her pegasus form, she now seemed convinced that it was a delicious snack when she was human as well.

"I'm getting worried." Diana scanned the nearby cabins, as though Connor could somehow be hiding from Callum's pegasus. "You haven't sensed him all morning. I wonder where he's gone?"

"Knowing Connor, to a bar." Callum took Beth's hands, trying to encourage her to stand up rather than continue ripping up the meadow outside his cabin. "I expect he got bored yesterday evening and flew off to find some entertainment."

"You really think he'd stay out all night?"

"I've known him to stay out all week. For Connor, staggering back mid-afternoon the next day would be making an early night of it."

"But he was so eager to meet Beth properly today," Diana said, her hands twisting together. "I'm worried that something might have happened to him. Maurice is still out there, after all. What if he's gone after Connor? What if he's managed to capture him?"

Privately, Callum thought that Maurice would find that Connor made a very poor hostage. In the unlikely event that Maurice *had* abducted Connor, by now the poor hellhound would probably be desperate to offer *them* a ransom to take him back.

But that was unlikely to reassure Diana. Callum found himself in the unusual—and not entirely comfortable—position of having to say something good about his brother.

"Connor is a fully-grown pegasus stallion. He can take care of himself." That was debatable in most contexts, but not this one. Callum knew only too well how good Connor was in a fight. "And he's had more than enough practice at brawling. He's a better fighter than I am, actually. Don't tell him I said that."

"I don't doubt that he's physically capable." Worry still creased Diana's brow. "But I got the impression he, um…"

"Has the common sense of a carrot?"

Diana shot him a reproving look. "I was going to say, doesn't entirely think things through."

"He doesn't *at all* think things through. He doesn't even start to think things through. His mind is a small dog in an infinite field of squirrels."

Diana folded her arms sternly, though he could tell she was smothering a giggle. "Be nice about your brother. He's my family too now, you know."

"I *am* being nice about him." Beth was tugging at his hands, demanding a cuddle. He picked her up, supporting her on his hip. "Anyway, he's probably just sleeping it off somewhere. Possibly the town drunk tank. If he hasn't turned up by dinner, I'll go looking for him."

Diana poked him in the shoulder. "Put it on your list. That way I know you'll do it."

Callum sighed, but obligingly pulled out his notepad and added it on to his to-do list for the day. Right at the bottom. He had more important things to do than chase after his idiot brother.

He ran a finger down his itinerary. "I have to get going. I'm behind schedule."

Diana's cheeks went pink, but her eyes sparkled. "So sorry for distracting you from your planned activities for the morning."

He caught her with his free arm, drawing her in for a long, lingering kiss. Beth squawked in protest, squished between them.

"I'm not," Callum said, releasing his mate again. "But I do have to go. Min-Seo still needs me to search for Maurice. And I have to talk to Rory and the others."

That was the most important thing. It hadn't entirely been Diana's lush, delicious body that had made him drag her back into bed this morning (though just thinking of it now made him tempted to throw his notebook into the bushes, abandoning all other plans for the day). Callum couldn't risk her talking to his friends, not until he'd had a chance to brief them on his…slight alteration of the facts.

His pegasus flattened its ears at him. *You mean your lies.*

He repressed his inner animal. At most, it was a white lie. For the good of everyone. Connor couldn't possibly want to be a father, after all. He would have thanked Callum for taking on all the responsibility, if he'd known the truth.

Callum's friends would agree that he'd made the right call. They'd go along with it. They'd understand. He'd *make* them understand—

Callum was abruptly jerked out of his train of thought by Beth twisting in his arms. She craned her neck, staring at the sky. Sensing what had attracted her attention, he froze too.

What's he doing here?

"What is it? What have you both sensed?" Diana shaded her eyes, following his gaze. "Oh! Is that Connor?"

"No." Callum passed Beth to her, a twinge of protective instinct prompting him to step in front of them both. "It's my other—"

He didn't get time to finish the sentence. Conleth came hurtling down in a streak of copper, flying so fast that Callum thought he wasn't going to stop at all. But at the last second Conleth flared his wings, shifting as he fell out of the sky. Conleth's human feet hit the ground right in front of him—and the next thing Callum knew, his jaw exploded with pain.

His pegasus surged up, taking control. Conleth shifted as well, rearing to meet him, front hooves clashing against his own. Instinct drowned all human thought. It wasn't his brother in front of him, but another stallion, a challenger, a *rival-!*

"Stop!" Diana shrieked. She was retreating, shielding Beth with her own body, but her voice was furious and unafraid. "Both of you, stop it, *now!*"

Her voice dragged him back like a lasso around his neck. Callum dropped down to four hooves, backing off. He kept his wings spread, ready to attack again if Conleth made the slightest move towards Diana and Beth.

Conleth, however, shrank into human form. His usually pristine business suit was creased and rumpled, tie askew, shirt sweat-stained. He looked like he'd been flying flat-out for hours.

"Ask him what dress you were wearing," Conleth snarled.

For a moment, Callum couldn't make any sense of the words.

Then he realized they weren't addressed to him.

"What are you talking about, Connor?" Diana said, sounding utterly confused—and then her eyes narrowed. "No, wait. You must be the other one. Conleth, right?"

Conleth's chin jerked down in a sharp nod. He never took his eyes off Callum. "Ask him what dress you were wearing, the night of the charity bachelor auction. *Ask him!*"

Everything stopped.

His breath. His heart. His whole world.

No. No. Impossible.

Conleth hadn't recognized Diana. Callum had shown Conleth her picture, and watched his face, and he hadn't so much as flickered an eyelid. It wasn't Conleth. It couldn't be Conleth...

Yet here he was, chest heaving, teeth bared in aggression, more furious than Callum had ever seen him.

Diana's eyes found his. She didn't ask him anything. She didn't have to. The mate bond told her everything.

Conleth took a deep breath, regaining a little of his usual air of confident composure. "You wore a green dress, knee length, embroidered with leaves at the hem. You had a necklace on, a little gold bird."

Every word hit the mate bond like an axe-blow. He could feel it fraying, parting, leaving him dangling by a single thread over a black abyss.

"You took me up to my room on the sixth floor," Conleth continued, relentless, ruthless, his eyes cold and unforgiving. "You made out with me all the way up in the elevator. And that is my daughter."

CHAPTER 25

"Hello, little one," Conleth murmured as Beth eyed him dubiously. "I'm your daddy. I'm here now. I'm here at last."

Conleth was down on his knees on the grass, heedless of his expensive designer suit. His soft, wonderstruck expression stabbed through Diana. It was the same way Callum looked at their daughter.

No. Not their daughter.

Her daughter.

And Conleth's.

Beth continued to regard Conleth owlishly for a moment, as though searching for hidden defects. Then, without warning, her little face broke into a broad grin. She held her hands out to him.

Conleth's breath caught in a dry, rasping sob. He hugged Beth tight, pressing his cheek to hers. Diana could see the bright gleam of tears leaking out from his closed eyes.

"I didn't know," Conleth murmured, so softly Diana almost didn't catch the words. "I didn't know what I was missing. Until now."

Beth, with a toddler's attention span, was already more interested in undoing Conleth's tie than participating in a heart-warming family moment. Conleth sat back on his heels, tugging off the strip of red silk so that Beth could play with it. He swiped the back of a hand across his eyes, then looked up at Diana.

"Thank you," he said, voice hoarse with emotion. "I only wish I could have been here for you earlier."

"You don't need to apologize. It wasn't your fault." Diana tried to smile at him, because it *wasn't* his fault. The mate bond lay like a stone on her heart, cold and heavy. "You—you had no way of knowing."

Conleth's gaze flickered to Callum. He'd retreated to the edge of the forest, half-hidden in shadow, to give Conleth space to meet Beth. The rest of the squad had gathered nearby too, in an uncomfortable, fidgeting huddle. Nobody seemed to want to approach Callum.

"I shouldn't have lied," Conleth said, still watching his brother. His jaw clenched. "He called me, you see. Last week. He didn't mention Beth, but he showed me your picture. Now I realize he was fishing for a reaction. If I hadn't pretended I didn't recognize you, he would have been forced to tell me the truth."

"Why did you do that?"

Conleth gave her a wry, disarming smile. It was bizarre, seeing the face she knew so well animated by yet another personality. His mannerisms were somewhere between Callum's tight restraint and Connor's bright exuberance; controlled, smooth, confident.

"Because at that point, I thought that I'd just made out with you," Conleth said. "And that seemed bad enough. I thought he'd never speak to me again if he knew I'd kissed his mate. There's enough of a rift between us as it is. The last thing I wanted was to make things worse."

"Wait, you didn't realise that we'd slept together?"

Conleth grimaced. "Please don't think that I'm trying to make excuses for my appalling behavior, but by the point you encountered me in the elevator, I was having a rather unfortunate drug interaction. I take a particularly potent medicine to control my ADHD, specially formulated for shifters, and it does *not* mix well with alcohol. I'm normally very careful not to drink when I'm on it. But before the auction, when I was impersonating Connor, I was carrying around a bottle of whiskey, in order to be more convincing.

And when I first saw you hiding behind the potted plants at the bar—"

"That was *you*? You're the one who gave me all that money, and asked me to bid on you?"

"Yes. I was buying time for Connor to sober up enough to actually appear at the auction. I couldn't go on stage myself. I'm not a firefighter. It would have been fraud." Conleth heaved a long-suffering sigh. "Which Connor *should* have realized before he'd emptied the entire minibar in his room. Never leave him alone with tiny food. Anyway, when I first saw you, my pegasus kicked up such a fuss that I thought you were *my* mate. I was so startled I actually took a swig from the bottle."

"I remember you drank a couple of times while we were talking."

Conleth looked a little embarrassed. "One slip leads to another. Or sip, in this case. I was very distracted by my pegasus yelling in my head that you were somehow important. That's why I gave you the money to bid on Connor. I thought perhaps you were *his* mate."

Diana remembered how 'Stallion' had looked at her strangely for a moment, when she'd won the auction. "I'm pretty sure Connor's pegasus recognized me too."

Conleth nodded. "Anyway, by the time you ran into me a second time, I was so out of my head that *everything* seemed like a great idea. Including kissing you. I thought perhaps you *were* my true mate, and my pegasus just needed a push to realize it. And…I don't really remember much beyond that."

She felt just as embarrassed as he clearly was. "I owe you a huge apology. I only meant to take you back to your hotel room. But I got to the elevator, and some stupid, *stupid* mad impulse made me turn around and go back to your hotel room. I'm so, so sorry."

"Neither of us was exactly our best selves that night." Conleth looked down at Beth. "And something wonderful came out of it all."

It was good, that he was looking at Beth with such adoration. It was good, to have everything explained at last. This was all good.

So why did Diana feel like her heart had shattered into a million splinters of glass?

Conleth cleared his throat, turning brisk. "There's so much we need to discuss. Money, for a start. I don't know if Callum mentioned this, but the Tiernach family is, shall we say, fairly well off. I'll start transferring assets over immediately."

"Oh, no. I can't accept—"

"Not negotiable," Conleth interrupted.

His eyes gleamed with amusement, but his tone made it clear that he wasn't going to take no for an answer. Diana suddenly realized that he was *very* used to getting his own way.

"I've been stuck managing this damn investment firm for years while my father and brothers flitted around playing fireman," Conleth went on. "It's about time I got some use out of all this money. Now, a proportion will be held in trust for Beth, of course, but I'll sign some investments over to you directly. More than enough to support you in comfort. As long as you don't need more than, say, two or three houses, I admit."

Diana's mind reeled. She'd been overwhelmed enough by Callum sharing his small cabin. Now here was Conleth casually talking about giving her multiple *houses?*

Conleth was already continuing on. "We will need to thrash out all the legalities as well. Access rights, shared custody arrangements, how we'll handle decisions about her education and so forth…I'll have my lawyers start drawing up the itinerary for discussion."

"Yes," Diana said faintly. "That sounds…sensible."

Conleth hesitated, eying her. "I'm sure we can make this an amicable process, but you'll need your own legal representation too. Though I trust you aren't planning to contest my claim of paternity?"

Lawyers and contracts and arrangements…it was all so different. So much more complicated than Callum's simple, quiet statement, back when he'd first told her his feelings: *I want you. I want to be with you. Not just as Beth's father.*

But Callum wasn't Beth's father. Conleth was.

Diana forced down the crushing wave of bleak despair that accompanied the thought. She couldn't let her own heartbreak get in the way of what was right for Beth.

Conleth *was* right. This was the sensible way to go about things, the adult way. Formal contracts and careful discussion. Not foolish trust in true love, and everything magically working out.

After all, she'd trusted Callum.

She swallowed, forcing a bright, optimistic tone. "Of course I'm not going to contest your paternity. You are Beth's father, after all."

"Yes. I am." Conleth glanced again at Callum. His mouth flattened. "And he tried to steal her from me."

"Cal—" His name stuck in her throat painfully, like a fishhook. "Callum's still my mate."

Conleth's face set in hard, cold lines. Suddenly, he looked nothing at all like Callum.

"Then you have a decision to make," he said. "Because Beth is coming back to England with me."

CHAPTER 26

"No," Callum said.

His brother folded his arms, glaring at him. "This is not open to discussion. Connor told me about the escaped hellhound, and all the other dangers targeting your squad. My daughter is not safe here. I will not permit this situation to continue."

Callum could feel the feral energy coursing under Conleth's skin, barely held in check. Conleth might appear as cool and collected as always, but underneath the surface he was poised to shift and fight.

Yes. His own pegasus bared its teeth, more than willing to settle this hoof to hoof, stallion to stallion. *Drive off the rival! Fight for our mate and foal!*

But Beth wasn't his.

And now he was losing Diana, too.

Diana stood in Conleth's shadow, holding Beth. Her whole body was tight and drawn, huddled protectively around her child. To his pegasus senses, she was a pale ghost of herself; all her bright strength smothered, leaving only faint flickering embers.

He'd done that to her. Broken her trust. Made her doubt all her decisions, leaving her vulnerable to Conleth's manipulation.

Conleth. Conleth with his smooth words that came so easily.

Callum had watched him talking to Diana, talking and talking. He'd been too far away to hear what Conleth had said, but he'd seen the effect on Diana. Seen how every sentence settled on her shoulders like a snowflake—so light, so reasonable—until she bowed and gave way to the cold, crushing weight of Conleth's logic.

He couldn't wield words like a weapon as Conleth did. Especially not now. Every life form for miles around grated against Callum's mind. His pegasus was raging, his guilt was a cavernous void in his chest, the mate bond was running through his fingers like sand from an hourglass no matter how he tried to hold onto it—everything was wrong and it was all his fault, and he couldn't focus, couldn't *think*.

All he could do was say again: "No."

"It is *over*, brother," Conleth snapped. "You know full well that the only reason you insisted Diana and Beth stay here was because you were trying to hide the truth. Well, that reason is gone now. I'm taking them back home, where they can be safe."

"They are safe here. With the squad."

"But they would be safer with their *family*," Conleth countered instantly. "Our parents are waiting back in Brighton, desperate to meet their first grandchild. And the city is a far better place for a child than this backwater wilderness. For pity's sake, Callum, Brighton is protected by the Phoenix Eternal! You think any enemy can get past him?"

Callum's feeble arguments died on his tongue, smothered by the inescapable truth. The Phoenix—Blaise's father—was one of the most powerful shifters in the world. There was no doubt that Diana and Beth would be safer under his burning wings.

No, no, his pegasus raged. *This is our home, our place to protect, and it is their home too! Our mate and foal belong here, with us! He cannot take them away!*

In desperation, he looked at Diana. "You didn't want to go to England, before. You didn't want to uproot your life."

"Diana only wants what's best for Beth," Conleth said before Diana could speak. He put a possessive hand on her shoulder, fixing Callum with cold, scornful eyes. "And if you were Beth's real father, you would too."

The words sliced across his throat like a knife. He couldn't speak, because what if that was true?

"Conleth." Diana touched his brother's arm. "Would you watch Beth? I need to talk to Callum."

"Of course." Conleth took Beth. It hurt, even more, to see how easily she went to him. "Please, beat some sense into my brother's stubborn skull. Take as long as you need."

Conleth walked off. Every instinct screamed at Callum to run after his brother, snatch back his child, claim what was his.

Instead, he turned to Diana. "This is really what you want?"

Diana nodded, her face pale and wan. It ripped his heart in half to see her look so defeated.

"Conleth is right," she said. She rubbed her arms as if she was cold, avoiding his eyes. "Going to England is the sensible thing to do, especially with Maurice on the loose again. There's so much Conleth and I need to sort out between us, and it will be easier to do back at his place. I do want Beth to meet her grandparents, as well. There's... there's no reason to stay here."

Me, he wanted to say. *I'm here.*

But he *wasn't* a reason for her to stay. Not anymore.

The words were ludicrously inadequate to express how he felt, but he had to say them anyway. "I'm sorry."

Diana lifted her head. She met his eyes at last, and the hurt in them was the worst pain of all.

"Sorry you lied?" she said. "Or sorry you got caught?"

"Both."

She made a small sound, a sob of mingled despair and surprise. "Well, at least you admit it."

"Only the truth from now on. I promise."

"You said that before." Diana shook her head, still holding his gaze. "Callum...I understand why you did what you did. But that doesn't mean I'm okay with it."

"I'm not asking that. You shouldn't be okay with it. I betrayed you.

I...I honestly thought that I might have been Beth's father. I took sleeping pills that night, and I don't remember any of what happened. I was clinging to hope that you'd somehow come into *my* hotel room by accident, since my pegasus kept insisting that Beth is mine. But even though we all know the truth now, I still...I still..."

Callum stumbled into silence. The mate bond was just a dim, flickering candle in the void of his soul. He reached for it, trying to reach *her*, to show her mere words could never convey.

Diana's eyes searched his face. He couldn't read her own expression, didn't know if he'd reached her or not. "You still what, Callum?"

"I still love Beth," he got out, though his chest felt like it was being squeezed in a vise. "I still want to be a father to her, even though she's not mine. I'm still your mate."

"And I'm still yours," Diana whispered. Her tears overspilled, making shining tracks down her cheeks. "But I have to be a mother first."

Then take me with you.

The words stuck in his throat, refusing to come out. But he *had* to say them. If she was going to England, then he had to beg her to let him come too. If that was the price of keeping his mate, he had to pay it.

Even if it meant leaving the gentle peace of the mountain for the screaming chaos of the city, with countless human lives shrieking in his awareness.

Even if it meant leaving his crew, his friends, the only place he'd ever truly felt he fit in.

Even if it meant—

"Diana!" Conleth interrupted. Callum had never before heard such pure joy in his brother's voice. "Look! Look at Beth! She's walking!"

Callum jerked round, just in time to see Beth take another toddling, wobbling step.

Towards Conleth.

Diana abandoned Callum without hesitation, pelting for Conleth and Beth. She reached them just as Beth teetered into Conleth's outstretched hands.

"Baby! Oh, my baby!" Diana flung her arms around both Conleth and Beth, hugging them indiscriminately. "Your first steps! I'm so proud of you!"

There was no place for Callum in that tight-knit huddle. He was on the outside, as he always had been.

As he always would be.

Callum stepped back, shifting. He took to the sky, and none of them even noticed he was gone.

CHAPTER 27

Callum didn't come back.

Connor joined them at dinner—it turned out he'd been hiding at the nearest bar to avoid getting drawn into his brothers' confrontation—but Callum never appeared. Diana stayed up long into the night, waiting for him to return. She fell asleep listening for his soft, quiet tread, and woke up to echoing absence.

Even now, she kept turning at every little noise, hoping it was him. She kept expecting the cabin door to open, for him to step through and...and...

Diana wasn't sure what she expected him to do. What she *wanted* him to do. Throw himself at her feet? Sweep her into his arms? Plead with her to stay? Beg to come with her?

Like that's ever going to happen, she thought bleakly. Callum would never return to his home city. Not while his brothers were there.

Diana had heard the old, unhealed hurt in his voice as he'd described how they'd tormented him as a child. She'd seen for herself the deep, bitter rift dividing him from Connor and Conleth.

And she was on the wrong side of it.

Conleth was Beth's father. He would be part of her life now, a big part, forever. How could she expect Callum to swallow all those old grievances and play happy families, just for her sake? Let alone endure fresh wounds as he watched Conleth claim Beth's love, claim the role of her father?

It was too much to ask of him. Too much to ask of anyone.

Maybe it was just as well he hadn't come back.

Diana packed the last romper into the cardboard box, and taped up the lid. She hadn't wanted to take much—Callum had paid for everything, after all--but she also hadn't wanted to just leave all the baby stuff cluttering up the place. The least she could do for Callum was to make sure he wouldn't be assaulted by bitter reminders of Beth when he *did* come back to his cabin.

"I think that's the last of it," she said, taking Beth back from Rory. "You'll see this gets put to good use, right?"

Rory hefted the heavy box under one arm without any apparent effort. "I'll put it in the storeroom. For when you come back."

"I'm not coming back." She handed him Callum's spare keys. "Give this to him when you see him, okay? And tell him...tell him..."

"I'll tell him he's being a bloody idiot," Rory rumbled. "And to get his sorry tail on the next plane to England."

"Don't." She laid a hand on his arm, looking up into those kind, sad golden eyes. "Please. Just...don't. Be here for him, as his friend. For my sake."

Rory's broad shoulders fell in a sigh, but he nodded, slowly. "I will as long as I can. Edith and I are going back to Brighton soon. And the others, too. We have a tradition of all our families getting together for Christmas. Callum...I'll do my best to persuade him to come. But the rest of us will see you there, at least."

"I'd like that very much." On impulse, she gave him a hug. "Thanks, Rory. Take care of him for me."

Diana had already said her goodbyes—or goodbyes for now—to the rest of the squad. Duffel bag over her shoulder, Beth in her arms, she headed for the cabin Conleth and Connor had borrowed.

"Hi Connor," she said as he opened the door. "Is Conleth here?"

He shot her a wry look, which tipped her off to her mistake a moment too late. "Actually, it *is* me."

"I'm sorry!" Flushing with embarrassment, she gestured at the Thunder Mountain Hotshot t-shirt he was wearing. "I just assumed from the clothes…"

His face split into a sudden broad, beaming grin that very much *wasn't* Conleth's. "Naw, I'm just messing with you. It's Connor."

Diana was starting to have a lot more sympathy for Callum. "Do you take *every* opportunity to do that?"

Still smirking, Connor shrugged. "Wouldn't you, if you had an identical twin?"

"Not as often as you do." Diana hesitated, studying him. "Connor? Why *do* you do that so much? You must know that Callum really hates it."

Connor's grin flickered, just for a second. "Yeah. But at least it gets his attention. And I…just like being someone else, sometimes."

Then his smile was back, with full mega-watt force. "Anyway, it's freaking *hilarious*. Conleth! Diana's here!"

"Thank you, I have not suddenly stopped being a pegasus shifter in the last five minutes." Conleth emerged from the cabin, pushing Connor to one side with a casual, brotherly shove. Diana still found it disconcerting to see two identical faces side-by-side like that. "What is it, Diana? Is something wrong?"

"No." She held up her packed duffel bag. "I just wanted to let you know that I'm ready to go when you are."

For the first time since she'd met him, Conleth looked less than entirely self-assured. "But Callum's not back yet."

"I don't…" Diana had to stop for a second, swallowing the pain. "I don't think he's coming to say goodbye. It'll be easier on him if we just go."

Conleth had the expression of a man whose day was suddenly not going to plan. "But he's supposed to come back."

"I *told* you you'd overplayed your hand," Connor muttered.

Diana looked from one brother to the other. "Am I missing something here?"

"Yes." Connor leaned on the doorframe, hooking his thumbs into the waistband of his jeans. "The fact that my brother is a pig-headed idiot."

"Callum isn't—"

"Not Callum." Connor jerked his chin in Conleth's direction. "*That* one."

Conleth glared at him, though worry still lurked at the edges of his expression. "I'm not the one who's currently sulking god-knows-where rather than coming back to where he clearly belongs."

Connor let out a long-suffering sigh. It was exactly the same sound that Conleth had made about *him* the previous day. "No. You're the one who's once again manipulating everyone into doing what you want, just so that you can avoid having to apologize."

"*I'm* not the one who needs to apologize!"

"Yeah, yeah, you never are. But for once you can't pin this on me, Conleth. You're the one that screwed the pooch this time." Connor glanced at Diana. "Uh. Sorry. Bad choice of words. No offence intended."

"None taken," Diana replied. "Is someone going to explain to me what's going on?"

Conleth started to pace in tight, anxious steps. Diana's heart twisted, because it was exactly the same way Callum moved when *he* was worried.

"He'll come back." Conleth ran a hand through his hair, searching the sky as though expecting to see flame-red wings appear at any second. "He *has* to come back. She's his mate."

Connor sighed again. "Sometimes I think that I got all the brains in this family as well as all the good looks. Not to mention all the charisma, moves, sense of humor and sex appeal." He turned to Diana, gesturing at his brother. "Conleth thought that he could use you to drag Callum back home at last."

Diana stared from Connor to Conleth. "You want Callum to come to England with us?"

Conleth looked at her as if this should have been self-evident. "Of course I do. He's my brother."

"But—but—" Diana struggled to make sense of this. "You said such terrible things to him yesterday. You acted like you were furious with him."

"I *am* furious with him. He tried to keep Beth away from me! Just like he's kept *himself* away from me, for years and years! Callum's a stubborn, selfish, proud..." For once, Conleth seemed to run out of words. His chest heaved, as though he was struggling to catch his breath. "And I...I..."

"He misses him," Connor supplied, when his brother didn't continue. "We both do."

Conleth's shoulders slumped. He sat down heavily on the cabin's front steps, burying his face in his hands.

"I just wanted him to come home," he said, muffled. "I just wanted my family back."

Beth was wriggling in Diana's arms, getting bored. Diana put her down on the cabin's porch, next to the railing so she could practice pulling herself up. She sat down next to Conleth.

"Have you ever told him that?" she asked softly.

Conleth dropped his hands again with a sigh. "I've tried. But he doesn't listen to me. He's the only person I can't *make* listen. Who I can't talk round."

"Maybe you should have tried different words," Connor suggested. "Like, 'I miss you, bro' rather than 'For heaven's sake, Callum, when will you stop holding onto these childish grudges?' Also, an 'I'm sorry' or two wouldn't go amiss."

Conleth shot him yet another glare. "I'm not apologizing to Callum."

"What *is* it with my brothers and the words 'I'm sorry?'" Connor asked the world in general. "I mean, it's not that hard to say. I do it all the time. Admittedly, because I fuck up all the time."

"Callum doesn't have any problem apologizing," Diana protested. "Not to me, at least."

"Huh. That's definitely not like the Callum that we know and love and frequently want to beat over the head with a whole frozen salmon." Connor cocked an eyebrow, casting her a significant look. "You may want to think about that."

Diana did, but it would have to wait. She turned back to Conleth. "I think you do owe Callum an apology. He's told me what it was like, growing up with you two. You must have realized how hard it was for him before you were diagnosed and got the help you needed."

For a second, Conleth's jaw set in a stubborn line, like he was going to argue further. Then Beth toddled into him. He caught her as she lost her balance, swooping her into his lap. Beth giggled, and Conleth's expression softened.

"I know," he said quietly, hugging Beth. "But I didn't want to. Because that would mean admitting that I was responsible for our estrangement. Not him. I wanted to believe that it was all Callum's fault, that he didn't work hard enough at trying to understand me."

"Did you ever work at trying to understand him?"

"Why would I?" Conleth's mouth twisted in bitter self-mockery. "Why should I have to *work* to have a relationship with my own brother? After all, I had one that I understood effortlessly."

"That's me," Connor interjected cheerfully, as though Diana might not have realized this. "And if you think I'm bad, you *really* need to see Conleth off his meds. It's epic. Remind me to tell you the apple story."

"We do *not* speak of the apple story." Conleth flung him an exasperated but clearly fond glance. "I had Connor, and Connor had me. But Callum didn't have anyone who understood him like that. To be honest, I don't know if I'll ever understand him. But I…I want to try. I just wish he would let me."

"Again, magic words," Connor put in. "'I'm sorry.' Try it sometime."

"Have you ever apologized to Callum?" Diana asked him, curious.

"Me? Fuck yeah. All the time." Connor shrugged. "Problem is, he knows I'm going to have to say it again five minutes later. I should probably just have it playing constantly on a repeating loop, like a personal soundtrack. Maybe with some dubstep, too. Or bagpipes!"

"Congratulations, brother mine," Conleth said dryly. "You have achieved the miraculous feat of working out how to make yourself even more annoying."

Connor polished his fingernails on his shirt and inspected them, modestly. "It's a gift."

"There's still something I don't understand," Diana said. "Conleth, if you're so keen to try to repair the rift between you and Callum, why do you still help Connor pull pranks on him? You were there, at the charity bachelor auction. You could have stopped Connor."

"Well, to be fair, no one can stop me," Connor said. "Believe me, many have tried."

Conleth snorted. "No, Diana's right. I *could* have stopped you, or at least not helped. I did lure Callum to L.A. for you."

"Why did you do that?" Diana asked him.

"Because at least then I could *see* him." Conleth's voice dropped, softening. "And…because it was like old times. Connor calling me up with this terrible, awful, hilarious idea, wanting my help…"

He trailed off into silence. Diana looked at him, the harsh, lonely lines of his face, and realized something.

"It's not just Callum that you miss, is it?" she said. "It's Connor as well. He's gone most of the time too, since he's a smokejumper. And you miss him."

"Huh?" Connor said. He laughed, as if the very idea was ridiculous. "Naw. People are actively grateful when I'm not present. Nobody misses *me*. Especially not Conleth. Do you?"

Conleth avoided his brother's eyes. He nodded, just the barest movement, as if even that tiny admission was something shameful.

Connor looked startled. "Hey. What? Really? You miss having me around?"

"Of course I do," Conleth said testily, all traces of vulnerability disappearing again. "Idiot."

"Well, you could have *said*." Connor punched his brother in the shoulder, not at all gently. "Idiot yourself."

Conleth shoved him in return, just as hard. "Why? It's not like you could do anything about it. You love smokejumping. What was I going to do, ask you to give it up? Move back to England and spend your time analyzing profit-loss pivot tables with me instead?"

"Well, when you put it like that…" Connor shuddered theatrically. "Not a chance. I love you, but not *that* much."

"Conleth," Diana said. "Callum loves his work just as much as Connor does."

Conleth stared down at Beth. "I know. And you're his mate. You can't leave him."

He said it so simply, as if it was blatantly obvious. And it *was* true, Diana realized. She couldn't live with this hollowness in her chest, the silence at her side where Callum should be.

Not even for Beth.

"I'm sorry, Conleth." She put a hand on his, squeezing it. "I promise, we'll work something out. You're still Beth's father, and I want you to be present in her life as much as you want to be. But I can't come to England with you."

Conleth's shoulders slumped, but he nodded. "I should never have asked you to. I shouldn't have tried to manipulate you like that, or Callum. I'm sorry."

"See?" Connor exclaimed triumphantly. "I *told* you it wasn't that hard. You really are a goddess, Diana. I'd ask you to marry me and have my babies, but even I can tell that would be a bad idea. There's enough confusion in the father-uncle area as it is."

Diana winced. "Oh God, that's still a mess. I feel like I should be on one of those trashy TV shows where they do paternity tests live on air and everyone screams and throws things."

Conleth sighed heavily. "Much as I want to be a father, I admit it would be a lot simpler if I really was just Beth's uncle."

"I still can't believe your pegasus didn't stop you," Connor agreed. "Even *mine* had enough sense to do that."

"Mine was yelling at me that it was a bad idea while I was just kissing Diana in the elevator." Conleth rubbed his forehead. "It's *still* yelling at me. It knows I'm not your mate, so it doesn't believe I can possibly be Beth's father. Despite all the evidence."

"That's weird," Diana said. "Because Callum said his pegasus *did* insist that he was the father. But that's impossible."

"Holy *fuck*," Connor said. He suddenly looked excited. "Conleth, you said you don't remember Diana coming back into your room, right?"

Conleth gave him a pained look. "Do we have to dredge through the awful night again?"

"Yes. Definitely." Connor bounced on his toes, as though he couldn't contain himself any longer. "Think about it. What hotel room were you in?"

"667," Conleth said promptly.

"No you weren't," Diana corrected. "It was 666. I remember seeing it as I fled in the morning."

Conleth shook his head firmly. "No, it was definitely 667. I booked the rooms myself. Connor was in 665, and Callum…"

He stopped dead. They stared at each other, wide-eyed.

"Callum was in 666," Conleth finished in a whisper. "You're really sure?"

"Completely," Diana replied, her mouth dry. "It's not the sort of number you forget. I remember at the time thinking that I should have known it was a bad omen."

"You said you started back to the elevator after taking Conleth to his hotel room, but then changed your mind and turned around," Connor said, beaming. "You went to the wrong hotel room! You went to Callum's room! Which means that Callum and Conleth's inner animals are right. Callum *is* Beth's father. You really did meet each other that night."

Diana laughed in pure joy—and then caught her breath, as a bolt of pain lanced through her chest.

"Diana?" Suddenly the brothers were on each side of her, holding her up, wearing identical expressions of alarm. "Diana!"

"It's Callum," she gasped. The mate bond was a fiery beacon of distress in her soul, silently calling to her. "He's in trouble."

CHAPTER 28

"I got him for you." The voice was rough, growling; the sound of a tough man trying to hide his fear. "I did what you wanted."

Callum knew that voice from somewhere. It penetrated the fog of pain, raising him back to consciousness. Thick ropes bound him to a tree, the bark rough against his back.

Quiet, his pegasus whispered. *Be still.*

Memory came back, in a rush like a dam breaking. He'd been flying randomly, heartsick and hurting, until every wingbeat was an effort. He'd tried to focus only on the life forms all around, casting his senses out like a net in search of distraction. Every life had stabbed him like a sword, because it wasn't Diana, wasn't his mate. He'd welcomed every wound, throwing himself further open…

And then Callum had sensed one that had him wheeling round despite his exhaustion. He'd told himself that there wasn't time to call for help, that he had to act before his enemy slipped away again…but that hadn't been the real reason he'd swooped to attack.

As the hellhound's fireball had hit him, as Callum had fallen into darkness, the last thing he'd felt had been relief. Because at least there would be an end to the pain.

Unfortunately, he seemed to have woken up.

Now one whole side of his body was in agony. Callum could feel his shifter healing burning through what little energy he had left, struggling to repair his injuries.

Quiet, his pegasus said again. Its wings wrapped around his mind, holding him close. *We must be very, very quiet now. So she will not hear us. So she will not come.*

She? Callum wondered. He held himself still as his animal commanded, trying to give no sign that he'd regained consciousness.

Since he couldn't risk opening his eyes, he concentrated on his pegasus senses instead, reaching out to feel the life forms all around. There weren't many. Beetles under the tree bark, a squirrel perched motionless on a branch overhead…as far as he could sense, all the little lives were keeping as still and quiet as himself. It was as if a shadow of some great predator had fallen over the forest.

Yet the only predator he could detect was the hellhound. Maurice was pacing around him, every movement agitated. The sharp reek of fear hung around him.

"I held up my end of the bargain," the hellhound said, apparently talking to himself. "I want out now. You can take it from here. You don't need me anymore."

Oh, but we do. This is just the first step. Your true task still awaits.

Callum started despite himself. That hissing, self-satisfied voice had come out of thin air. His senses flailed, fruitlessly searching for who could have spoken.

"Look, this is a fucking dumb plan," Maurice said to his mysterious conversational partner. "Stalking and ambushing 'em one at a time, okay, that I can do. But this is gonna draw down a fucking lot more fire than that. They'll *all* come to rescue their buddy. The griffin, the unicorn, all of them. You expect me to take on a fucking *sea dragon* all by myself?"

The queen has summoned her scion. Lupa is willful, but she cannot ignore the queen's call. Callum realized that he was hearing the voice with his mind, not his ears. He still couldn't tell where it was coming from. *Even now, she brings the pack.*

"Then let *them* do your damn dirty work."

The other voice hissed angrily. *The queen cannot rely on Lupa or her craven hounds for this. Only you have the heart—or lack of it—to do what the queen requires.*

"Well, I got the brains to *not* do it," Maurice retorted. "Not like this, at least. Yeah, I can step out of hiding and kill one weak, helpless human before the rest of 'em can react, but after that the shit is gonna hit the fan. Those damn firefighters have got their own hellhound, and he's the size of a fucking bear. If I try to duck sideways again afterwards, he'll pull me back by my tail and the rest of them will rip me apart in revenge. This is suicide. I ain't doing it."

You have no choice, the other voice hissed. *You pledged your soul to the service of the queen. You do not want to feel her displeasure.*

Maurice made a strangled, pained grunt. Callum risked opening his eyes, just a fraction. Maurice was standing right in front of him, pale-faced, cradling his left arm against his chest as if it was broken. Some kind of mark glowed on the back of his hand, throbbing with a sickly red light. Callum only caught a glimpse of it before Maurice closed his other hand over it, hiding it from sight.

Our prisoner is awake, said the other voice. *Good. It is time. Look at me, little shifter. Look at me, and know true fear.*

Since there was no point in further pretense, Callum lifted his head. He stared around, but he still couldn't see anyone other than Maurice.

Up here, little shifter.

The squirrel dropped out of the tree, landing on Maurice's shoulder. The hellhound twitched, a look of pure revulsion contorting his face, but he made no move to brush the creature away. The squirrel sat up, folding its front paws neatly. Its eyes glowed like red embers.

Do not show fear, his pegasus said urgently. *Do not feel fear. It wants us to be afraid. Stay calm.*

That was easier said than done. Callum did his best to keep his breathing steady and unchanged, holding the demon's malevolent gaze without flinching.

"This won't work." Callum's voice came out hoarse and croaky. His chest and shoulder burned where Maurice's fiery breath had caught him. "Even if you possess me, it won't do you any good. My friends won't be fooled. And we know how to deal with your kind."

The demon stretched the squirrel's mouth into an unnatural grin, showing long, pointed fangs. *Oh you do, do you, little shifter? Will your one true mate come to save you? Will she feel me gnawing away at your soul? Will she reach down and cast me out with the bright power of her love? Is your bond so strong? Are you so very sure of that?*

"Yes. Yes, I am."

And he was. Because despite everything he had done, all the ways he had failed her, he could still feel Diana's love shining in his soul. It had just taken the utter darkness of rock bottom for him to see it.

His heart lifted, despite the pain, despite the demon. Diana loved him, as he loved her. No matter what, they were mates. If he needed her, she would always come—

NO! His pegasus reared up, kicking him away from the mate bond. *DO NOT REACH FOR HER! THAT IS WHAT IT WANTS!*

His breath froze in his chest as he finally realized the demon's true goal. Because Maurice had been talking about ambushing and killing just one person...

One helpless, *human* person.

The demon-squirrel laughed, a horribly human sound from that animal throat. *Excellent.* Now *you are afraid.*

It leaped from Maurice's shoulder, landing on his own. Callum felt the pinprick scratch of its claws as it curled around his neck. Its teeth pressed against his flesh, not quite breaking the skin.

And you will be more afraid, the demon crooned in his mind. *You will not be able to stop yourself from screaming for your mate, once I am inside you. Once you feel me nibbling away at your soul, one tender bite at a time. You will scream. And she will come to save you. And then, she will die.*

"No," Callum whispered. He pulled at the ropes, heedless of the pain that shot through his burned side, struggling to break free. It didn't make sense, Maurice had only gone after Diana as a way to get to *him*, why would the demons want to kill her...? "No! I swear, I won't fight. Possess me, do whatever you want with me, just leave Diana alone! You don't need her! You have me already!"

You? The demon laughed again, as its teeth sank into Callum's neck. *Oh, little shifter. This was never about* you.

CHAPTER 29

Diana gasped, clutching at her chest. Not because of pain, but because of a sudden *lack* of pain. No matter how she reached for Callum, he evaded her touch. She had an odd sense of him retreating, slamming up thick shields, trying to hide from her.

Which meant that something was very, *very* wrong.

She tugged at Connor's streaming red mane. He turned his head, ears tilting quizzically in her direction.

"Something's happened!" She had to shout at the top of her lungs against the rush of the wind. "Callum needs us now. We have to go faster!"

Connor snorted to show that he understood. He made eye contact with Rory, who was flying at his wingtip in griffin form. Diana couldn't hear their telepathic communication, not being a shifter herself, but she knew that Connor must be relaying her message to Rory.

"Diana!" Edith called from Rory's back. She had her hands cupped round her mouth, balancing easily despite the griffin's surging wing-beats. The wind snatched most of her words away, leaving only fragments. "Rory can't—too dangerous—stick together!"

You're only going to get yourself killed, Gertrude whispered. *You only escaped from Maurice before by sheer dumb luck. You're weak and useless. You should have left this to the shifters. What can* you *possibly do to save Callum?*

Diana set her jaw, ignoring that poisonous background murmur. She crouched low over Connor's neck, redoubling her grip on his mane.

"How fast can you fly?" she said into his ear.

Connor's eye rolled to look back at her. There was a distinctly wicked gleam in those dark depths. She felt his muscles bunch under her thighs.

Edith yelled something—but they were already streaking ahead. Risking a backward glance, Diana could see Rory clawing at the air to try to keep up, but the griffin was no match for a pegasus. In mere seconds, he was just a distant dot behind them.

Diana faced forward again, squinting against the wind. She scanned the mountains below, looking for any sign of Callum. The mate bond was cold and silent in her heart, giving no indication of which way they should go…but she wasn't the one navigating.

"Are we getting close yet?" she yelled to Connor.

The pegasus tossed his head in a nod. Diana had to throw her arms around his neck as he dropped without warning into a steep dive. She scrunched her eyes shut, Connor's mane lashing her cheek, and held on.

She felt the jolt of Connor's hooves touching down. His headlong flight turned into a gallop, far faster than any horse could run, weaving round tree trunks. Diana clung to his back as branches whipped past her head.

Connor slowed, prancing to a halt. Sitting up, Diana immediately realized why he'd had to land and run the last stretch. This was old, dense forest, trees crowded together too closely for a pegasus to fly between. Leaves and branches made a thick roof above their heads.

"*Diana!*"

Callum was alone in a small clearing, tied to a tree by thick ropes wrapped around his chest and legs. His t-shirt was in tatters, exposing burns and bite-marks across his shoulder, but he didn't seem to be seriously injured.

Callum's eyes met hers in the dimness of the forest, and the mate bond burst like a firework in her heart. He wasn't trying to hide from her any longer—and yet immediately something else slammed between them, a horribly foreign presence. Dark, scaled coils snatched him away from her again, hiding his soul.

She could practically *see* the horned serpent that had possessed him, like a physical presence wrapped around his body. But Callum was fighting it, as fiercely as he was fighting the ropes that bound him. She could feel how terrified he was.

But not for himself.

"Trap," Callum choked out. His head jerked, that demonic force trying to gag him, trying to stop him from warning her... "*Hellhound! Run!*"

Too late.

A flame-eyed, black-furred shape leaped out of thin air, slamming into Connor, knocking him over. Diana was flung off his back. She hit the ground hard, all the breath driven out of her.

A wall of flame speared past her, separating her from Connor. She could hear him shrieking like a furious bird of prey, struggling back to his feet to come to her aid. But the hellhound was already leaping for her, jaws open wide, hellfire boiling in its throat...

Time seemed to collapse. She was seven years old again, helpless and terrified, scrabbling backward with mud under her palms. And the *thing* was lunging, fire dripping from its fangs, lunging at her mom—

Who faced it, calm and unafraid. Who raised her hands...

Diana saw it as clearly as if her mother was here now, standing in front of her once again. Her mother's spirit flooded through her, warm and protective, backed by the strength of all their ancestors. She could feel them all, as she produced her own hands.

She clapped, once.

A shockwave blasted from her palms with a sound like thunder. The hellhound was thrown back, head over tail, his snarl becoming a startled yelp. Then Connor was on him, kicking and biting, and the hellhound abruptly had bigger things to worry about.

Diana was already racing across to Callum, trusting Connor to keep the hellhound off her back. She could sense that alien force sliding through her mate's mind, like a snake trying to slither down a hole.

Well, she wasn't having *that*.

"Get out!" she snarled at the demon in Callum. She seized his face between her hands, pressing her whole body against his, her whole soul blazing down the mate bond with righteous fury. "That's *my* mate! Get out of him!"

Callum twisted in his bonds, gagging. He wrenched his head to one side, and a torrent of darkness poured out of his mouth. Diana held onto him, refusing to let go, until the last wisp of smoke streamed out of him.

Callum sagged in his ropes, panting. The newly-ousted demon was a formless, shifting mass of shadow, twisting on the ground. Even as Diana watched, it started to solidify, taking on the form of a monstrous horned serpent.

"It'll reform and attack," Callum gasped. "My knife. Quickly!"

Diana found his utility knife, holstered as ever at his belt. She sawed through the ropes, silently blessing Superintendent Buck for insisting that his firefighters were always prepared for an emergency.

No! The demon's soundless voice shrieked across Diana's mind like fingernails on a blackboard, making her flinch. It was still foggy and half-formed, but it had burning red eyes now, blazing with hate. It turned toward the hellhound, who was still locked in battle with Connor. *Attack her, kill her now, before it is too late! Leave the other one!*

The hellhound turned, his form starting to blur into invisibility. Lightning-fast, Connor locked his teeth in the hellhound's leg, dragging him back into solidity. No matter how the hellhound snarled and snapped, the pegasus held on grimly, stopping the beast from escaping him.

Callum fell free at last, into her arms. For a heartbeat, he just leaned on her, holding her as tightly as she clutched at him. Then he was pushing her back, behind him.

"Whatever you just did," Callum said to her, his wary eyes fixed on the writhing demon. "Can you do it again?"

"I have no idea!" Her fingertips were still tingling with that electric surge of energy, but that strange sense of calm certainty had deserted her. "But I'll try!"

Diana held up her hands threateningly, hoping the demon couldn't tell how they were shaking. She clapped.

Nothing happened.

The demon let out a cold laugh. It coiled, head rising into the air, taking solid form at last. It was huge, far bigger than any real snake, dwarfing them all.

Too late, little thunder-kin, it hissed in triumph. *Too little, too late. You never learned how to summon your power. We killed your mother, as we killed all the rest of the Storm Society, before they could teach you. You slipped through our fangs all those years ago, but now we have you at last. No one can help you now.*

"Connor!" Callum called, as the demon gathered itself to strike.

Still wrestling the hellhound, Connor locked eyes with his brother. Diana could sense some brief, wordless flicker of understanding pass between them. *She* understood, and cold terror gripped her heart.

"No!" She grabbed hold of Callum's arm, digging her fingers in. "I'm not leaving you!"

"You have to. I can't fly." Callum twisted free, despite her effort to hold onto him. He stepped forward, shielding her body with his own. "But I can hold them off long enough for you to escape."

Callum shifted into pegasus form, rearing up. He was scorched and wounded, many feathers burned down to charred stumps, but he still spread his wings in a show of threat. He screamed like a hawk, proud and defiant.

She had only seconds. Connor was already tossing the hellhound aside, racing for her. Diana closed her eyes, reaching deep into herself, looking for that spark of connection once more.

Because the demon had said that no one could help her now…but that wasn't true.

Thunder-kin, it had called her.

"Wakinyan," she whispered. "Thunderbird. Come."

CHAPTER 30

The sky split open.

A hammer blow of wind drove Callum into the ground. For an instant, he thought that the demon had already struck, faster than he'd been able to react—but the horned snake had been thrown aside by the shockwave as well.

All around, trees snapped and splintered, trunks cracking like matchsticks, falling outward. Callum shifted back into human form, throwing himself over Diana to shelter her from the storm as best he could. A little way off, he glimpsed Connor also shifting, curling into a ball with his arms over his head to protect himself from the flying debris.

Shadow fell over them. Huge wings unfurled, blocking out the sun. Electricity crackled, leaping from feather to feather like lightning.

Diana pushed him aside. Alone out of all of them, she rose to her feet, unaffected by the storm winds screaming all around, undaunted by the massive talons hanging over her head. She lifted her arms in welcome.

"Wakinyan!" she called out, her face shining with joy and wonder.

The Thunderbird responded with a rumble of thunder that shook the ground. Its burning white gaze moved from Diana to the cowering demon. The geometric patterns on its wings brightened, seething with an ominous electric glow.

The demon moved in a streak of black. With the speed of desperation, it struck.

Callum reacted instinctively, grabbing for Diana—but she wasn't the horned snake's target. He'd moved in the wrong direction, and now there was nothing he could do to stop the demon's attack.

Its fangs closed on Connor.

"No!" Callum shouted, echoed by Diana—but it was too late.

The demon disappeared, pouring itself into Connor. He convulsed as it entered him, dropping to his knees. Callum knew all too well what his brother would be feeling. The cold running through his blood, black coils wrapping round his inner pegasus…and Connor had no mate bond glowing in his soul to help him resist.

"No!" Diana screamed again, but she wasn't speaking to the demon. She twisted out of Callum's grasp, running forward to fling herself between Connor and the Thunderbird. She stretched out her arms as though trying to shield Connor, head tipped back to meet the Thunderbird's pitiless white stare. "Stop! He's my friend!"

"Yessss," hissed Connor—except it wasn't Connor. His green eyes were wide, panicked, the only part of him left under his own control. His teeth bared in a horrible parody of his usual grin. "Sssstrike me now, and this host dies as well."

Thunder rumbled again. Lightning hissed and spat from the Thunderbird's outstretched claws.

"You can't just kill him!" Diana shouted up at the Thunderbird. "There has to be another way!"

"Let me go, and perhapssss I will release him." The demon was backing away, stumbling in jerky, graceless steps, manipulating Connor like a puppet. "You have no other choice. You cannot force me out. You are not *his* mate."

"No," Callum said, stepping forward. "But I'm his brother."

He lunged, grabbing hold of Connor's wrist. And the pranks didn't matter, the differences between them didn't matter, the old hurts and misunderstandings and arguments didn't matter.

Because, beneath all that, they were family.

Callum seized hold of that connection, the bond that he'd tried to deny for so long. He plunged into Connor's bright kaleidoscope of a soul, chasing away the shadows that sought to smother it. The demon recoiled from him, unable to comprehend such fierce, irrational love.

Connor's fingers closed on his own wrist. His brother coughed out a last shred of demonic smoke, and lifted his head to meet his eyes.

"Hey, bro." Connor's voice was weak and hoarse, but his grin was as cocky as ever. "Didn't know you cared."

Callum held him up, shoulder to shoulder. "I'm the only one who gets to kill you."

"Ditto." Connor looked past Callum, his eyes widening. "And on that topic—*duck!*"

The world went white. Callum just had a momentary sense of Connor tackling him to the ground as heat roared over them both, and then everything seemed to glitch.

When he came to, he found himself staring up at his own face, ears ringing. Connor gave him a rueful grin, his body still covering his own protectively. His hair was standing on end, crackling with static electricity.

"Always wondered what it would be like to get hit by lightning," Connor said, too loudly. His brother rolled off him, rubbing at one ear with a pained expression. "Gotta say, it's not as much fun as I expected."

Where the demon had been was nothing but a smoking, blackened crater. Fallen branches burned fitfully around the rim. On pure reflex, Callum scrambled up, kicking the flaming debris into the charred area so that the fire couldn't spread. Out of the corner of his eye, he saw Connor doing the same thing.

"I got this," Connor shouted, still talking far too loudly. He waved Callum off. "You take care of *him*."

The hellhound must have been knocked unconscious in the Thunderbird's initial attack, lapsing back into human form. Now Maurice was stirring groggily, starting to push himself to hands and knees.

Callum pinned him down, twisting one arm behind the hellhound's back so that he wouldn't be able to shift.

"Surrender," Callum growled. Inside, his pegasus wanted to trample the man to a bloody pulp, but that would just be sinking to Maurice's level. The hellhound would receive more than enough punishment at the hands of the law. "It's over. You've lost."

"So have you, little shifter."

That crooning, amused voice raised the hair on the back of Callum's neck. When the demon had been using Connor's tongue, it had still sounded like his brother...but this didn't sound *anything* like Maurice. It wasn't even a male voice.

The whites showed all around Maurice's eyes. It was clear the hellhound didn't have any clue what was happening either. The mark on his hand was glowing brighter, pulsing like a heartbeat.

"You don't yet understand the cost of your so-called victory," continued the foreign voice coming from Maurice's mouth. The evil red light ran further up the hellhound's arm, under the skin, spreading like an infection. *"Look to your mate, little shifter. Look to your mate, and despair."*

It had to be a trick, but Callum couldn't help glancing in Diana's direction. While he'd been distracted, the Thunderbird had landed, mantling Diana in its wings. She had her head tipped back, revealing her pale, set face. Callum couldn't hear anything himself, but it looked like Diana was listening to something.

A throaty female laugh came from Maurice's throat. The hellhound was writhing now, fighting—not Callum's hold on him, but whatever force had taken over his body. His skin was cold as ice under Callum's hands.

"You have lost her," that evil voice murmured. Red light veined all through Maurice's flesh now, consuming him from within. *"The storm will take her, and change her, and nothing of her own mind will remain. You should have let my servant kill her, little shifter. It would have been kinder."*

Maurice gave one last gasping breath, going still. Callum jerked away as the hellhound disintegrated in a flare of light. There was nothing left of him but a patch of frost in the exact shape of his body.

"Diana." Callum ran for her, pushing through the Thunderbird's storm-gray feathers, that last cold laugh still ringing in his ears. "*Diana!*"

She didn't turn at his call. Even when he grabbed her shoulders, pulling her round, her gaze stayed fixed on the Thunderbird.

And her eyes burned white with lightning.

CHAPTER 31

CHANGE

The thunderous voice swept through Diana with the force of a hurricane. A storm of imagery and emotions assaulted her, too much for any mere human mind to comprehend. She could only grasp snatched fragments—darkness welling up out of the ground, lightning striking between clouds, fury and fire and a terrible, aching loneliness…

And through it all, a single insistent, irresistible command.

CHANGE

Its voice shook her body, her mind, her very soul. Lightning coursed under her skin, struggling to break free, to unfold into stormcloud wings. Her human self was just an egg, cracking, shattering.

"Diana!"

Callum's voice was just a whisper in the raging storm. But his love wrapped round her, sheltering her from the storm that sought to sweep her away. He held her, held her together, fighting the force that was trying to rip her apart and remake her into something new.

CHANGE, the Thunderbird demanded, in a voice that could not be denied.

But Diana knew how to handle inner voices.

She opened herself to the storm—not fighting it, not trying to resist, but not giving way to it either. She let the power flow through her, acknowledging it without surrendering to it, just like she did with her anxieties. She was a tree, storm-tossed, bowing to a greater power…but not breaking.

She was strong. And her roots went deep.

CHAPTER 32

In Callum's arms, Diana let out a long, slow breath. When she opened her eyes again, they were her own once more—dark brown, soft, human. And yet...not entirely unchanged. There was a calmness to them, a sense of hidden power, that hadn't been there before.

But she was still his Diana, still his mate. She smiled at him, reaching up to touch his face.

"Callum," she whispered. "I heard you. I heard you calling to me."

He tightened his arms around her, heart still pounding with terror and relief. "I thought I'd lost you. Whatever the Thunderbird was doing, I could feel it tearing you away. Tearing you apart."

"He wasn't trying to hurt me. He's just so alone."

"He?"

Diana nodded, her expression serious. She turned in his embrace, tilting her face upward. The Thunderbird still loomed over them both, motionless as a mountain.

"I'm sorry," Diana said softly to the vast bird. "I'll do what I can, but I won't come with you. This is where I belong."

The Thunderbird bowed its head. Callum tensed, but Diana just laid her hand on the enormous hooked beak.

"Yes," she whispered, as though it had spoken to her. "I will. I promise."

The Thunderbird closed its eyes for a moment. Then it straightened again, spreading its wings. Wind whipped their clothes and hair. Callum held Diana close, protecting her from the downdraft.

"What did it want?" Callum asked Diana, as the bird took off.

Diana's gaze tracked the Thunderbird as it soared into the sky. "Help. And not just fighting Uncegila and her brood. He's lost, he can't find his way home—"

Then Diana gasped, clutching at his arm. "Callum! He needs our help *now*!"

Callum was already thrusting her behind him, his pegasus senses screaming as a dozen blood-red lives appeared out of nowhere. Fierce, feral barks split the air.

"Oh, goodie. More fun." Connor was abruptly at his back, sandwiching Diana between them. "Who else is joining this party?"

"Lupa's pack," Callum replied grimly, eyes fixed on the dark forms running through the sky. "She must have detected the Thunderbird's presence. They've come to hunt it."

The hellhounds raced around the huge bird, running on thin air as though it was solid ground. They were far smaller than the Thunderbird, but more agile, and more numerous. They mobbed the struggling bird like crows harassing an owl.

"Hellhounds fly now?" Connor sounded personally offended by this, as though he felt the hellhounds were somehow cheating. "Without wings?"

"These ones do. Something to do with Lupa." Callum stayed tense and ready, in case any of the hellhounds noticed their audience. "The Thunderbird's been caught off-guard. Look, it can't break free."

The Thunderbird was struggling to gain height, hampered by being so low to the ground. Hellhounds darting in to snap at it with burning jaws, then fled before it could bring its lightning to bear on them.

"We have to help him!" Diana's face was pale, but she raised her hands. "The wakinyan unlocked something inside me. I didn't want to try to use it again until I understood it better, but—"

"It's all right." Callum caught her wrist. "Don't risk yourself. Other help is here."

With a fierce cry, a golden griffin dove from the clouds, scattering the pack. Rory wasn't alone, either. Edith clung to his back, firing shots from a flare gun. Shan's winged tiger flew at Rory's wingtip, roaring and swiping at hellhounds with massive claws. Min-Seo rode him, cackling with wicked glee as she used her power to make hellhounds scramble away from Shan in terror.

And, behind them all, came the shark.

"What the actual fucking fuck?" Connor yelped, ducking low as the shark swooped down, swimming through the sky as if it was water.

"It's Seren," Callum explained. "And Joe. It's a long story."

Connor shot him a pained look. "Is there *anything* that doesn't fly around here?"

"Me," Joe said, hopping off Seren's back. He grinned round at them all as his mate soared off to join Rory in the fight. "Hi bros! We left Wystan and Blaise back with Conleth to guard Beth, but the rest of us thought we'd better come rescue you. Picked up some old friends of yours on the way, Cal."

"Glad to see you," Callum replied, with feeling. "All of you."

"About time, bro!" Connor was hopping from foot to foot, nearly beside himself with impatience. "Take over guarding my brother's sorry ass for me? *Someone* has to show these jumped-up dogs what real flying is."

"On it, bro." Joe high-fived Connor. "Go get 'em!"

Connor shifted and took off, plunging into the melee with glee. With his arrival, the tides of battle were definitely shifting. Callum's friends were still outnumbered, but any one of them was a match for at least three hellhounds.

But hellhounds weren't all that they faced.

Callum threw his mind open, casting an urgent telepathic message to his friends. *Be careful! The wendigo is here!*

Even as he sent the warning, a huge white shape separated from the rest of the pack, plunging toward them. Joe shifted instantly, wrapping protective coils around them. The sea dragon roared at the wendigo as it landed, spreading his talons wide in warning.

The wendigo roared back, ice crystals hanging in the air, facing the sea dragon without any sign of fear. The skull-faced monster was bigger than a polar bear, with antlers ten feet across. It was far smaller than Joe, but size wasn't everything. Callum tensed despite his injuries, ready to shift and fight.

A woman perched on the wendigo's hulking shoulders. Callum had never seen her before, but he knew instantly who she was. Lupa was just as Joe had described her—beautiful, arrogant, midnight hair blowing across her cold, angry face. To Callum's pegasus senses, she was a black hole in the world.

"No." Lupa's hard voice carried clearly to his ears, but she didn't seem to be talking to them. "She has a child. I won't."

Lupa paused as though listening to something. The wind caught her hair, tugging it back from her forehead. With a jolt of shock, Callum saw a glowing red mark there—a twisting, horned snake, identical to the one that had been imprinted on the back of Maurice's hand.

The red glow from the mark brightened, pulsating. Lupa bared her teeth, eyes glittering in anger.

"She didn't change! She's no threat to us." Lupa kneed the wendigo, wheeling her monstrous steed round. "The Thunderbird is our real—"

A huge black shape appeared out of nowhere, knocking Lupa off the wendigo's back. The beast roared in fury, turning—but Joe lashed out, sweeping it away with his finned tail.

Have her! Fenrir's telepathic voice was a howl of triumph. He pinned Lupa down with his massive bulk *Caught the Bad Bitch!*

Callum expected Lupa to shift to hellhound form to fight, but to his surprise she stayed human. She twisted under Fenrir, struggling— and abruptly went still, staring into his burning eyes.

"You," she breathed.

Callum dragged Diana further away, every life form shrieking in his senses. He had to get his mate to safety, but there was too much to keep track of, too much pulling at his attention.

Joe and the wendigo were a tangle of teeth and claws, the sea dragon fighting to keep the wendigo away from Lupa and Fenrir. Above, the Thunderbird had broken free from the pack at last, winging up safely into the sky. Now the hellhounds were turning, charging down, trying to come to their alpha's aid. And Fenrir—

Fenrir was just standing there, frozen.

"No!" Callum shouted, as Lupa scrabbled out from under the hellhound. "Don't let her get away!"

It was too late. The wendigo flung a blast of ice at Joe that made the sea dragon recoil, then ran for Lupa, snatching her up in its boney jaws. Never slowing, it disappeared into the forest. Lupa twisted, staring backwards at Fenrir, until the trees hid her from sight.

Fenrir threw back his head and howled, forlorn and lost.

CHAPTER 33

Min-Seo patted the matte gray side of the armored prisoner transport. "Well, we may not have got Lupa, but at least we've pulled her fangs. She'll be a whole lot less dangerous without her pack at her back."

"You'll make sure none of them escape this time?" Callum asked.

Min-Seo wrinkled her nose, looking pained. "That was embarrassing. But at least we can learn from our mistakes. Shan won't let any of the prisoners out of his sight until they're all safely locked away in a high-security facility. No more demons are going to slip past us, I promise."

Callum nodded, reassured. "And you'll let us know what you find out from interrogating Lupa's pack?"

"Of course. As long as *you* promise to share information too." Min-Seo poked him in the ribs, making him wince. "Ooops. Sorry, forgot about the bruises. Anyway, keep in contact this time, okay?"

"Don't worry," Diana said, slipping her arm around his waist. She smiled at the shifter agent. "I won't let him disappear into the wilderness again. Metaphorically or literally."

Min-Seo beamed back at her. "You take care of this big goofball, you hear? And as for you, Callum, don't you dare let this one get away, or I'll hunt you down and eat your liver."

"I won't." Callum clasped her hand. "Thank you for all your help."

Min-Seo yanked him into a hug, jarring his injuries again. "Anytime, beanpole. Don't be a stranger."

With a final wave, Min-Seo hopped into her car. The vehicle pulled away, closely followed by the prisoner transport.

"Come on, you." Diana propped her shoulder under his, steering him toward the hotshot base's infirmary. "You need to lie down before you *fall* down."

Callum leaned on her gratefully. "In a minute. There's someone I need to see first. Two someones."

He could sense them, of course. And they could sense him in return. Callum lengthened his stride despite his weariness, heart lifting with anticipation.

Diana made a little cry of pure happiness as she caught sight of them. "Beth!"

Beth shrieked in excitement, thrashing in Conleth's arms. To Callum's slight surprise, Conleth knelt, putting her down. The instant he released her, Beth shifted. She charged toward her mother on four tiny hooves.

Diana laughed as Beth barreled into her. She hugged the baby pegasus tight, burying her face in Beth's soft mane. "Oh, baby, my clever, clever baby! Look at you!"

Callum's breath caught in his throat. He clasped Diana's shoulder, making her glance up at him. "Yes. Look at her. Really *look* at her."

On cue, Beth spread her small wings, revealing the bold markings on the underside of her feathers. She pranced, preening herself, inviting them to admire her.

Diana's eyes widened. "Oh. *Oh.*"

Conleth looked between them all, his expression puzzled. "What? What is it?"

"Her markings." Callum touched Beth's feathers, tracing the intricate geometric shapes laid out in black, white, and red. "They're the same as the Thunderbird's."

"The Thunderbird?" Conleth stared at Beth too. "What does that mean?"

"That she's special," Diana said softly. She gathered Beth into her arms again, pressing her forehead against her daughter's. "Even more special than I thought."

Beth rubbed her soft muzzle against Diana's cheek, then wriggled free. She bounced over to Callum, leaping up at him. He caught her, and found himself with an armful of warm, cuddly baby rather than horse.

"Hello," he murmured to her. "I'm sorry I went away. I won't ever leave you again. That's a promise."

Beth looked up at him, her little face very serious. "Dada."

Callum's heart missed a beat. He stared over Beth's head at Diana, who looked equally stunned.

"Callum," Diana whispered. "Did she just say…?"

"Dada," Beth announced again, firmly. She snuggled against his chest, fisting her hands in his torn shirt. "Dada."

A flicker of movement caught Callum's eye. Conleth was easing backward, away from them all.

"Conleth," Callum said—and stalled.

On the long drive back to the base, Diana had told him about her conversation with his brothers. What they'd worked out, that he really *was* Beth's father…

Callum wasn't good with words at the best of times. Now, face to face with his brother again, Callum found he had no idea what to say. What he even *wanted* to say.

Conleth's shoulders set, as though in preparation for a fight. "I… I'm sorry."

Caught off-guard, Callum could only blink at his brother.

"For…" Conleth grimaced, making a vague, embarrassed gesture at himself, then Callum. "For driving you away."

"That was my mistake. And you were only trying to do the right thing, taking responsibility for Beth. I shouldn't have—"

"No," Conleth interrupted. He shoved his hands in his pockets, shoulders hunching. "I meant…earlier. Much earlier. I'm sorry."

Callum looked at him, and for the first time in a long time—maybe ever—he saw Conleth. Not a ghost from the past, or a better, more confident version of himself. Just Conleth.

His brother.

Callum went over to him. Conleth twitched a little, as though expecting a punch—and then started in surprise as Callum held Beth out to him.

"Look," Callum said to Beth, because words came easier that way. "Can you say 'uncle?'"

Beth beamed, reaching out for Conleth as well. "Gagabagaga!"

Conleth snorted, though his eyes were suspiciously bright. "You'd better not all start calling me that."

"She'll work it out." Callum cuddled his daughter. "We all will. That's what family does."

∽

"Absolutely motherloving not," Buck said flatly.

"Oh, come on, chief," Blaise cajoled. "It would explain so much."

"You should at least consider the possibility," Wystan added.

"I'll give it all the consideration it deserves." Buck folded his arms across his chest. "There. Done. No."

"It was only a suggestion," Diana said quickly, before any of the crew could continue badgering the surly Superintendent.

They were all gathered in the mess hall—the squad, Buck, Connor and Conleth. Beth had been passed around everyone at least twice, over the hours it had taken to explain what had happened. Now Beth was sound asleep on Callum's shoulder, her head nestled against his neck.

Diana's throat was hoarse from talking so long. She took a sip of her now-cold coffee before continuing, "I just thought, since you said that my mother and your sister were close friends, they might have had...well, more in common than we thought. Which means you might be like me."

Buck scowled as though she'd viciously insulted his entire family. "I am *not* a motherloving shifter."

"I don't think I am either, exactly." Diana fumbled to explain the connection she'd felt to the Thunderbird. "The horned serpent called me *thunder-kin*. There's this story my mom used to tell me, about a Lakota woman who was so brave and true-hearted that a Thunderbird fell in love with her. Their children were great warriors, blessed by the storm spirits. I think my mother was telling me about my ancestors. I was too young to understand at the time, but she must have been preparing me to be claim my birthright."

"We know now that hellhounds attacked Diana as a child," Callum said. Under the table, his hand found hers. "At the command of the horned serpents. And later, they managed to murder her mother. You told us that your sister and her family also perished in a mysterious fire, Superintendent. That can't be a co-incidence."

Buck's expression closed down, going hard and tight. His hands clenched together, knuckles whitening. He didn't speak for a long moment.

"Wanda did drop a few hints about being in some kind of secret club," Buck said at last in a low, defeated voice. "This 'Storm Society' you say the demon mentioned? It rings a bell. I thought she was just winding me up, the way big sisters do, but maybe…maybe there was something more to it."

"I'm so sorry." Diana wanted to reach out to him, but even shadowed by old grief, the Superintendent was still a fearsomely intimidating man. "It seems like the horned serpents made a concerted effort to wipe out their enemies, all those years ago."

Buck rubbed his forehead, surreptitiously swiping at his eyes. When he looked up again, his glare was as fierce as ever. "Well, no overgrown dog or damn horny snake went after me. And *I* wasn't some little kid they could've just missed. Whatever Wanda might've been, I'm not."

"Maybe you are, and just don't know it yet," Joe suggested. "Diana didn't realize her awesomeness right away, after all. Not until she was in imminent danger."

"I've been in imminent danger more times than you've had hangovers," Buck retorted. "I was a Marine. Believe me, there's been more than once in my life when I've prayed for anything to come to my rescue, even if it was motherloving Tinkerbell. I still never knocked anyone on their ass by clapping my hands. Maybe it's a girl thing."

"I think Buck's right," Blaise put in. "He's been face-to-face with the Thunderbird before, remember? And it just stared at him. Admittedly in kind of a weird way, but it certainly didn't give him any magic powers."

"He," Diana corrected. "The Thunderbird is a he."

Blaise shrugged. "If you say so."

"What did he say to you, Diana?" Wystan asked curiously.

"I can't really put it into words." Diana shivered, in mingled fear and joy, remembering that powerful communion. "*He* doesn't think in words. Or at least, he mostly doesn't. There was a moment, right at the end, when I thought…"

"What?" Edith said, when Diana didn't continue.

"I thought I heard a voice," Diana said softly. "Though the storm. Just the barest whisper. A man's voice. He said, 'Help me.'"

Rory's forehead creased. "What do you think that means?"

"I don't know," Diana replied. "But I have a hunch he wasn't just talking about his fight with the horned serpents. When I first felt the power of the wakinyan coursing through me, it was…overwhelming. It was only thanks to Callum that I wasn't swept away entirely."

Callum's fingers tightened on her hand. "Not just me."

She squeezed back, smiling at him. "You steadied me long enough for me to find my own feet. If you hadn't been there…well, I don't want to think about what would have happened. But I wonder if maybe it *did* happen. To someone else, who didn't have that kind of bond."

"You think the Thunderbird might be a person?" Edith asked. "Someone stuck in the wrong shape, like Fenrir?"

Fenrir, who'd been lying silently by the door all evening, lifted his head at last. His lip wrinkled back, showing his fangs. *Not stuck. Not wrong.*

Edith looked mortified. Her hands made a short, jerky motion. "I'm sorry—I didn't, didn't mean—"

"He knows you didn't mean it like that." Rory put an arm around his mate, shooting Fenrir a warning glance over the top of her head. "Don't you, Fenrir?"

Fenrir's only response was a low, surly growl. He lay back down, pointedly facing away from them all.

"Hey." Blaise wadded up a napkin and tossed it at the hellhound, hitting him in the rump. "What's gotten into you?"

"I'd like to know that too," Buck said, eyes narrowing. "And I'm your boss, even if I do pay you in meaty bones. According to Callum, you had Lupa pinned down. And then you let her go again, meek as a lamb. Care to explain yourself?"

Fenrir stood up, abruptly shifting into his true, huge shape. Without a word, he faded into a shadow, and was gone.

Buck made an exasperated sound. "I'll take that as a no. Motherloving shifters."

Joe cocked an eyebrow, casting a significant look around at the rest of the squad. "We're all thinking the same thing, right?"

"I don't know," Edith said. "But *I* think that Lupa's his mate."

"Me too." Rory sighed, rubbing his forehead with his thumb. "Now there's a complication."

Wystan looked thoughtful. "Or possibly a solution. Love is a strange and powerful force, after all."

"Undoubtedly." Seren's expression was grim. "But even so, I would not wish such a mate on my worst enemy."

Edith nodded, her hands fluttering a little. "Poor Fenrir."

"Well, all we can do is wait until he's ready to talk about it." Rory sighed again. "However long that takes. I just wish he *hadn't* let her go. Lupa may have lost her pack, but I doubt we've seen the last of her. Or the horned serpents."

"Probably not," Joe agreed cheerfully. He gestured round at them all. "But look on the bright side. We're alive!"

"Despite my idiot brother's best efforts," Conleth muttered.

"Hey!" Connor objected. "I didn't do anything."

"Not you. Him." Conleth pointed at Callum. "By the way, congratulations, Callum. For flying off and nearly getting yourself killed, you are now officially my most bone-headed brother."

The corner of Callum's mouth twitched up, very slightly. "Considering the competition, I'm honored."

"*Hey!*"

"Oh, don't look so wounded, currently-second-most-idiot brother mine," Conleth said to Connor. "No doubt you'll manage to reclaim your crown tomorrow."

Connor rubbed his chin, looking uncharacteristically thoughtful. "Huh. There's a challenge. What could I do?"

"I'm sure you'll think of something," Callum and Conleth said together, in exactly the same dry tones.

Connor let out a loud groan, as his brothers exchanged identical startled glances. "Great. Now *I'm* the odd one out. You two had better not start ganging up on me."

Callum and Conleth were still eying each other, a little warily. Then, slowly—first Conleth, then Callum—they smiled.

It was only a tiny hint of connection between the brothers, but it still made Diana's heart soar. Under the table, Callum squeezed her hand again. She knew he could feel her joy and relief, just as she could feel his quiet, tentative wonder.

Diana cleared her throat, trying for a normal, casual tone, as though what had just happened had been no big deal at all. "Well, it's getting late. We should get Beth into bed. Did you remember to unpack the cot and put it back in your cabin, Callum?"

Callum exchanged a sly, secretive glance with Conleth. "Not exactly."

～

With a final satisfied moan, Diana collapsed onto his bare chest. She lay there for a moment, limp and panting, then propped herself up on her elbows to grin at him.

"Okay," she said. "I have to say, it would be nice if Conleth didn't live on the other side of the Atlantic. It's great having a handy uncle to look after Beth overnight."

Callum chuckled, pushing his fingers through her tangled hair. He kissed her, luxuriating in her soft mouth, the little hum of pleasure she made, everything about her.

She kissed him back with equal enthusiasm. Her hands ran over his bare shoulders, sending fresh heat through him despite their just-finished lovemaking.

"Mmmm," Diana purred. She shifted her hips, deliciously. "You didn't tell me shifters had superhuman stamina as well as strength."

He nuzzled down the soft line of her neck, inhaling her scent. "Would you like a demonstration?"

She giggled, but tugged him back up again by his hair. "You're supposed to be resting."

"There's no need. I'm fine." Thanks to Wystan's unicorn friend Sunrise and her healing abilities, he didn't even have bruises now. "Anyway, I *am* resting. I'm flat on my back."

"Well, even if you aren't tired, *I* am." She rolled off him, stretching with a yawn. "And we have to get up early tomorrow. There's a lot to do."

With a grudging sigh, Callum desisted despite his rising interest. He spooned around her, folding her in his arms. "I know. I'll need your help to make a list."

"You and your lists," Diana said fondly. "You know, it makes me wonder..."

She fell quiet. Something about the feel of the mate bond made Callum lift his head, studying her as best he could in the dimness.

"You're thinking about something." He brushed her hair back from her face, trying to interpret her expression. "What is it?"

"Nothing bad, I promise. It's just..." She rolled in his arms so that she was facing him, nose to nose. "Callum, have you ever considered whether you might have ADD?"

He stiffened a little—this time, not in the good way. Even with the new, tentative bridges he'd started building with his brothers, he still had a knee-jerk reaction to being compared to them.

"You've seen Connor off his meds," he said. "You really think I'm like him?"

"That's not what I said. ADD, not ADHD. Attention deficit disorder, without the hyperactive part." Diana touched his face tentatively, laying her palm against his cheek. "I had a friend at school who had it. For a long time, teachers just thought she was quiet and dreamy. They were always scolding her for being off in a world of her own. They didn't realize for ages that her grades were so bad because she *couldn't* focus, not because she didn't want to."

"I didn't get bad grades."

"No." Diana's thumb caressed his jaw. Her eyes were deep and warm and gentle. "You found ways to cope. But Callum, I've seen how hard you work to stay on top of everything. Most people don't have to do that. Maybe…maybe you shouldn't have to either."

Callum reflexively started to shake his head…and then stilled, seeing himself through her eyes. The mate bond showed him exactly how she felt, how much she loved him. Just as he was, quirks and all.

She was his mate. She *knew* him.

Perhaps better than he knew himself.

Diana kissed him, very gently. "Think about it, okay?"

"I will." He drew her closer. "I…already have, sometimes, if I'm honest. But I never wanted to admit that I might have more than skin-deep similarities to Connor and Conleth. Not even to myself."

"You don't have to prove to anyone that you're different." Diana kissed him again, more deeply. "Especially not me."

He closed his eyes, savoring the sweetness of her mouth. His mate, his incredible, perfect mate. All his, as he was hers.

"I'll talk to Conleth," he said, when their lips had parted again. "About the meds he takes, the ones for shifters. If…if there's anything that could help me focus, help me to not get distracted by the lives I can sense, I want to try. I'm going to have to spend more time in cities, after all. We need to take Beth back to Brighton, to see my parents. We might end up spending off-season there."

Diana sighed, her expression turning more serious. "We still have so much to work out, don't we? Where we're going to live, what I'm going to do while you're away during fire season, how to fight the horned serpents…"

"Yes." Callum kissed her again, cutting her off. He rolled onto her, pinning her underneath him, as her legs opened in welcome. "And we will. But not now."

EPILOGUE

It was bizarre.

He was standing in a crowded room, in a crowded pub, in a crowded city...and yet, it didn't bother him. It wasn't that he wasn't *aware* of the lives all around. He could just...not pay attention to them.

He could *choose* not to pay attention to them.

Conleth was watching him with a knowing air. "It's like suddenly acquiring a superpower, isn't it?"

"One that it turns out everyone else had all along," Callum said ruefully. "I should have done this years ago."

"True," Conleth agreed. "Still, at least by waiting this long to get treatment, you got to go straight onto a known, shifter-appropriate formulation rather than suffering through every side-effect under the sun while the doctors tried to work out the right drug combination."

Callum shook his head, still astonished at how easy it had all been. "*Are* there any side-effects I should know about?"

"Not really. Just make sure you stay off the booze. One secret baby is quite enough." Conleth raised his glass of mulled apple juice in a toast that was only slightly sarcastic. "Welcome to the Stone-Cold Sober Club. Membership, two."

Callum clinked his glass against Conleth's. "The benefits are worth the price of admission."

Conleth snorted as he drained his drink. "Now if only we could persuade Connor of that."

Callum sipped his own warm, spicy apple juice more slowly, still watching the crowd. Before, he'd always avoided the annual private party at the Full Moon pub in Brighton. Being crammed into a small space with so many shifters, with colored lights twinkling and carols playing and the air filled with the scents of pine and beer and gingerbread…he would have been frozen in misery, not knowing which way to turn.

Now, however, it was actually enjoyable. It gave him a strange, warm feeling inside, to look around and see so many familiar faces. Not just his own family and hotshot squad, but others too. His father's fellow firefighters and their mates; their grown children, even some of *their* mates. All entangled in a complicated extended clan, more like uncles and aunts and cousins than mere friends.

He'd avoided them all for so long, he'd been nervous about seeing them again. He shouldn't have worried. They'd all welcomed him back as though he'd never gone away at all. As though nothing, not even his own mistakes, could ever break those intangible connections.

As though they were family.

"Hi boys!" Blaise's mother Rose, the owner of the Full Moon pub, bustled up with a jug in each hand. "Having a good time?"

"Your Christmas party is as legendary as ever," Conleth declared, toasting her as well. "I do believe that this one is your finest yet."

"I agree, but I don't think I can take the credit for that." Rose smiled, casting a glance at Callum. "I came over to ask if one of you could tell me where my daughter's gone. I need her help with the mince pies."

Callum reached out with his pegasus senses, marveling once again at how *simple* it was to focus on one particular life rather than being blasted with all of them at once. He found Blaise's compressed, shadowy energy—and another soul nearby. There was no mistaking *that* incandescent power.

"She's out back," Callum reported. "With her father."

Rose pursed her lips. "In that case, I won't interrupt them. They have a lot to catch up on. By the way, watch out. I've already kicked Connor out from behind the bar six times. I do believe he's made it his mission in life to spike your drinks."

Conleth let out a long-suffering sigh. "Thanks for the warning, aunt Rose. Let me know if he becomes too much of a pest."

"Just don't lock him in the cellar again," Rose said with pained shudder. "We don't want a repeat of last year."

Conleth winced. "In my defense, I had no idea he could tap a beer keg with his bare hands."

"Did you want help with those pies?" Callum asked Rose.

"Oh, no, don't trouble yourself." Rose patted his arm. "You two have a lot of catching up to do as well. I'll rope in some of the other kids. Wystan! Leonie! I have a job for you!"

Conleth sighed again as Rose headed off. "I swear, that brother of ours is going to make me prematurely gray."

Callum laughed under his breath. "At least then you'd stand out."

"Bros!" Connor himself appeared, looking somewhat wild-eyed. He gave them a swift, assessing glance, and beamed. "Thank fuck you both have the same predictably boring lack of style. Callum, undo your top button. Conleth, roll down your sleeves. Hurry!"

Conleth made no move to adjust his shirt. "Connor, this had better not be what I think it is."

"*Please.* Otherwise I'm so dead." Connor was already pulling his flashing LED Christmas jumper over his head, revealing a white dress shirt that was nearly identical to the ones Conleth and Callum were wearing. "Consider it my Christmas present?"

"Connor, you walloping arsehole! *What did you do to this beer?*"

With a yelp, Connor raked a hand through his mussed hair to flatten it. He straightened, adopting a bland, neutral expression—just as Rory's twin brother Ross stormed up with a thunderous expression.

"All right." The griffin shifter folded his tattooed arms, raking them all with narrowed golden eyes. "Which one of you is the bloody idiot who thinks he's so funny?"

Connor promptly pointed at Callum. A heartbeat behind him, Conleth pointed at Connor. On sudden impulse, Callum pointed at Conleth.

Ross gave them all a deeply disgusted look. "I liked it better when you all hated each other. Well, if I catch *any* of you carrot-headed mingemunchers so much as *breathing* on my kegs, I'll roast *all* your chestnuts over an open fire."

The brewer stalked off, muttering to himself. Connor maintained his perfect poker-face until Ross had disappeared into the crowd once more. Then he grinned, slouching back into his own persona.

"Thanks, bros," Connor said, punching them both in the shoulder simultaneously. "I owe you one. Ooo, cookies!"

Conleth gave Callum a curious sidelong look as Connor bounced off again. "Why'd you do that?"

Callum shrugged, not quite sure himself. "It *is* kind of amusing, when one isn't on the receiving end. Never tell Connor I said that."

"Your secret is safe with me." Conleth smirked. "At least until I next want you to do something."

Callum started to reply, but was interrupted by Conleth's phone going off. With a grimace of apology, Conleth pulled the device out of his pocket. He glanced at the screen and scowled.

"Work?" Callum asked, recognizing *that* expression.

"It is the *day after Christmas.*" Conleth jabbed the 'decline call' button so hard, Callum was surprised the screen didn't crack in half. "I refuse to go into the office unless it is actively on fire. And if it *was*, I'd send Dad and you two. Putting out literal flames is not my job."

"Maybe it should be. You hate your job."

"We have enough firefighters in this family as it is." Conleth shoved his phone back into his pocket. "There are other careers, you know."

"Yes. And there are careers other than investment banking." Callum had been looking for a way to steer the conversation onto this topic. "Conleth, you could just stop. It's obvious your work makes you miserable. How much money do you need, anyway?"

Conleth shrugged. "Work keeps me busy. It's not like *I* have a mate and daughter."

"No, but you have a niece. And when summer comes, I'll have to be away from home a lot. Diana and I have been talking about how to make that work." Callum met his brother's wary eyes. "And we have a proposition for you."

~

At Diana's side, Callum's mother Connie chuckled. "I'm not sure who's enjoying the kids' area more. The children, or the grandads."

Diana laughed as well, watching Beth clamber all over Chase. The pegasus shifter was lying flat on his back in an inflatable ball pit, long arms and legs sprawling over the edges, beaming from ear-to-ear as Beth giggled and tipped balls over him. Nearby, little Charlie was energetically knocking down oversized foam bricks as fast as his own grandfather, dragon shifter Dai, could set them up.

"Now I understand why Rose set aside so much space," Diana said, looking round the lavishly-decorated nook. Rose had turned one corner of the pub into a veritable Santa's grotto, overflowing with toys to keep the children amused. "I thought it seemed like overkill for two small toddlers."

Connie grinned, her green eyes sparkling. "You just wait. Before the end of the evening, I bet the whole fire crew will be in there."

"Both crews," Joe interjected, overhearing. "Thunder Mountain Hotshots aren't about to let Alpha Team have all the fun. Uncle Chase! When are you going to stop hogging the ball pit?"

"Respect your elders!" Chase called back. "You young would-be alphas can just wait your turn!"

Diana giggled at Joe's pout. "Maybe we should ask Rose to rent *two* ball pits next year."

"Good idea," Rory agreed, putting his arm around Edith. He

exchanged a strange, secretive look with his mate. "We might need even more toys by then."

The way Rory's hand curved protectively around Edith's middle caught Diana's attention. She put two and two together, and gasped.

"Rory! Edith!" she exclaimed. "Are you…?"

Rory's grin widened, turning distinctly smug. "We weren't going to tell anyone yet, since it's so early. But yes. We're pregnant."

"*I'm* pregnant," Edith said indignantly. "I'm doing all the work here. I'm claiming the credit."

"Oh! Oh!" Diana was so excited, she nearly tipped her glass of wine over Connie. "I'm so happy for you both!"

"Congratulations," Wystan agreed. He glanced at Candice, who was eying him with an odd, small smile playing around her lips. Wystan smiled back, looking a little wry. "You may now say 'I told you so.' I really should have learned to listen to you by now."

"I told you so," Candice said promptly. She tucked herself under Wystan's arm, still smirking. "And yes, you should."

"You'd already guessed?" Edith asked, looking a little confused.

"Not exactly." Candice flattened a hand against her own stomach. "But I'd guessed that you and Rory were trying. I told Wystan we should make our *own* announcement before you beat us to it. But he wanted to wait."

This time, Diana *did* spill her wine, though thankfully over her hand rather than her mother-in-law. "*You're* pregnant too?"

"Oh, thank the Sea," Joe exclaimed, before Candice could respond. He pointed at both Edith and Candice. "Don't move. I'll be right back."

Candice raised her eyebrows at Seren as Joe dashed away. "What's all that about?"

Seren looked just as baffled. "I have not the faintest idea."

Joe came panting back a few minutes later, interrupting the mutual congratulations and exclamations. His arms were full of bags.

"Christmas was yesterday," Rory observed, as Joe started pulling out wrapped presents and handing them round.

"Yes, and I was expecting you both to tell everyone the happy news *before* then." Joe tossed a parcel to him. "Do you know how hard it's been to keep my mouth shut all these months?"

"Joe!" Edith had just opened her own present. She held up a familiar sparkly pink romper, with When I grow up, I want to be just like Mommy! printed on the front. "You knew all the way back in the autumn? Before we even started trying? And you didn't *tell* us?"

Joe winked. "Nobody likes spoilers."

Wystan shook his head in amazement. "And to think we all thought that *you* were desperately broody."

Joe shrugged. "Well, I knew I wouldn't be able to keep my mouth *completely* shut for so long. I had to do something to throw you all off the scent."

Diana noticed that Seren had gone rather quiet. She caught Joe's eye, and looked pointedly at his mate.

"Oh, yeah." Joe's expression turned more serious. He took Seren's hands, gazing down at her earnestly. "I'm really sorry, Seren. I didn't dare tell you, since as a Knight you're honor-bound to always tell the truth. I didn't want to put you in an awkward position if any of our friends asked you what was up. I know I freaked you out, going on about babies so much."

Seren was even paler than usual. "So...it was all an act?"

"Well, not totally," Joe confessed. "I do really, really want to have kids with you. I mean, *really*. But I'm totally happy to wait until you're ready. And if you don't want them at all, that's okay too."

Strangely, Seren did not look reassured by this. "But you wouldn't be upset to, ah, *not* wait?"

Joe grinned down at her. "Hey. I'd be thrilled to have a baby with you tomorrow."

"Not tomorrow." Seren bit her lip. "But...in just under nine months?"

"If that's when you want to start trying—" Joe began...and then stopped dead.

Rory stared from Joe to Seren and back again. "Wait a second. I thought sea dragons weren't, uh, fertile unless they did a special ritual first."

"Yes," Seren said. "So did I."

"We're *all* having babies?" Edith exclaimed.

"We're all having babies," Joe repeated, sounding utterly stunned. "We're all having babies. *We're all having babies!*"

Rory chuckled, pulling Edith out of the way as Joe swept Seren up, spinning her around. "So much for your visions, Joe. Guess fate can still surprise you."

"I love surprises." Joe put Seren down, but didn't let her go. "I love *you*, my incredible mate. I love everyone in this bar! Also, I need all my Christmas presents back."

The mate bond tugged at Diana's attention. She stepped away from the rest of the group, turning. A moment later, Callum came round the corner. He smiled as he caught sight of her, then cast a curious look at his squabbling squadmates.

"Did I miss something?" he asked Diana in a low voice.

"A sudden outbreak of baby fever," Diana replied, smothering a giggle. She stretched up on her toes to kiss him. "Let's just say that at this rate, Buck's going to have to set up a staff creche."

Callum's eyebrows rose. "Maybe *that* could be Conleth's new career."

"Oh! Did you talk to him? Did he say yes?"

Callum nodded, his mouth curving in a small smile. "He said he'll have to think about it. But I'm certain he'll agree to spend summers in Montana with us."

"I'm so glad!" Diana flung her arms around him, hugging him in joy. "It'll make things so much easier, to have him around to help look after Beth. I'll be able to keep up my research."

"That reminds me." Callum pulled a folded paper out from his back pocket, handing it to her. "This is for you."

"A list?" she said, a little surprised. She hadn't seen him write one since he'd started taking his ADD medication.

Callum's smile widened. "Yes, but not one of mine. Buck emailed that over earlier today. It's the names he can remember his sister mentioning. All the people who might have been involved with her and your mother in the Storm Society. Maybe some of them escaped the horned serpents too."

"I'm sure of it. Many groups have tried to silence my people, over the centuries." Diana ran a finger down the column of names. "But we're still here. And we still have our stories. One way or another, I'm going to carry on my mother's work."

Callum pressed a kiss to the top of her head. "I think she'd be very proud of you."

Diana smiled up at him. "I know she is."

"Diana! Callum!" Joe called to them. He waved a bottle over his head. "Come over here! We're drinking a toast!"

They rejoined the others. Joe passed out glasses of champagne—and sparkling grape juice, for Callum and the pregnant women—then raised his own.

"To family," the sea dragon declared, beaming. His arm tightened around Seren. "Old and new."

"To family," Diana echoed, gazing up at her mate.

Edith sighed, lowering her glass again. "I wish Fenrir was here," she said wistfully. "It's not the same without him."

"He still isn't talking?" Rory asked Wystan and Candice.

The unicorn shifter shook his head. "We've barely seen him all winter. He's been sleeping at our ranch, but he spends all his time roaming the mountains. I think he's looking for something. Or someone."

⁓

Alone in the wilderness, he ran.

There was no scent to guide him. No paw print, no fur caught in bark, no bent leaf or disturbed grasses. But he didn't need them.

They were pack. And pack knew pack. Pack *always* knew pack, no matter how long it had been.

Nose to the ground, Fenrir ran on.

Following the trail of his sister.

Fenrir's true nature is revealed in WILDFIRE HELLHOUND - coming soon!
To be notified as soon as it's released, join my mailing list.

Have you read the first Fire & Rescue Shifters series, featuring the parents of the Wildfire Crew?
If not, binge the complete series starting with Firefighter Dragon

ALSO BY ZOE CHANT

Fire & Rescue Shifters

Firefighter Dragon
Firefighter Pegasus
Firefighter Griffin
Firefighter Sea Dragon
The Master Shark's Mate
Firefighter Unicorn
Firefighter Phoenix

Fire & Rescue Shifters Collection 1

Fire & Rescue Shifters: Wildfire Crew

Wildfire Griffin
Wildfire Unicorn
Wildfire Sea Dragon
Wildfire Pegasus
Wildfire Hellhound (coming soon!)
Wildfire [SPOILER!] (releasing in 2020)

… and many more! See the complete list at www.zoechant.com

WRITING AS HELEN KEEBLE

Author's Note: These are YA paranormal comedies, not adult romances. No sex, no swearing, lots of laughs!

Fang Girl

No Angel

"Keeble's entertaining plot contains action and suspense coupled with a witty protagonist and a great cast of secondary characters. A funny, refreshing novel." (School Library Journal)

"Quirky and fun. The authentic teen dialogue is refreshing and reminiscent of Louise Rennison's Confessions of Georgia Nicolson series." (Voice of Youth Advocates (VOYA))

"Likable voice, well-drawn characters and dead-on humor."--Kirkus Reviews

Printed in Great Britain
by Amazon